WILDFIRE

"Guess I should claim my reward for rescuing you, shouldn't I?" Jim said huskily, looking into her eyes, then at her mouth.

They had been through too much together in less than twenty-four hours for Brandy to feel self-conscious. She raised herself up on tiptoes as Jim's hand cupped the back of her neck. Her fingers spread across his chest to balance herself.

She felt the rough brush of his whiskers first, then the warmth of his mouth closing over hers. The kiss was gently firm, nothing tentative or uncertain about it, just like the man who gave it.

When the kiss came to an end, Brandy wished silently that it hadn't ended so soon. She gazed into his eyes, veiled by sooty lashes, their expression unreadable. The hand at the back of her neck slowly tightened, drawing her to him.

She didn't need the pressure of his hand to tip her head back to receive his kiss. The hard demand of his mouth ignited a wildfire of desire.

from "Bluegrass King"

FOREVER

Janet Dailey

ZEBRA BOOKS
KENSINGTON PUBLISHING CORP.

http://www.kensingtonbooks.com

ZEBRA BOOKS are published by

Kensington Publishing Corp.
850 Third Avenue
New York, NY 10022

All Kensington titles, imprints and distributed lines are avail-
able at special quantity discounts for bulk purchases for sales
promotion, premiums, fund-raising, educational or institu-
tional use.

Special book excerpts or customized printings can also be
created to fit specific needs. For details, write or phone the
office of the Kensington Special Sales Manager: Kensington
Publishing Corp., 850 Third Avenue, New York, NY 10022.
Attn. Special Sales Department. Phone: 1-800-221-2647.

First Printing: July 2004
10 9 8 7 6 5 4 3 2 1

Printed in the United States of America

CONTENTS

BLUEGRASS KING   7

SONORA SUNDOWN   175

BLUEGRASS KING

CHAPTER ONE

The horses stomped restlessly in their stalls, straw rustling under their hooves. Sleek chestnut and bay heads looked over the weathered doors as they whickered softly at the rising crimson sun.

Dani Williams glanced over the back of the gray stable pony she was saddling, her hazel eyes watching her father making his last-minute inspection of the tall, cedar-red thoroughbred. Tension crackled in the air as the big horse bared his teeth and nipped at her father's shoulder.

Muscles rippled in the powerful hindquarters as the horse edged away from the man, hooves moving lightly over the ground. A groom clung to the halter of the animal's bobbing head, nearly pulled off the ground occasionally by the raising of the strong neck.

This was The Rogue, fierce and wild. Misbehaving for the sheer love of it. A fighter. But more important, The Rogue was a racehorse. Dani's father had often said that if a man was lucky, he would see a horse like this once in his lifetime.

The marvel was that they owned him. The two-year-old stallion stood nearly seventeen hands at the shoulder and was still growing. Yet it wasn't only The Rogue's size that promised greatness. There was the wide flare of the nostrils to drink in the wind, the broad chest to let his lungs fill to the limit and most precious of all, the inborn desire to race.

The Rogue had raced three times as a two-year-old and won easily three times. The fourth time he went to the post, he never got out of the starting gate. Always fractious, always strong-willed, at race time the big horse was an explosive keg of dynamite. His impatience had surfaced in his fourth race when he tried to open the starting gate himself and injured his right front leg in the process.

For a horse of The Rogue's caliber, no injury was slight. For two months they had babied, pampered, and nursed him along, taking no chances that would aggravate the bruise and muscle strain into something more serious. Today was the day The Rogue was to be tested.

A movement caught Dani's gaze, and she looked at the lean man walking towards her, a racing saddle over the arm that carried the riding crop. She gave him a tentative smile of greeting.

"I almost forget what it's like to get up at the crack of dawn," he said, stopping beside her. The top of his brown head was several inches below hers, but that was a good height for a jockey.

"It's a nice quiet morning," Dani murmured, smoothing her sweating palms over the sides of her faded jeans before preparing to tighten the saddle cinch. "What do you think, Manny? Is he ready?"

The jockey's deep brown eyes turned to Dani; like his dark skin, they revealed Manuel Herrera's Puerto Rican ancestry. He gave her no answer. And Dani, who had spent nearly all of her nineteen years in the company of fragile racehorses, knew there was no certain answer to her question. At some point in a horse's full stride all his thousand-plus pounds is balanced on one leg, its ankle no bigger around than a ballet dancer's.

She sighed, trying to let go of the tension that gripped her. With a fluid movement born of long habit, Dani swung herself into the saddle of the stocky gray horse and walked him slowly to the larger fidgeting thoroughbred. The Rogue blew softly through his nose, nuzzling the neck of the more sedate horse, calming somewhat while still moving nervously under the ministering hand of her father.

Her eyes searched Lew Williams's drawn face, missing none of the strain and tension that had him on edge, too. Lew Williams had once been a jockey like Manny, before he lost the battle with his weight and height. But racing was in his blood. A few years after Dani was born, he had turned to training without much success, then, twelve years ago, had picked up his first horse in a claiming race.

But, as her father had often grumbled, it cost as much money to keep a loser as it did a winner, and most of the horses they'd owned had been losers. Besides The Rogue, they owned a string of six third-rate horses. The only money winner in the lot this year had been an aging racing mare. But The Rogue—every dream her father had ever dreamed was wrapped up in this horse.

The bridle was on and the saddle was cinched. Her father boosted Manny into the saddle, then stared at the rider crouched like a monkey on the big horse's back.

"Once round the track at a canter to loosen him up," Lew Williams instructed, looking anxiously at the jockey, who nodded. "Then a slow gallop, and dammit! I mean slow!" His swift glance encompassed his daughter Dani still mounted on the stable pony. "Take Nappy around, too. The Rogue will keep pace with him."

The mouse-gray pony was his stablemate and the only horse The Rogue didn't attempt to outdistance. There was a brisk nod from Manny, who directed a sharp glance at Dani, plainly saying she was to lead the way. Seconds later, the pair were walking their horses onto the empty racetrack. For a furlong they trotted, paying no attention to the beautiful rose gardens in the infield. The famous twin spires of the Churchill Downs clubhouse kept watch. Churchill Downs, home of the Kentucky Derby horse race, was more than a century old, patterned after the equally famous Epsom Downs in England.

Neither rider said a word as Dani nudged the gray into a rocking canter and The Rogue followed suit. Around the oval track, the pair traveled clockwise once. Dani's stomach knotted as she urged the gray into a steady gallop, straining to see the slightest sign that the Rogue was favoring his right leg, but the big cedar-red stallion galloped effortlessly beside her, his ears erect and forward as he tugged at the tightly wrapped reins without really attempting to increase the pace.

As they drew level again with the stand where her father stood, Manny raised his whip to signal that all was well and Lew Williams motioned them to circle the track once more. At the end of the third route, he waved them to the gate.

Unconsciously Dani held her breath while she watched her father run his hand along the right front leg of the stallion. There was a watery brightness to his brown eyes as he looked up, a grin splitting the weathered lines around his mouth.

"He ain't even warm," he said gruffly. And she knew the tightness in his voice was caused by the lump of relief in his throat. "You might as well get down, Dani. The Rogue doesn't need a babysitter anymore."

She nodded and slipped from the saddle, reaching out to stroke the silken neck of The Rogue, stopping when the magnificent head swung toward her hand, prepared to nip.

"You bad boy," Dani crooned softly, smiling into the darkly intelligent yet mischievous eyes. "I'd almost let you bite me just to see you run again the way you were born to."

But she stepped back, out of reach of his teeth, marveling again at the beauty and strength of the animal before her. The perfectly carved head of The Rogue swung away from his admiring audience. Both Dani and her father turned to see what had captured his attention.

A golden chestnut with a flaxen mane and tail, a white blaze down his forehead, and four flashing white stockings was sidling toward them. Dani's smile hardened as she recognized Easy Doesit, the pride of Coronet Farm. She waved to the apprentice jockey astride the horse, Jimmy Graves, but her eyes rested coldly on the man striding effortlessly beside the trainer who led the animal. His confident, cocky grin annoyed her.

"Hello, Lew," the man greeted her father. "How's The Rogue today?"

"Barrett." Her father's smile was broad and welcoming, the complete opposite of his daughter's expression. "He's sound and healthy, everywhere."

"He can take that movie horse of yours any day," Dani declared, not attempting to hide the sarcasm in her voice.

"Hello, kid." Barrett King's cool green eyes flicked over her indifferently. "Still as sassy as ever, I see."

She half expected him to ruffle her hair, which was cropped in a very feminine version of a boy's cut. As always, her hair prickled along the back of her neck as she stared resentfully at Barrett King, but he was already ignoring her.

"Are you working this horse today, Lew, or are you only letting him get warm?" He was studying the restive movements of the horse, a glint of admiration in his gaze.

An exultant light glittered in Dani's eyes; she guessed how much Barrett King still wanted the stallion he had tried to buy from them as a yearling. To this day her father declared that he had never considered selling The Rogue, but Dani knew how tempting the offer had been, especially considering the steadily mounting feed bills, stable fees, and entry fees and four months without one of their horses finishing in the money.

Twice he had picked up the telephone to accept Barrett King's offer, but she had managed to talk him out of it both times. Then the racing mare, Riding High, had providentially come in second. With that money in his pocket, the offer wasn't as tempting as the promise of the big stallion.

Dani couldn't help but gloat a little, knowing they had a horse that all the King money couldn't buy. And the King family, an old established Kentucky clan, had money to burn. Most of it wasn't tied up in racehorses, but the ones they owned were the best. The fillies and colts from their stud farm in the heart of Bluegrass country brought top dollar. So Dani took secret satisfaction in watching Barrett King look at the stallion he couldn't have.

"I'm letting him go all out today, Barrett," her father was saying. "The Rogue works better with competition. What about it? Are you going to let Easy Doesit have his head?"

"Simms is the trainer," Barrett shrugged, turning his easy smile to the man holding the golden chestnut. "Do you want to run him alone or work him with The Rogue?"

"If you're afraid The Rogue is too much horse for yours," Dani said softly, "we'll understand."

"Danielle." The muttered reprimand from her father was meant only for her ears, but her taunt brought Barrett King's gaze back to her. It angered her to notice that her words seemed to amuse him.

"We'll lead your horse once around the track," Simms answered, chuckling as he spoke.

"We'll see who leads who!" Dani snapped, spinning abruptly on a booted heel and shoving her hands deep into the pockets of her faded jeans.

Anger spurred her on as she walked quickly to the stand. Her father and Barrett King followed at a more leisurely pace. Her smoldering eyes were narrow as she looked at them, momentarily disliking her father for showing so much deference to the man at his side simply because he represented money.

She'd been on her guard from the first day she'd seen Barrett King almost five years ago, as if instantly recognizing an enemy. Most people didn't see beyond his charming smile and good looks, but Dani did. And she studied him again as he walked beside her short, paunchy father.

He was tall, more than six feet, much taller than most of the men around the racetrack. The breadth of his shoulders and chest tapered sexily to lean hips, in keeping with his height.

Deep lines were etched in the sides of his mouth, amounting to masculine dimples. A grin quirked the corners of his mouth, despite the set of the powerful jaw and chin. His sternly handsome face was dominated by long, dark-lashed eyes of vivid green. Yet his cool, reckless gaze always seemed to have little devils of laughter just under its surface. But Dani knew they were devils that could quickly become anything but funny. Barrett King could be ruthless if he chose.

His thick, wavy hair shone with a touch of fire in the morning sun. As always, he wore his expensively tailored clothes with careless grace. Her father classified him as a man's man, but Dani considered him a ladies' man, and the beautiful women who chased him proved it.

At nineteen, Dani felt very worldly—not from experience but exposure. She had traveled the racetrack circuit almost since she was born. For the first five years she had been accompanied by her mother, not that she remembered much about her. Her mother had hated the unpredictable life of horse racing and had abandoned her husband and child. Dani was twelve when the word reached them that her mother had been killed in a car crash a few months before. Her father had grieved quietly, but she'd felt nothing, a fact that had haunted her with overtones of guilt.

A frown creased her forehead. She loved racing. She loved horses. She didn't want the security her mother had craved. So they weren't wealthy like Barrett King, Dani thought angrily. So they lived out of the back end of a pickup truck. This was her life and she loved it.

Up with the sun, she found that mornings were a joy. The scent of hay tickled her nose. The warm smell of horses. The fragrance of leather and saddle soap that always clung to her hands. The accelerated beat of her heart when the call to post was sounded. The mostly good-natured competition between horse owners. As for friends, she had hundreds scattered across the East Coast from Florida to New York.

So what if her clothes could all fit in one small

suitcase and she didn't have a dress to her name? The jeans and simple tops that clothed her slender figure made her look more like a young boy than a girl, but she didn't care. No one had to know that the only education she had was for-credit courses on the Internet. And if she pretty much lived on hamburgers and Cokes, that was her business too. None of that made Barrett King any better than she was.

These last thoughts were the reason the glint in her eyes was so openly defiant when her father and Barrett King joined her. There was a puzzled question in King's eyes as he met her gaze, but as usual his glance never lingered very long on her. Barrett King saw her as a child, at most a teenager. That rankled Dani, too. She wanted to declare that she was his equal, but the apprehensive look on her father's face made her hold back the scathing comment.

Clamping her lips shut, she turned her gaze to the two horses slowly circling the track counter-clockwise. Without the quieting influence of his stablemate, The Rogue was showing his eagerness to run, fighting the steel muscles of Manny's arms holding him in tight rein.

"He looks good, Lew," Barrett commented.

"He looks more than good. He looks great!" Dani said firmly, the lukewarm praise irritating her. "When he's a three-year-old he's going to take the Triple Crown—the Kentucky Derby, the Preakness, and then the Belmont."

"You're pretty sure of yourself," Barrett cautioned with a hint of mockery. "The Rogue is only a horse."

She spun around to glare at him angrily. "You can say that because you haven't seen him run. When The Rogue's in full stride, nothing can touch him. Nothing!" A brow was raised at her vehement declaration. "You knew he was good, Mr. King, that's why you tried to buy him, but he belongs to Lew and me!"

For once there were no devils in his gaze. "It isn't good to get too attached to a horse, especially a working thoroughbred. It can only lead to heartbreak—it almost has already."

"You'd like to see him crippled, wouldn't you?" she accused, her hazel eyes flashing fire. "If you can't have The Rogue, you don't want anyone else to have him either."

"That's enough." Her father's voice was a low growl and just as menacing but the effect was dampened by the apologetic look he tossed to Barrett. "You'll have to excuse my daughter. Tough to teach them respect in this kind of environment."

"I respect people who deserve it," Dani retorted.

Her chin tipped upward defiantly at his cool look. Mentally she braced herself for the taller man's anger.

Instead Barrett said calmly, "The horses are at the starting line."

The decision had been made not to use the starting gate since The Rogue hadn't been worked out of it since his injury. At the signal from the trainer, Simms, the two horses were off.

The flashy chestnut immediately leaped to the front, a big agile horse except when compared with The Rogue. As they passed the trio in the stands, the cedar-red thoroughbred was at the chestnut's heels. Both horses were at a run, yet neither hit their top speed. The mile-long track meant races were won at the end, not the beginning.

"That's a tight wrap your jockey has on those reins." Simms had joined them.

"The Rogue doesn't like other horses in front of him," Lew explained, not taking his eyes off the racing horses now circling the track. "He tends to want to get in front too soon. We haven't been able to rate him."

Around the first turn they ran, the pounding of their hooves overshadowing the pounding of Dani's heart. Along the backstretch, The Rogue's nose pulled even with the saddle of the golden chestnut. In a sense, it was a match race between the horse that the newspapers declared was the best three year-old and the horse that Dani knew was better than any three- or four-year-old. From under her thick brown lashes, she glanced surreptitiously at Barrett King.

"The Rogue's going to take your horse, you know," she said softly and more than a little triumphantly.

His cool green gaze swept her face briefly but arrogantly, although he made no reply. As the horses came out of the final turn into the homestretch, Dani leaned forward, her hands closing over the railing, wanting only to scream "Go, Rogue, go!" All thought of the big thoroughbred's past injury vanished from her mind. The chestnut's jockey was showing his horse the whip, flicking it near the side of the horse's head, but Manny had only relaxed his hold and was hand-riding The Rogue, urging the horse to full stride.

The chestnut quickened his stride to attain top speed, like most horses. But The Rogue, a strider, lengthened his. Easy Doesit seemed to be giving it his all when The Rogue stretched out, magically flying above the ground, seeming to pass him with one bound. Each effortlessly gliding movement carried him farther ahead.

"I don't believe it," Simms murmured as The Rogue drew nearer the finish line five, then six lengths ahead of the flashy chestnut, still pulling away with his ears pricked forward, under no strain at all.

"I told you!" Dani exclaimed, and turned away from the rail, an exultant light in her eyes. "I told you nothing could touch him!"

Then came the sound, a short, explosive pop like no other—a small, insignificant sound that turns the blood of horsemen to ice. Only one thing made that sound—the snapping of a bone.

With a stifled cry, Dani spun back to the track, her wide, terrified eyes seeing the still galloping Rogue, his gait strange and uneven, the frantic efforts of Manny to pull the horse to a halt. Vaguely she was conscious of the three men vaulting over the railing and her own race to follow them as they dashed down the dirt track to the gradually slowing horse and rider.

"He was sound. I swear to God he was sound. The leg was healed," her father kept mumbling in what amounted to a desperate prayer.

By the time they reached the horse, Manny had dismounted and was attempting to quiet the awkwardly prancing horse. The Rogue's large, intelligent eyes were glazed as he struggled against the efforts of the four men to aid him. With nightmarish clarity, Dani watched Barrett King attempt to use his belt to cradle the leg of the dangling right ankle and prevent further damage.

Shock rooted her to the ground until his piercing green eyes turned to her. "Get a vet, dammit!" Barrett commanded.

When she first turned to race toward the stables, her legs almost crumpled beneath her and for one horrified moment, Dani thought she was incapable of action. Then she was running, fighting back the sobs to gasp for breath.

There was no reality in the next thirty minutes. She didn't exactly remember reaching Doc Langley's office on the race grounds, nor his clipped orders that sent his assistants scurrying to get the special horse van on the track. Dani did recall the large hypodermic needle puncturing the cedar-red coat of The Rogue to sedate him, so she must have accompanied the vet to the track. Snatches of conversation were jumbled in her mind, talk of X-rays and consulting Doctor Hamilton. Mostly there were grimly foreboding expressions.

When the daze lifted, Dani found her unseeing gaze was watching the slowly twirling racing goggles in the swarthy hand of Manny Herrera. A film of dust darkened his face except where the goggles had been. She was seated in a chair beside him, her fingers digging into the wooden arms. How she got there she had no idea. With an effort Dani raised her eyes, wrinkling her nose at the medicinal scent of the vet's office. Then she saw her father's bowed head.

"Lew?" Her voice was a plaintive whisper. She

couldn't remember the last time she had called him dad or father.

When his graying head lifted, Dani saw the shattered, broken look in his eyes, the look of someone who had suffered the final defeat, his spirit broken and his soul gone, leaving only an old man.

"His leg is broken," his flat voice answered.

A violent shudder racked her slender body. With difficulty she swallowed the lump in her throat.

"That doesn't mean he has to be destroyed," she said vehemently. Acid tears suddenly burned her eyes. "Broken legs can be healed. It isn't hopeless!"

But her father only looked at her blankly and lowered his head in his hands.

"Remember when Swaps broke his leg." The words were a plea not to give up. "The doctors can fix The Rogue, too. You'll see. He'll race again, I know it. I know it!"

The door opened and Doctor Langley walked in. "Lew." The vet's gaze settled immediately on the man hunched forward in his chair.

"Yes." Her father's voice seemed to come from some deep, empty cavern as he acknowledged the man without raising his head.

"Hamilton and I studied the X-rays thoroughly. There isn't any hope." The blunt sentence was deliberately clipped as the raw edges of his tone sawed through the air.

Dani stared at the elderly doctor in disbelief. Her head moved in a sharp negative movement to the side as if to shake off his verdict. Then her father's tight voice sliced the room.

"Do what you have to do."

Dr. Langley started to turn back to the door. Dani bounded to her feet.

"No!" she shrieked. "There must be something you can do. You aren't going to destroy The Rogue . . ."

"I'm sorry." The vet's expression was sadly firm as he reluctantly brought his gaze to bear on Dani. "There's nothing left of his ankle bones but a thousand tiny fragments."

A trembling rage took possession of her. She refused to accept his statement. Her breath was coming in quick, painful spasms as her head kept moving from side to side.

"I don't believe you," she said hoarsely.

The pitying glances of the others in the room were unbearable. There was a movement in the doorway and Barrett King entered the room, tall and compelling. Resentment boiled as she saw the rueful nod of the vet in Barrett's direction, answering the unasked question that was evident in the green eyes.

"It's your fault." Dani turned her anguished fury on him. "How much did you pay him to have The Rogue destroyed? You tried to buy him and we wouldn't sell." Her shaking legs carried her to stand in front of him, her head thrown back, tears glimmering in the corners of her eyes. "You got your revenge, didn't you? They're going to kill him! They're going to kill him!"

Her tight fists began pummelling his chest, beating against the solid wall with all her strength. Lights exploded around her, then hands closed over her arms, trying to pull her away. Distantly, she heard Barrett King's voice saying, "Let her be." And the hands let her go.

Slowly her cries of anger and hatred gave way to sobs of pain and anguish. Beneath her, Dani felt her knees begin to buckle before a pair of strong arms slipped around her in support and she was drawn against that hard wall she'd tried to knock down.

"Go ahead, kid," a comforting voice said near her ear. "Cry it all out."

She sobbed wildly, hearing nothing but his steady heartbeat and the racking sounds in her throat. As the force of her grief began to subside, she heard a door close. Opening her tear-drenched eyes, she focused her gaze beyond the arms that held her and on her father. A man was standing beside him. She couldn't say how she knew, but some inner voice told her he was the consultant vet, Dr. Hamilton.

Dani didn't need to see her father suddenly crumple to the floor to know that the man had come to tell him it was over. The Rogue was dead. Her hands crept to her ears, as if covering them would prevent the news reaching her. She heard someone scream "No!" then realized it was she who was screaming. Then there was a strange buzzing in her ears and waves of blackness washed over her, while Barrett's strong arms tightened their hold.

CHAPTER TWO

The bed was uncomfortable and totally unfamiliar. Dani blinked and glanced around the room, trying to remember which hotel they were staying in this time. One glance at the sterile walls and the crisp sheets covering her told her she was in a hospital. Mentally she checked out her body to discover where she was hurt, only to decide that the only thing troubling her was the throbbing in her head.

Had The Rogue kicked her? she wondered. A wave of nausea hit her as she remembered The Rogue was dead, mercifully destroyed because he had shattered the bones in his ankle. With a painful moan, she turned her head into the starched pillows and let the tears slip from her hazel eyes. But she didn't cry or sob, despite the dull, disbelieving ache in her heart.

Twisting her head back, she stared unblinkingly at the snow-white ceiling, not bothering to wipe the fresh tears from her cheeks and not caring how tousled her short brown hair was because of the way she had pushed her head back against the pillow. Footsteps sounded near her door—slow, defeated footsteps. Before they entered her room, she knew they belonged to her father.

"Hello, Danielle," her father said quietly. No smile turned up the corners of his mouth and there was no light in his eyes.

"Hello, Lew," she answered.

An uneasy silence fell. A week ago she wouldn't have given a thought to how old her father was. Now, looking at the small, broken man, she tried to remember if he was fifty-six or fifty-seven. He looked much older than that.

"Why am I here?" she asked finally.

"You collapsed. The shock of . . . of . . ."

His voice broke again and Dani didn't force him to say the words. "I see," she murmured. "When can I leave?"

"They want you to stay overnight. It's the best thing—considering," he sighed.

"Considering what? I'm all right now."

"You might as well take advantage of the peace and quiet while you can," her father said cryptically, his face unnaturally pale. He caught her questioning look. "There were a bunch of newspaper reporters at the vet's. Your picture and Barrett King's are plastered all over the paper."

Then Dani remembered those strange explosions of light that had seemed so much a part of the nightmare of her memory. Obviously they had been flashbulbs. She winced inwardly at the recollection of her attack on Barrett King and the wild accusations she had made.

She could justify her attack by her need to strike back—at anyone. Her total dislike of Barrett King had made him the likely choice. She felt no regret for what she had done, only that outsiders had witnessed it. She tried to catch her father's gaze, but he refused to meet hers.

"Why do you hate him so much?" he asked.

Her quick retort was instinctive. "Because he breathes." Normally a reply like that would have brought a reluctant smile to her father's face, but this time his head moved wearily in despair. "I'm sorry, Lew," Dani spoke hesitantly. "He just rubs me the wrong way."

"I wish we had sold The Rogue to him."

"What are you saying?" She gasped at her father's traitorous statement. Her head jerked upward as she tried to fathom the blank expression of the man gazing sightlessly at the drawn curtains of the hospital window.

"Your mother was right about me." He ignored her question and continued speaking in that same emotionless tone. "If I entered a one-man race, I'd lose. I'm a loser. I wasn't any good as a jockey. Only fools hired me to train their horses. Those hayburners we own aren't fit to be called thoroughbreds. A man like me had no right to own The Rogue."

"No!" But her whispering protest was ignored.

"It's the truth." His eyes turned to Dani. There was no reflection, just deep, bottomless pools of brown intensified by the sunken hollows surrounding them. "I never raised you right, Dani. I gave you free rein. I never tried to curb you or control your fiery temper. You aren't to blame for the way you acted today. I am."

Tears began to scald her eyes again. "Don't say things like that!"

"What do you know, girl? Horses, that's all," he answered for her. "You eat, sleep, and smell like horses. You don't know any other world. That's my fault."

Dani watched in horrified silence as a shaking hand reached inside the jacket of his worn suit. He pulled out a crumpled wad of bills and pushed it toward her, shoving his cold fingers into her resisting palm.

"When you leave the hospital tomorrow morning, I don't want you to come to the track. I don't want you to go near one ever again." His voice was trembling as badly as his hands, but the emotion in it was undeniable. "Take this money and make a new life for yourself. Get an apartment, a job, or go to school. Dress like a woman, not a boy. You'll never get ahead looking like that. Unless you want to muck out stables for the rest of your life."

"Where did you get this?" she demanded hoarsely as the folded bills flipped open and she realized there was at least ten thousand dollars in her hand.

"I sold the horses . . . all except the mare. All I know is racing. I don't know anything else," he mumbled brokenly. "But you're young. You can make a new start, a new life." A tear trickled out of the corner of his eye, unnoticed. "You're a fighter—like The Rogue. You can be somebody.

But not if you stick with me. I'll drag you down and you'll be a nothing, a loser just like your old dad.''

"No, Daddy, no!" She scurried forward, her hands reaching out for him, unaware that she hadn't called him Lew, but he drew back from the bed.

"Promise me you won't have anything to do with horses. They'll break your heart and your spirit. Promise me.''

"I promise." She shook her head firmly, almost blinded by tears.

"I'm leaving tonight. I don't know where I'm going or when I'll see you again," he continued absently. "The track is crawling with reporters. I can't stand to talk about . . .'' For a long minute, his eyes rested on her bewildered face. "Goodbye, Dani.''

Before she realized it, he had left the room. She tried to call him back, but she couldn't get anything past the knotted muscles in her throat. Clutching the money in her hand, she pushed back the sheet and scrambled to her feet, the bottom of the hospital gown flapping strangely around her bare knees. No longer stunned by his announcement, she felt the need to go after her father and convince him that nothing he'd said was true.

Racing toward the small closet in the room, Dani was stopped by the sight of a slender girl in a white gown hurrying toward her. It took a full second before she realized it was a mirror reflecting her own image.

Her short hair glowed a rich brown in the over-head light. The cinnamon shade of her hazel eyes was enhanced by her thick but not long lashes. Ignoring the boyish style of her hair, Dani noticed for the first time the clean lines of her face, oval with nicely prominent cheekbones, a small and straight nose above a well-shaped mouth and naturally arched eyebrows. Her neck was long and graceful, like a racehorse's. The skin of her arms and face was a light golden color, showing no inclination to freckle.

But her legs were pale white beneath the gown, never having been exposed to the sun the way her face and arms were. They were slender, yet well muscled. In fact, she thought, as she hitched the hospital gown up near her thighs, her legs and the rest of her looked a lot like the half-naked girls on the calendars at the stables. This was the first time she had ever thought about having a figure, and the sight of her gently rounded hips and small waist was almost surprising.

"You have great legs. How old are you?"

At the sound of the masculine voice, Dani let go of the gown, letting the hem fall down around her knees as she spun to face the man leaning against the doorjamb.

"Who are you? What do you want?" Her cheeks flamed as she encountered the unabashed interest in his dark brown eyes.

"Marshall Thompsen," the stranger replied smoothly. An eyebrow as thick and as black as his hair arched as his gaze traveled lazily over her. "Barrett said you were a kid."

Dani put her hands behind her back to hide the money she still clutched, unaware that the action tightened the thin cotton gown across her front, outlining the upward thrust of her breasts.

"I'm not a kid!" she retorted.

"I can see that," he murmured with a smile that was obviously meant to charm.

"What are you doing here?" She began to edge warily toward the bed. "If Barrett King sent you, then you can just turn around and leave."

"Oh, Barrett King and I aren't friends, not by any stretch of the imagination. Acquaintances, enemies even, but never friends." The man straightened and stepped further into the room. "I was curious about you. Telling Barrett off took guts."

"Are you one of those reporters?" Dani accused, her fingers reaching for the telephone at her bedside.

Her obvious resistance to his practiced charm didn't seem to disconcert him. "No. I'm a syndicated columnist. I write about the lives and loves of the rich and famous."

"That still doesn't explain what you're doing here," Dani persisted.

"I thought I'd already explained." A gold business card case materialized in the hand that had been in the pocket of his impeccably tailored blazer. "Barrett King is always good material, and that was quite a scene the two of you had this morning."

"Were you there?" she demanded.

"Read about it. If you'd like to tell me more, here's my number." He handed her a business card. "Or we can talk now." From under his arm, he withdrew a newspaper and handed it to her. "Have you seen the article?"

"No." She accepted the paper, sliding onto the bed and discreetly slipping the money beneath her pillow.

Her father had told her about the article, but Dani had imagined some small write-up, possibly with a picture tucked in some corner of the paper. She hadn't expected the story to monopolize nearly one entire page. There were three photographs. The largest was of her attempt to beat up Barrett King. The second picture must have been taken after she collapsed because it showed her being carried in his arms. But the last brought a tight knot of pain in her chest. It was a magnificent photo of The Rogue, rearing and fighting off a groom who was trying to hold him. Dani remembered it had been taken some months ago, before his third race. He looked invincible. It hurt unbearably to remind herself that The Rogue was dead.

She fought back scalding tears as she glanced at Marshall Thompsen. "Why?" she asked huskily. "Why all this? Nobody's even heard of The Rogue before."

"Oh, a combination of things, I guess," he shrugged. "A lack of any other noteworthy news, the human interest angle of a possibly great horse being destroyed, and the name of Barrett King. I don't suppose there was any truth in your accusations?"

Dani's chin lifted defiantly, her eyes sparkling with anger and unshed tears. "He wanted The Rogue. He tried to buy him, but we wouldn't sell. My father—" She trailed off, unwilling to repeat what her father had said—that they should have

sold the thoroughbred to Barrett King, that they
had no right to own a horse like The Rogue.

"Yes, I saw your father slipping out of your room
and down the back stairs. That's how I guessed
which room was yours." The man smoothly filled in
the gap left by her uncompleted sentence, allowing
her time to collect herself. "Guess he was trying
to avoid the reporters by the entrance. He isn't
taking The Rogue's death very well, is he?"

The quiet question struck a responsive chord in
Dani and she was suddenly overcome with a need
to confide the confusing events that had taken
place. Her words tumbled over each other as she
explained how severely depressed her father was,
his insistence that he was a failure, a loser, even
his assertion that they should have sold The Rogue
to Barrett King. She glossed over the part about
how he hadn't raised her right and didn't mention
the money tucked under her pillow. She ended by
saying that Lew had pushed her out on her own
while he left town that very night. The only reaction
from Marshall Thompsen was a sharp look that
glittered in his dark eyes.

"You never did say how old you were," he commented.

"Nineteen. I'll be twenty, in November."

"Okay, that's old enough to leave the nest. What
do you plan to do?"

"I thought," Dani took a deep breath, "I thought
I would go after my father. He shouldn't be alone
at a time like this."

"I think you're wrong," Thompsen said bluntly.
"He's convinced himself that he's a failure as a

father as well as a man. Your well-meaning pity would only make him feel worse."

"So you think I should do as he asked?" she said thoughtfully, appreciating the logic of his reasoning. "There's only one problem," she sighed, "What am I going to do? Lew made me promise I wouldn't have anything to do with horses, and that's all I know."

"Has anyone ever told you—Dani, isn't it?"

"Yes, short for Danielle."

"I like that name," Marshall Thompsen murmured. "It has class. Has anyone told you that you're photogenic?"

"What does that mean?" Again the wariness crept into her voice.

"It means you photograph well." He looked at her short hair. "Even with that chopped-off hair and those boys' clothes you wear, your face is very expressive in pictures. You could model. Ever thought about it?"

"Are you offering to make me one?" Dani asked, looking skeptically at the handsome man now.

"Oh, I have the right connections," he answered without the slightest hesitation. "I could set up a meeting—"

"And what kind of a meeting would that be? And when? Your apartment around midnight?" she demanded sarcastically.

"No." He chuckled softly.

"I'm not that naïve, you know."

"Danielle, an evening at my apartment wasn't what I had in mind, although I'm sure it'd be fun. No, I have an even better plan, one that Barrett King may not like, but I think you and I will."

"What is it?"

He glanced at his watch—his large, gold and expensive watch. "The nurse is on her way and your room is strictly off limits. I don't have time to explain it now. You'll be released in the morning, right?"

"Yes." Dani nodded, puzzled by his conspiratorial air and curious about what he had in mind.

"You have my card. Call me tomorrow after you've left the hospital and we'll get together to discuss it." White teeth flashed when he smiled. "At a restaurant. In public," he added with a wink as he started toward the door. "It would be better if you didn't mention my visit to Barrett when you see him."

"I won't be seeing him, so he won't find out," Dani replied crossly.

"Don't you know?" The dark brow arched again in a mocking movement. "This is an exclusive private hospital and Mr. King is picking up the tab for your stay. You can be sure he'll be in to see you before you're released."

With that bombshell, Marshall Thompsen left the room. Dani fumed silently, wishing she had someone to vent her rage on, then settled back against the bed as she planned what she would say to Barrett King when she saw him. The money stashed beneath her pillow reassured her that she wasn't a charity case and she intended to inform Mr. King of that fact.

"Well, you've finally woken up. How are you feeling?" A white-uniformed nurse walked briskly into the room, a smile fixed on her round face.

After her initial start of surprise, Dani recovered and answered calmly, "I'm fine, thank you."

Silently she endured having her temperature, pulse and blood pressure taken. The nurse worked with businesslike efficiency, for which Dani was grateful.

"You slept through lunch and dinner," the nurse said after she had entered the results on Dani's chart. "Would you like some sandwiches and milk?"

Sandwiches and milk. Dani couldn't hide the wry smile that tugged at the corners of her mouth. Why not milk and cookies? The nurse seemed to think that she was speaking to a child. But the suggestion made her realize there was an empty gnawing in her stomach.

"Okay. I'm hungry," she admitted.

"I'll be right back with a tray." The nurse smiled, and returned a few minutes later. Before she left again, she showed Dani how to operate the buzzer at her bedside and added, "If you have trouble getting to sleep, the doctor authorized us to administer a sleeping pill. I'll come back later to pick up your tray."

Dani unwrapped the first sandwich and began eating hungrily, spreading out the newspaper to read the article beneath her pictures. The first few paragraphs referred only briefly to The Rogue's previous winning record and the muscle injury that had kept him out of the bigger races.

The sandwich became tasteless as she read Manny's account of this morning's workout. He made it clear that the track had been in excellent condition and The Rogue had shown no effects of his previous injury. His best guess: a freak misstep by the thoroughbred. Her throat tightened at the jockey's glowing words of praise when he described the supreme effort The Rogue made to keep from falling. Yet Dani knew that the very fact that The Rogue hadn't gone down had contributed to the irreparable damage done to his ankle.

There was a synopsis of her father's career in racing, including his stint as a jockey before his forced retirement. The track people interviewed said Dani was an emotional and sensitive young girl and blamed that for her blow-up at Barrett King when she'd learned that The Rogue had to be destroyed.

Lew Williams had refused to comment on the reporter's questions, a fact duly noted in the article. But there were quotes from Barrett King, and Dani read them with a grim sort of eagerness.

Asked for the truth behind her accusations, Barrett had admitted that he'd tried to buy the colt as a yearling because he thought it had potential. He'd added that Dani said The Rogue wasn't for sale, and her father had told him the same thing. She read the next quote with mixed feelings. ''I don't know exactly why she lashed out at me today. She was in shock—I wouldn't hold her responsible for her actions.''

He'd added a few comments on The Rogue's ability. ''My horse, Easy Doesit, faced some pretty stiff competition this year and came out on top most of the time. Today The Rogue crossed the finish line six lengths ahead, still pulling away easily. He might have been the horse of the decade, but that's something we'll never know.''

The article concluded with the bitter reminder that The Rogue had been injured during a workout and was destroyed without ever reaching his prime.

Dani gulped down her milk, trying to swallow the lump in her throat at the same time. She shifted her gaze to the photographs again, studying them a little longer this time as she tried to gauge Barrett King's reaction by his expression.

In the first picture, the strong line of his jaw seemed clenched. There was an arrogant tilt of his head and the look in his eyes was indecipherable, but his arms were at his side as he allowed himself to be subjected to her pummeling.

In the second, he was carrying her in his arms, effortlessly striding toward the camera. This time there was no mistaking the grim expression on his face—whether from concern or anger, Dani had no way of telling. In that picture she did look awfully young, passed out in his arms, her head resting against his chest.

The memory of the warmth and the strength she'd felt in those arms just before she'd lost consciousness came rushing back, an embrace that had seemed to absorb some of her anguish. The low voice that had urged her to cry held so much comfort.

Comfort? She nearly laughed aloud. What a strange word to associate with an overbearing guy like Barrett King. She couldn't possibly be comfortable in his arms, unless she was unconscious.

She thrust the newspaper angrily away, refusing to think about him anymore.

CHAPTER THREE

After breakfast the next morning, Dani scrambled into her boots, faded jeans, and a shapeless blouse that pretty much hid her slender, feminine figure. At the sound of firm footsteps in the hallway outside her door, she remembered Marshall Thompsen's warning that she would see Barrett King before she left the hospital. When his voice greeted her from the doorway, her face didn't register any surprise.

"Good morning," she replied crisply, throwing him a defiant look before reaching in her back pocket for the comb she always kept there. The hairs along the back of her neck were tingling.

"Feeling better?"

Dani refused to let the warmth in his voice charm her as it did so many others. She could see through him.

"Oh, recovered, I guess," she answered.

To her relief, a young nurse walked into the room—and instantly apologized to Barrett for the interruption. When she glanced at Dani, it was almost an afterthought.

"We need some additional information, Ms. Williams, that we weren't able to obtain when you were admitted yesterday," the nurse explained. "Just for our records, in case you have to come here again."

The last was obviously meant as a small joke, since the nurse laughed after she said it. But Dani didn't smile as she glanced at Barrett, wishing he would leave and knowing he wouldn't.

"What do you need to know?" she asked instead, her mouth tightening as she watched Barrett walk to the window.

The nurse asked routine questions about her date of birth, childhood diseases, permanent residence—she wrote down "none," along with the other answers on a notepad. Dani couldn't help noticing the way the young woman's gaze continued to stray to Barrett. Only once did she herself look to see if he was watching them, but he was still staring out of the window, the sunlight streaming in to accent the coppery shade of his thick hair. It irritated her how easily he could dominate a room.

The nurse smiled. "That's everything. The doctor will be here in an hour to sign your release."

Dani knew the smile was really meant for Barrett, and she pitied the nurse for being taken in by his striking looks and not seeing the ruthlessness in those green eyes.

"Why did you lie, Dani?" Barrett demanded as he turned a disapproving look on her.

There was a flash of anger in her eyes. "I didn't lie! You wanted The Rogue for yourself!"

"I'm not talking about that." The edge was out of his tone, but the underlying hardness was still there. "I mean just now. I know it must seem like an incredibly long time before you're an adult, but lying about your age won't get you there any faster."

"I wasn't lying. I am nineteen and I'll be twenty in November! Sorry I can't produce a birth certificate on the spur of the moment to prove it," she retorted sarcastically.

There was something unnervingly insolent about the way his level gaze swept her from head to toe. It was all she could do not to reach out for the pitcher of water and throw it at him.

"You don't look a day over fifteen," he murmured.

"Spare me the sweet-sixteen-and-never-been-kissed remarks," she snapped. "I am not sixteen and believe me, I've been kissed."

"Not very thoroughly." There were wicked devils of laughter dancing in his eyes.

Her hands moved defiantly to her hips, reminding her at the same moment that her pocket was full of money—the money her father had given her. Marshall Thompsen's statement that Barrett intended to pay for her hospital stay came into her mind. But before she could mention it, and her intention to cover her own medical bills, he spoke again.

"Have you seen your father?"

"Why?" she asked suspiciously.

"I stopped at the track to talk to him this morning and discovered he was gone. Seems he left last night. Do you know anything about it?''

"Yes," Dani answered simply.

A muscle jumped along his jawline and Dani knew her lack of further explanation angered him. She had to admire the self-control that kept his temper in check.

"Will he be here this morning when you're released?" he asked with marked patience.

"No."

"Instead of playing Twenty Questions, why don't you explain the situation?" His penetrating gaze was difficult to meet.

"Is that what we're playing?" she asked innocently. "I'm never sure what your game is." She knew the snide comment didn't go unnoticed as she hurried on. "It's simple enough—my father left town last night. He left me enough money to cover the hospital bill." She pulled off several hundreds from the roll in her pocket and waved them in the air.

"That's already taken care of." Barrett spoke with ominous quietness.

"We don't need your charity—or is it really a twinge of guilty conscience?" she asked softly.

He took two quick strides forward, suddenly looming over her. "It was a gesture of sympathy on my part. I don't feel guilty about what happened to your horse. You know it wasn't my fault."

Dani had the honesty to redden at his reference to her accusation the day before. "No, I know it wasn't," she said, hating to admit that he was right about anything. "Guess I should apologize for the things I said."

His anger vanished. "Don't apologize if you don't mean it."

"Well, I do," Dani asserted, her chin lifting rebelliously. "Even though I don't want to."

"I accept your backhanded apology," Barrett smiled.

His head moved in a mocking nod and she was forcibly reminded of his magnetism. Barrett King was a potent combination of looks, wealth, and charm. Dani turned away, silently grateful that she was immune to such things. She fought the slight breathlessness she felt under his gaze.

"Are you planning to meet up with your father immediately?" he asked quietly.

"Why?" Her question was wary.

"Might be best if you waited a couple of days before you travel." Indifference lined his voice.

"There's nothing wrong with me. I only fainted," she reminded him.

She had no intention of telling Barrett that she had no plans to join her father, nor was she going to mention Marshall Thompsen, mostly because it was none of Barrett's business. However, she realized that as long as Barrett was asking questions, the chances of her accidently revealing her plans increased.

"Why are you here?" she demanded with a suddenness that was supposed to catch him off guard.

"To help," he answered without any hesitation.

"What do I need your help for?" She did her best to ignore the feeling that he was winning their imaginary battle.

"For starters, there are a couple of reporters waiting downstairs—"

"And you're afraid I'll say worse things about you, I suppose," Dani said.

"You can say anything you like," Barrett said quietly. "I thought that since your father was avoiding them, you would, too."

"My father wasn't avoiding reporters," she said angrily. He gave her a sharply questioning look. "And I can deal with a few nosy men without any assistance from you, so you can leave whenever you want. The sooner the better as far as I'm concerned."

"Okay," was his clipped reply as he turned away and started for the open door.

"And, Mr. King"—her eyes glittered with defiant triumph as his head turned in answer to his name—"I'm paying for my stay here. You can cancel whatever arrangements you've made."

There was a grim set to his mouth as he surveyed her with unnerving thoroughness. Her heartbeat quickened.

"I'm sure you've seen an unruly horse saddled and bridled," Barrett replied. "I wonder how it would work with a headstrong brat like you."

While she gasped in outraged anger, Barrett King walked calmly from the room. Seething with fury, she stalked about the room, muttering a few curses and kicking at the chair and bed, suffering the consequences of a stubbed toe. When the doctor arrived to release her formally, she barely spoke to him.

At the payment office on the first floor, Dani drew herself up to her full height of five foot four inches and demanded her bill, fully prepared to argue. But the elderly clerk produced it without comment, taking most of the wind from Dani's sails. Tucking the receipt in her pocket with the rest of the money her father had given her, Dani entered the hospital lobby.

All hope that she could slip past the reporters unnoticed fled when she saw them waiting. She didn't exactly look her best in her faded blue jeans, boots, and disreputable blouse. Everyone's attention focused on her immediately. Squaring her shoulders, Dani started to walk across the tiled floor, but three men and a photographer surrounded her, bombarding her with questions and denying her a clear path to the door.

"Could you tell us where your father is, Dani?"

"What's your reaction to what Barrett King said about The Rogue? Do you agree with him?"

"What are your plans now, Dani?"

"Hey, look this way!"

Her hand shielded her eyes from the flashbulbs. "Please let me through." She was forced to raise her voice to make herself heard over their barrage of questions. "No comment!"

Her requests were ignored and she looked around wildly for some other means of escape, but the men had her blocked at every turn. Over the shoulder of one man, Dani saw Barrett King leaning against a far wall, obviously amused at her predicament. For a split second, she silently begged him for his help before she turned determinedly away.

"Let me through," she repeated in a desperate tone as she tried to push her way around one of the men, who only took a step backward without giving her an opening.

In the next second, Dani felt a firm hand grip her elbow.

"Come on, guys, give her a break," Barrett said. "She was just released from the hospital. Back off."

"We only want to ask her a few questions, Barrett," one of the reporters said in a wheedling tone.

"Do you want to answer them?"

From the direction of his voice, Dani knew Barrett had bent his head toward her. "I just want to get out of here," she muttered into his shirt front.

"You heard the lady, Fred," Barrett said lightly, his arm moving around her shoulders as the reporters stepped aside, grumbling a little but well aware of the steel in his voice.

Dani wanted to run out the front door, but Barrett's arm around her shoulders kept her firmly at his side as they walked unhurriedly across the lobby and through the doors. Once outside, she turned to thank him for his help even though she resented the need to do so. But he guided her down the steps in the general direction of the parking lot.

"I can make it on my own now, thank you," she said, shrugging free. "I don't need your help anymore."

His fingers slipped to her wrist, holding her when she wanted to walk away. His superior strength forced her to stay.

"In two minutes those reporters will find you again." His mouth curved in a humorless smile as he studied the mutinous expression on her face. "I know it rankles you, but if you want to avoid them, you'll have to accept a ride from me."

She glared at him, angry that she hadn't been able to get away from the reporters without his help. And he knew it. He was much too sure of himself.

"Where's your car?" Dani snapped, feeling small and silly.

He gestured toward a new sportscar parked next to the curb, sleek and low to the ground, and Dani knew she would be forced to sit disgustingly close to this arrogant man. His attitude, as he ceremoniously opened the car door for her, was gentlemanly, a jibe at her own lack of manners. She hugged the door as tightly as possible while he walked around to the other side.

"Where do you want to go?" he asked, giving her an amused glance as he started the car and put it in gear.

The muscles in her body tensed as she tried to think of a destination. Asking him to leave her at a bus stop would only make him curious about her reluctance to tell him where she wanted to go. And so would hesitating too long before answering him. So she told him the name of a small café near the racetrack.

"Don't you want to go to your hotel?" he asked.

"Not right away." Dani kept her gaze firmly fixed on the road ahead. "I . . . I planned to meet a friend at the café."

Under the cover of one hand, she crossed her fingers. It was close to the truth, since she intended to phone Marshall Thompsen to arrange a meeting with him. She sensed that Barrett didn't really believe her and expected him to ask more questions. Ready to put him firmly in his place if he did, Dani was surprised when he fell into a thoughtful silence that lasted the short distance from the hospital to the café.

When he pulled up to the curb, her hand automatically reached for the handle of the door, anxious to be away. But his quiet voice stopped her.

"I'm sorry about The Rogue. I hope you believe me," Barrett said.

She glanced over her shoulder at his face, openly doubting the sincerity of his comment. Why did he have to be handsome and powerful, reckless and ruthless—and compelling?

"I don't need your pity," she retorted, refusing his sympathy.

Fire flashed momentarily in his expression, then Barrett shrugged, reaching into his pocket for a piece of paper and pen. Suspiciously Dani watched him write on the paper and hand it to her.

"This is the phone number at my apartment," he said.

Dani stared at it, making no move to take it. "Why would I want that?"

"If you need me in the next couple of days, feel free to call me," Barrett replied patiently.

"Well, I won't. I'm not a child. I can handle anything that comes along," she told him sharply.

"The way you handled the reporters?" he mocked softly.

"I know you think you rescued me, but I could've gotten away without your help," Dani snapped. "Thanks for the lift. My friend is waiting for me."

"Oh, I'd forgotten about your friend." Open doubt and amusement was written on his face.

Dani tossed a last glare at him before she shoved open the door and stepped onto the concrete sidewalk. As she slammed the door shut, she heard her name called. A triumphant smile lit her face as she saw Manny Herrera walking toward her. Good. Barrett King would assume she'd intended to meet Manny, and she purposely made small talk with the jockey while the sports car pulled away.

The instant Barrett drove out of sight, she excused herself and hurried into the café, going to the old-fashioned enclosed phone booth where she dialed the number Marshall Thompsen had given her.

Impulsive as she was, it never crossed Dani's mind to think twice before contacting him. Her father had pushed her out on her own, extracting a promise that she stay away from horse racing, which was the only life she knew. She'd never had any interests outside of horses. At this point she was open to any suggestion.

Marshall's hints about making her a model were intriguing, especially if there were no strings attached. He'd added that Barrett King might not like what he had in mind, which only added to her curiosity. Whether she was photogenic enough, tall enough, or thin enough to become a model, Dani had no way of knowing, but she had picked up the confidence in the columnist's tone. Besides, he looked like a man who knew what he was talking about and he had connections. Dani was confident that she would be able to tell if he was only trying to take advantage of her.

Half an hour after her call, Marshall Thompsen walked into the café, taking in the clean but uninspiring interior with disdain. As he slid into the booth seat opposite her, she began a discreet study of him.

Hanging around racetracks all her life had taught Dani to spot the difference between the professional gambler and the average Joe or Josephine, a wealthy person from a merely well-dressed person, a confidence man and an honest man. She was rarely ever wrong.

Marshall Thompsen was dark and handsome, that much she remembered from last night. Now she noticed the softness in his chin and jaw and the sulkiness of his mouth. Not altogether unattractive, yet he couldn't compare with the strength in the lines of Barrett King's face. Thompsen's even tan probably came from a sun bed, while she was positive Barrett's was the result of many hours spent outdoors. And there was no suggestion of muscular hardness beneath the well-tailored jacket.

In a thoroughbred, some of these faults would have revealed a lack of stamina and heart. With humans, Dani had learned to be more broadminded. So the faults she noted were balanced by the intelligence of the wide forehead and the sharply observant dark eyes. She tried to guess his age and decided Marshall must be a couple of years younger than Barrett King, which would put him in his late twenties or early thirties.

As the waitress placed a cup of coffee for Marshall on the table, Dani decided that she could trust him, as long as their relationship was based on business.

"I wondered if you would call me this morning." He glanced at her briefly as he stirred sugar into his coffee. "I was almost sure you would."

"I was curious about your proposal. You were a little vague," Dani said.

"I never reveal my cards all at once," Marshall smiled. "If you were the skittish type, frightened by your own shadow, you wouldn't have been any use to me and you wouldn't have phoned me. So now I know—if you agree to my offer, you'll carry it out."

"Exactly what is your offer?" She forced him to meet her gaze. "You said last night you could make me a model. How would you go about doing that?"

"First, I'd take you to a hairstylist and fix that crew cut of yours, then get you some better clothes. There's a professional photographer who owes me a favor. But I can't promise to make you a top model on my own. Being photogenic doesn't open the door to success. And Louisville, Kentucky, isn't the fashion capital of the world."

"However?" Dani prompted, knowing there was something more behind his offer.

His smile broadened at her wariness. "Well, I'm a well-known columnist. I could make you a minor celebrity, especially since you've already made the papers."

Dani clasped her hands around the coffee cup in front of her, her nails short but curved and rounded. Her hands were slightly callused from grooming and saddling horses, carrying water buckets and hay, and mucking out stalls. The idea that she could ever become a glamorous model was almost funny. There was a wry twist to her mouth as she thought of what she really needed: a fairy godmother with a magic wand.

An inner voice questioned her unspoken

agreement to his proposal. But there were two things that provided a formidable argument—her own discovery last night that beneath her ill-fitting clothes was a great figure and her father's statement that she looked more like a boy than a woman. If there were only the slimmest chance that she could succeed, Dani knew she had to take it. Not for the money or the possible success as a model, but to prove her father wrong.

Yet her impulsiveness was now tempered with caution. There were a few more things she wanted to find out.

"Okay, I get new clothes, a new hairstyle and makeup, and your photographer friend agrees that I have potential, then what?" Dani challenged.

"I get you into A-list parties attended by the right people. Kentucky is full of zillionaires. Who knows? You may be able to bag yourself a rich husband," Marshall shrugged. "It's really up to you."

"I'm not interested in men."

"Men will be interested in you," he said dryly.

But Dani had already dismissed the idea. "What are you going to get out of all of this? What's in it for you?"

"Didn't your dad ever teach you not to look a gift horse in the mouth?" he mocked.

"You didn't answer my question," she countered.

"Would you believe me if I said it was merely an act of kindness?" Marshall asked lightly.

"No." There was a suggestion of a smile in the upturned corners of her mouth.

"I thought not," he murmured with a soft

chuckle. "You and I are going to get along well. Your honesty is refreshing."

"Which still doesn't answer my question."

"No, it doesn't." There was a significant pause as Marshall hesitated. "Perhaps some people need to find out that things are not always what they seem."

"Would one of those people be Barrett King?" Dani suggested.

"Maybe." Marshall smiled and pushed his cup away from him. "Well, what do you say? Ready to give it a try?"

"Yes," she said firmly without any qualifications or explanations.

"Then let's get started."

CHAPTER FOUR

Half an hour later, Marshall parked his car in front of an elegant one-story building bearing the name "Giorgio's." Nothing on the outside indicated the type of business within, but it looked expensive somehow.

As Marshall escorted her inside, she knew her guess was correct. There was an imported crystal chandelier in the waiting area and a pastel blue carpet with dainty antique chairs in matching blue velvet. But it took her several seconds to realize that she was in a beauty salon. The beautiful woman who came to greet them glanced rather contemptuously at Dani and looked quizzically at the darkly handsome man accompanying her, obviously doubting that they had come to the right place.

"I'm Marshall Thompsen. Giorgio's expecting me," Marshall said.

The name Giorgio worked its magic and the woman immediately smiled. "Of course, Mr. Thompsen, this way, please."

She led them down a carpeted hallway, rapped lightly on a door, and opened it only after a voice inside replied. Announcing that Mr. Thompsen was here, the woman smiled again at Marshall and started back to the reception area. A hand on her elbow firmly pushed Dani inside the room.

"Hello, George," Marshall greeted the man who turned at their entrance.

Giorgio, or George as Marshall had called him, was a small man with dark hair winged with silver-gray. His bright, dark eyes appraised Dani in an instant.

"Marshall, you said you were bringing me a challenge, not an impossibility. Is this a boy or a girl?"

"Allow me to present Danielle Williams. Danielle, this is Giorgio Caprio, a close friend of mine and a master stylist." The introduction was made with exaggerated formality.

But before Dani could reply, Giorgio nodded and said, "Of course, it is a girl. The boys wear their hair much longer, unless they shave it off or spike it up with gel."

Without wasting any more time with chitchat, Giorgio took her hand and led her to a large chair in front of a lighted mirror and a counter crowded with bottles and hair rollers. He ran his fingers experimentally through her short brown hair, checking its length and fullness.

"What crime did you commit, Ms. Williams," he demanded, "to prompt someone to chop your hair in such a barbarous fashion?"

Under his critical eye, Dani felt ashamed of her appearance, something that had never concerned her in the past. A pale pink blush colored her cheeks.

"I did it myself," she admitted in a low voice. "It was easy to take care of this way."

She wished Giorgio wouldn't just stare at her with silent disapproval. Through his eyes, she could see how unflattering the side part was, not to mention the way she had combed her hair carelessly behind her ears. It took all her willpower not to sink into the cushions of the blue chair.

"Okay, work your magic," Marshall said. "I'll see about some clothes."

"Earth tones and simple lines. No ruffles or frills," Giorgio stated firmly. "No grunge. No retro hippie stuff. No Goth."

The look the stylist shot Marshall plainly said he was in charge of the makeover. Dani swallowed nervously as the door closed behind the other man. As Giorgio brushed, combed, and arranged her hair in various ways, she kept quiet until she saw the scissors in his hand.

"Are you going to cut it?" she protested, surprised. Then, in a quieter tone in case he thought she was trying to tell him what to do, "You did say it was too short already."

"It is too short," he admitted even as the scissors snipped around the back of her head. "But it needs shaping. Since I cannot make your hair longer, I must do what I can with the little you have. Is that all right?" The last was added with deliberate sarcasm.

Firmly reminded that he was the expert, Dani fell silent, observing his every move when she could.

After her hair had been shaped and shampooed, the short strands were somehow twisted on tiny rollers. Then she was placed beneath a dryer where a manicurist appeared and began repairing the years of neglect to her nails and hands. When the last application of nail polish was applied and had dried, the hair dryer also stopped.

Instead of leading her to the chair and having the rollers removed, Giorgio took her to another, smaller chair with a lighted mirror, where he gave a stern lecture on the care of her skin. Cleansing creams, astringents, moisturizers, makeup bases, blushers, eyeshadow, eyeliner, mascara, eyebrow pencils—she was instructed in the use of them all. Then he demonstrated how to use them, cautioning against a heavy hand.

"Wearing too much makeup is a greater crime than wearing too little," he reminded her impatiently for the fourth time as he made her dab away most of the shadow on her eyelids.

Finally he was satisfied with her efforts, but he refused to let her dawdle in front of the mirror, staring at the surprisingly attractive face that looked back. She was taken back to the first chair where the rollers were removed and a stiff brush raked through the short curls, almost flattening them completely.

The chair Dani sat in was turned away from the mirror so she couldn't see the results of his work as Giorgio combed, fluffed, and flattened. Before he was finished, Marshall walked into the room, his dark eyes lighting with pleasure when he looked at her. Whatever fear she felt vanished at his reassuring admiration.

When the stylist was finally done, he started to turn Dani around, but Marshall's upraised hand stopped him.

"Not yet, George. When Danielle sees herself, I want the transformation to be complete." The barely noticed packages he'd piled in another chair were picked up and handed to Dani. "Change into these and promise not to look in the mirror until you're dressed," he ordered.

Excitement tightened her stomach as she promised, her eyes glittering at the pleased expression on both men's faces when they left the room. Before she could give in to the almost overwhelming curiosity to see herself, Dani burrowed through the bags and boxes.

He'd brought everything from silk underwear to new shoes, but the sexy little suit in a shimmering material was the thing that really caught her eye. With fumbling fingers, she stripped free of the suddenly distasteful jeans and blouse and slipped eagerly into the new clothes.

When she was finally dressed, Dani was torn by uncertainty, afraid that she might be disappointed by what she saw. So instead she flung open the door and stepped into the hall. Marshall and Giorgio were a few feet away, deep in conversation, but turned together when she appeared.

"Fantastic!" Marshall breathed.

"Do I look all right?" Dani pleaded, feminine enough to need more than one word of reassurance.

"Do you mean you haven't looked?" The sternness left Giorgio's face as he smiled.

"No, I thought . . . maybe . . . ."

"Go," the stylist prodded gently, turning her around and pushing her into the room. "See for yourself."

With a mixture of awe and disbelief, Dani looked at the new woman in the mirror. Feather-soft waves of rich brown hair curled about her forehead and ears, accenting the perfect oval of her face and the strong cheekbones. The clinging material of the fitted jacket set off her slenderness, making the most of the gentle swell of her breasts and her narrow waist, while the color, like ripened wheat, brought out the sensual darkness of her hair and eyes.

Dani frowned. "It doesn't really seem like me."

"Get used to that image," Marshall chided, "because the old one is gone for good. You'll never be able to go back to your old ways without seeing yourself as you are today." To Giorgio, he said, "Throw her old clothes in the trash. She doesn't need them anymore."

"No," Dani protested as she stepped quickly toward the small pile of clothes, knowing the money was still in the pockets of her jeans. "I . . . I want to keep them!"

"Why?" Marshall asked sharply. "Nothing but rags when it comes right down to it."

"I still want to keep them," she asserted, prepared to do battle if it came to that.

"Let her," Giorgio said gently. "They'll remind her of what she used to look like."

Dani glared at him, and then at Marshall.

"Okay," Marshall gave in ungraciously. "Stuff them in one of those bags and take them out to the car. I'll be right out."

Dani did as she was told before Marshall changed his mind and hurried to the car, missing the startled glance of the receptionist. Marshall had a satisfied smile on his face when he slid behind the wheel a few minutes later.

"I knew I was right about your potential," he commented as he pulled the car out onto the street. "But I didn't expect you to look this good. I'm going to have to revise the schedule."

"The schedule? For what?" Dani asked.

"For your unveiling," Marshall replied complacently. "Which reminds me, I made another appointment for you with George this Saturday morning."

"So soon?"

"Yes, so soon," he chuckled.

Dani leaned back into the comfortable bucket seat, realizing just how much work it took to look this good.

"Tell me, Marshall, how did you become friends with a guy like Giorgio? I mean . . . he doesn't seem like the type you'd associate with." She was well aware that Marshall was a bit of a snob.

"Dani," he laughed, "more secrets are revealed in a beauty salon than any where else. George passes a lot of fascinating information on to me. In return, I occasionally mention his salon in my column. In other words, he scratches my back and I scratch his. The same goes for the boutique where I got that outfit and all the other clothes I had sent to your apartment."

"You mean you didn't pay for this?" Dani gasped, fingering the lapel of the jacket in surprise.

"In this case, because you needed so much, there was money involved, but I didn't pay full price. Not even close," he admitted. "Danielle, you're going to be billing a thousand an hour when you start. Then I'll present an itemized account of the money I've invested in you."

"You said something about my apartment?"

"Well, you need a place to stay. There was a vacancy in the complex where I live, so I rented it." He winked. "Your apartment isn't next to mine, don't worry."

"Will you be doing the landlord a favor, too?" Dani said cynically.

"Unfortunately not. This place is very exclusive. The management doesn't like publicity," Marshall sighed with mock regret.

"What happens if none of this turns out the way you planned? You're putting a lot of time and effort and money into this with no guarantee that I'll be able to pay you back," she asked.

"You aren't very trusting," he teased.

"I grew up around racetracks. Not everyone has a heart of gold." Her mind instantly thought of Barrett King, a man she wouldn't trust any further than she could throw him.

"Hey, my plan will work. But if it fails, I'll chalk it up to bad judgment on my part and cut my losses. I promise, Danielle," he said with obvious laughter in his voice, "I won't sell you to the highest bidder to recover my investment. I told you there would be no strings attached. The gamble is mine and the loss will be mine, if there is any. Does that satisfy you?"

"Yes," Dani nodded, adding with an impish twinkle, "so long as you're stuck with the bills if your plan does fail."

"Great minds think alike." Marshall smiled. "Where to now?"

Dani was eager to begin her new life, despite the nagging thought that things would have been quite different if The Rogue were still alive. She refused to admit that she would miss the bustling routine and comaraderie around the stables. This was her father's wish and she couldn't let him down.

"The photographer's," Marshall answered, "then somewhere for lunch."

During the next few days, Dani was swept up in a whirlwind of constant activity. It made the loss of The Rogue easier to bear and the strangeness of being away from her father a little less overwhelming. Still there were times when she wanted to see a familiar face, even Barrett King's, that would link her new life with the old.

Every minute of her day was organized. Marshall took her to art galleries, sessions with the photographer, aerobics and yoga to improve her already supple body, and even taught her about wine and haute cuisine to enable her to choose intelligently from the menus of the finest restaurants.

Even her so-called free time was controlled. Marshall was determined to teach her an appreciation for music and books that he deemed important.

Most nights, Dani tumbled into her luxurious bed exhausted, too weary to think about the abrupt about-face her life had taken. But she couldn't break the habit of rising with the sun. Every morning she wished for the sweet smell of hay and the impatient whickering of horses waiting for their grain. She had spent many contented hours rhythmically running a currycomb over sleek, shining coats. Yet through all her wistfulness over those uncomplicated days ran the painful memory of her last morning at the track and the fateful breakdown of The Rogue on the home stretch.

Before the anguish of that moment overwhelmed her, Dani would recall her father's last visit and the real reason why she was here in this empty apartment. And whatever plans Marshall had made for each day, she threw herself into them, driven to succeed—and to please her father.

As she got out of the taxi bringing her back from Giorgio's, Dani saw Marshall's car parked in front of her building. With a sigh of regret for the loss of a precious free hour, she hurried inside to where Marshall stood impatiently waiting.

"You're early," she said, leading the way to her apartment and unlocking the door. "Where are we off to this time?"

"Absolutely nowhere," he replied, as he followed her into the apartment.

Darting him a disbelieving look, Dani wondered if she was in for another session of self-improvement. She sincerely hoped not, because she simply didn't feel up to it.

"I stopped by to tell you that John was called out of town this morning and your afternoon session with him was canceled." John Henning was the photographer, a real pro, and not easily impressed. He didn't seem to be as confident as Marshall that Dani could have a career as a model, although he was willing to do her portfolio shots and never seemed displeased with the results. "And"—Marshall went on, the pause attaching importance to his next words—"to help you pick out what you're going to wear to your unveiling tonight."

"Unveiling?" Dani stopped in the center of the living room and gave him her complete attention. "How dramatic."

"Yes, I took the liberty of accepting an invitation on your behalf. Just an informal party, but it's being given by *the* Whitney Blakes."

"This is it, then," she murmured. "The first real test."

He must have caught the nervousness in her voice because his big smile was obviously meant to instill confidence. "Don't worry. You'll come through with flying colors."

As Dani finished dressing that evening and fussed with the long folds of her skirt, she couldn't convince herself it would be as easy as Marshall seemed to think. The full extent of her inexperience had been drummed into her head this last week.

Fingering the large topaz pendant that matched her earrings, she scrutinized her appearance. The sophisticated young woman in the mirror was still a stranger to Dani, but she had to admit she was practically perfect—except for the apprehension in her hazel eyes.

Marshall arrived promptly at seven. His talent for idle conversation helped her forget the upcoming party during their dinner at a local restaurant. Not until they were nearly at their destination did he mention it.

"Are you nervous?" he asked gently.

"A little," Dani admitted, breathing in deeply, grateful that he was looking at the road and couldn't see the tightness of her smile.

"You'll do fine," Marshall assured her. "There are only a few things for you to remember. Don't try to show off. If you don't know what someone's talking about, admit it. However, if someone asks your opinion about something you do know, give it. Just be your charming self and don't worry. Pretty women get photographed, but interesting women get quoted."

"I hope I don't let you down," she murmured, her eyes widening as Marshall turned into the long driveway leading to an elegant white mansion.

"You won't let me down because you won't let yourself down," he answered shrewdly, slowing the car to a stop near the entrance as a uniformed attendant sprang forward to open the doors.

They circulated for over an hour, hearing conversations that ranged from gossip to horse racing to politics. Sometimes they paused to chat since Marshall was instantly recognized and included. But he took care to draw Dani into the conversation, bolstering her confidence until she finally relaxed.

A lively debate was going on in a mixed group not far away and Marshall steered her to them. They stood on the fringe for a few minutes, until Dani figured out that they were discussing the merits of a certain book.

"Marshall, you're just the man to settle this," one of the men declared as he tapped him on the shoulder.

"Settle what?" Marshall asked dryly, tucking his hand securely under Dani's elbow so that she came with him as he was drawn into the group.

"What's your opinion of Michael Crichton's latest thriller? I just loved it. Don't you think he's a genius?" asked a woman who'd clearly had too much to drink.

"I really couldn't say." Marshall glanced speculatively at Dani. "But you were reading it the other day, Danielle. What do you think?"

She smothered a smile. He knew very well she'd hated it. It was one of the best-sellers he'd insisted she read, if only to have something to talk about.

"Well, I tried to read it," she said calmly, addressing her reply to the woman, determined to follow Marshall's advice to answer honestly. "But I spent half the night with the dictionary on my lap looking up scientific words. I finally ended up reading the dictionary. It was much more interesting."

A moment of silence followed her words and Dani began to think she had said something unforgivably stupid. Then the man who had drawn Marshall into the conversation began to laugh.

Then he turned to the woman, who scowled unattractively. "If you ask for an opinion, Katherine, you'd better be prepared for a real answer. Marshall, I insist that you introduce me to this gorgeous girl. She's a breath of fresh air."

Marshall did the honors and included the others in the small group, but in the wave of names, Dani only recalled those of Katherine Alberts, who smiled grudgingly after the man called Dru Carmichael nudged her on the sly.

There was a brief but good-natured discussion of Crichton before Dru turned to Dani, a bright twinkle in his blue eyes.

"Did you read that book about Seabiscuit?" he asked. "It was a best-seller about a year ago, especially in Kentucky. *An American Legend,* I believe it was called."

"Yes," she said without thinking. "A lot of people around the racetrack were reading it . . ." She trailed off, casting a worried look at Marshall.

Katherine Alberts made a whinnying noise and finished her vodka. "Dru, get me another Stoli."

But Dru Carmichael ignored her. "The racetrack? Is that where I've seen you before? You do look familiar."

"There was a write-up in the newspaper about Danielle recently," Marshall replied with deliberate casualness. "And her horse, The Rogue."

"With Barrett, of course!" The man snapped his fingers as if switching on a light in his mind. "You're the girl who collapsed in his arms. I stand corrected—young woman. Although you certainly didn't look it in those newspaper photographs."

"Yes, Ms. Williams is something of a mystery." The low, deep voice prickled the hairs on the back of Dani's neck. She turned with a start, and looked up into Barrett King's eyes, her heart racing.

"Barrett, what a surprise," Marshall said. But Dani had the distinct impression he wasn't surprised at all. In fact she was convinced he'd expected Barrett. "Sherry told me yesterday you were going to be spending the weekend at the farm."

"Really?" Barrett's dry voice and the crooked smile he gave Dani didn't hide the coldness in his green eyes. "Well, I'm surprised to find you here, Dani."

"Should I apologize?" she retorted, tossing a resentful look at Marshall.

"What for?" Barrett asked. "I was curious about where you'd disappeared to."

"I really don't know why you should be." Dani stiffened instinctively, knowing how she had deliberately deceived him. "It's none of your business where I go or what I do."

"Okay," Marshall raised his hands, palms out. "This is a social gathering. No scenes, please."

"Of course not," Barrett said blandly, looking indifferently at the man standing beside Dani, not missing the slightly possessive hold Marshall had on her arm. "In fact, I was about to ask Dani to dance with me."

His statement caught Dani off guard, and Marshall as well. She glanced at him quickly, almost beseeching him to interfere as she watched the hesitation in the dark eyes.

"Come now, Marshall," Barrett said sardonically at the continued silence. "Can't you see tomorrow's paper? *Dueling Duo Dancing Cheek to Cheek.* But maybe you're trying to protect Dani because you think she's afraid of me. You're not, are you, Dani?"

"Of course not!" she answered sharply, and immediately knew he'd backed her and Marshall into a corner.

"Then let's dance," Barrett said.

The look that Marshall gave her indicated that she had no choice but to agree. Reluctantly, Dani placed her hand in Barrett's, fighting the desire to pull away.

CHAPTER FIVE

"I don't want to dance with you, you know," Dani muttered as Barrett moved her away.

"I never would have guessed by your enthusiastic response." He had the nerve to smile as he guided her to the room where the music was playing.

"If you knew I didn't want to, then why did you ask?"

"All the usual reasons a man asks a beautiful woman to dance." The crooked smile deepened the lines around his mouth as the devils in his green eyes mocked her.

She couldn't think of a thing to say to that, so she clamped her mouth tightly shut.

The impromptu dancing area consisted of a space cleared of chairs and tables with the music furnished by an elaborate, club-style sound system. A heavy beat was coming from the speakers. Dani halted at the edge, forcing Barrett to do likewise as she stared at the hip-hop gyrations of the dancers, a younger group than Marshall had introduced her to so far.

"Something wrong?" Barrett asked lightly.

"Yes," she hissed, and his head had to bend to catch her words. "I don't know how to dance that way."

"That's a relief, because neither do I." That silent laughter was back in his gaze, but Dani had to admit it was more at the situation than at her.

She refused to be mollified. "Since we aren't going to dance, you can take me back to Marshall."

"Oh, but we *are* going to dance," he assured her softly.

Her hand was still firmly clasped in his as he led her away from the dance area. The house was large and guests seemed to be scattered all through it, clustering here and there in talkative groups. His long stride never slackened, maintaining a momentum that drew her along while he moved through the house.

"Where are we going?" she demanded, but he didn't answer.

As they turned down a corridor, the other guests were left behind. Dani didn't have to be told that they had entered a private wing of the large home. Its emptiness was explanation enough.

"We shouldn't be here," she protested as Barrett opened a door and pulled her somewhat unwillingly into the room. "I'm sure we aren't supposed to be in this part of the house."

"The Blakes are my godparents. They won't

mind," Barrett shrugged, closing the door behind them and releasing Dani's hand for the first time.

Rich mahogany paneling gleamed on all sides except for one wall of library shelves filled with books. The homey atmosphere of the study appealed to Dani, with its leather-covered furniture and polished wood. She barely noticed Barrett walk away until soft music filled the room. Then she saw the sound system and looked uncomfortably to the tall figure making his way back across the room toward her.

"I've changed my mind," she said through the tight lump in her throat. "I don't want to dance."

"But I do." Already he was standing in front of her.

"You can't make me," Dani asserted, cocking her head at a defiant angle.

"Oh?" Barrett replied quietly—too quietly.

His level gaze was daring her to challenge him. She was instantly reminded of the newspaper photograph of him carrying her so effortlessly in his arms and knew his muscular strength was infinitely superior to hers. And she knew she was irresistibly attracted to it.

With an exaggerated show of reluctance, she placed her hand in his and allowed him to put his arm around her waist, staring at the buttons on his shirt rather than at the triumphant gleam in his eyes.

For several minutes she stayed stiffly unyielding in his arms until the soothing music began to ease her tension. Close to the hard chest she had hammered on, it wasn't the anger that she remembered. It was the comfort and warm support that had closed around her when a pair of arms had drawn her against that chest. Gradually, without conscious thought, Dani allowed herself a moment of sweet surrender.

As the last notes of the song faded away, a reluctant sigh slipped from her throat. She drew her arm down to press a hand against his chest and push herself away. As she raised her head, his tender, probing kiss touched her lips, like summer lightning, white-hot and fleeting.

Her eyes widened accusingly. "What did you do that for?"

"To say thank you for the dance, of course," he replied smoothly. "Does a kiss have to have a reason?"

"No," Dani said slowly, trying to guess what was going on in his mind and failing.

"You did tell me you'd been kissed before," Barrett reminded her. "I didn't think that little peck would scare you."

"No, it didn't. I'm a big girl." Which was the truth. She wouldn't admit that she had found it disturbingly pleasant. "You surprised me, that's all."

"The next time I kiss you, I'll be sure to warn you." His mouth crooked into a half-smile as his arm fell away from her waist. Before she had a chance to say there wouldn't be a next time, Barrett walked away, adding almost indifferently over his shoulder, "Want to get back to the party now?"

"Why do you ask?"

"I don't care for parties myself. I prefer the peace and quiet of a room like this," he commented, settling himself into a leather chair and stretching out his long legs on the footstool. "Do you like parties?"

"I haven't been to very many," Dani hedged, still not totally trusting his motives.

"They're pretty much the same."

"If you feel that way, why did you come?" she asked curiously.

"As I said, the Blakes are my godparents. They expected me to attend and I didn't want to disappoint them," Barrett replied evenly. "Unless you absolutely have to return to Marshall, I'd like to stay here for a little while and relax."

Dani had no idea what Marshall expected, but the prospect of nestling in the overstuffed cushions of the leather chair next to Barrett's was inviting. It seemed like a very long time since she'd sat and relaxed.

"I can stay for a few minutes," she agreed, missing the amused light that gleamed momentarily in Barrett's eyes as she leaned back in the chair beside him.

A companionable silence fell between them for a few minutes before Barrett spoke.

"When are you planning to see your father again?"

"Not anytime soon," Dani answered, turning her head to look at him.

She expected to see a piercing sharpness in his expression, but his air of lazy contentment convinced her he was only making conversation.

"You knew that the day you were released from the hospital, didn't you?"

The amiable look he gave her indicated that he wasn't offended by the way she had fooled him.

"Yes." Her mouth curved into a smile at her admission. "Lew and I talked the night before and decided to go our separate ways."

"Your father was in favor of it?"

"Of course." Dani stiffened, not liking the hint of reproof in his tone.

"Sorry." He shrugged, as if saying silently that it was none of his business. "The few times I saw you and your father together, you always seemed so close. You two had a great relationship."

His compliment dissolved her momentary resentment. "I never thought you noticed us, besides as the owners of The Rogue, I mean."

"Are you serious?" he chuckled softly, a pleasant sound that ran over her shoulders and down her spine. "Do you honestly think I could forget a beautiful brat who kept sassing me every time I saw her?"

"I do get carried away sometimes," Dani admitted ruefully.

"I guess Marshall is going to change all that. By the way, how did you meet him? He's not your run-of-the-mill newspaper reporter."

She suspected something more behind his questions than simple curiosity, but she couldn't be sure.

"He saw the article in the paper and came to see me at the hospital," she answered. The truth was always the best. "It was after Lew and I had our talk. Marshall offered to help me find a job."

"So he's responsible for your transformation from a child to a woman." His gaze slid over her appraisingly. "Did he pick out the clothes and the hairdo, too?"

Dani didn't miss the underlying note of disapproval. "I'm going to pay him back. I already have a job." She didn't add that it was temporary or that John Henning had taken her on as a model with the proviso that if she didn't work out she was out of a job, and had little chance of getting another one.

"As a model, of course."

"Why do you assume that?" she demanded.

"That's Marshall's type."

"Why? Because he likes beautiful women? So do you."

"Don't believe everything you see in the papers. I don't expect a woman to be perfect," Barrett offered dryly.

"Neither does Marshall!"

"Then why has he already changed you to fit his standards?"

"That's ridiculous!" Dani protested. "Before tonight would you have considered asking me to dance?"

"No," Barrett admitted with a twinkle in his eyes. "I thought you were too young."

"You knew that morning in the hospital how old I was, and you still didn't consider me worthy of your attention," she reminded him tartly.

"As I recall, I waited around to rescue you from the clutches of those reporters." The lines deepened around his mouth.

"That may be so," Dani acknowledged grudgingly, "but it was still Marshall who recognized that I was actually an attractive woman, not a brat. And he's also the one who did something about it!"

"Is that what's important to you?" There was a

fractional narrowing of his gaze. "Before tonight, I saw you as a long-legged filly. A bit high-strung and fractious with certain people, but with a big heart. A natural beauty. This stuff—the designer clothes and phony talk—just isn't you. I much preferred the old Dani to the one sitting beside me."

Her mouth opened and refused to close as she bounded to her feet, incapable of believing that he actually meant what he said.

"I'm curious, Dani, what you hope to get out of this act. I wouldn't have thought money was important to you," Barrett mused.

"It isn't!" she protested.

"Then what is your goal?" Slowly and casually, Barrett straightened to his feet, towering over her. "Do you want to be mentioned in gossip columns? Spend most of your time being Marshall's arm candy? He'd like that. Oh, I'll agree your honesty is refreshing, as Dru said, but is that all you want out of life—photo opportunities?"

"How dare you!" Dani spluttered.

"Anyone could see how much you loved working with horses," he went on. "You were happy with the life you and your father led. I can't believe The Rogue's death changed you so much." His voice was quiet, but his disapproval was clear.

"Do you want to know why?" Dani was angry now. "I'll tell you! And it was because of The Rogue! Do you know what my father said at the hospital? That he should have sold The Rogue to you, because he didn't deserve to own a horse that good."

Barrett said nothing in reply.

"And the way I attacked you made him decide that he was a failure as a parent, too. He wanted me to be somebody, and that's exactly what I'm going to do!" Dani finished.

She spun on her heel and would have stalked from the room if a strong hand hadn't pulled her up short and turned her around.

"Wearing expensive clothes and jewelry, being up on the latest best-seller or whatever, and being invited to exclusive parties doesn't make you somebody, Dani," Barrett told her sternly. "Marshall will never be able to teach you that."

"How do you know?" she demanded sarcastically.

"Because he's a nobody, when you get right down to it. He doesn't do anything worthwhile. He gossips for a living, for Pete's sake—"

"Why do you resent the fact that Marshall is helping me? You're just trying to turn me against him!"

"You don't know very much about Marshall Thompsen," he said grimly.

The tautness of his jawline, the fire in his eyes, the impression of muscles tensed to spring were all warning signals.

But Dani ignored them. "I bet you can hardly wait to enlighten me about Marshall!"

Lean fingers closed over her bare arms, tightening when she tried to pull free. Then the grim line of his mouth relaxed into a very masculine smile that reminded her sharply of his virility.

"Look, I don't want to quarrel with you," Barrett murmured. His low-pitched, husky voice felt almost like a physical caress. "Why can't we have a civil conversation?"

"Because I don't want to. Save your famous King

charm for someone else." Not for the world would she admit that it had any effect on her.

"You obviously like and respect Marshall. I shouldn't have tried to force my opinion on you. It's natural to defend a friend."

"You don't really mean that," Dani accused him. "You're only saying that because you think it might make me like you."

"Maybe I just don't want you to dislike me so much," he suggested, bending his head and brushing her lips lightly with his own, igniting that pleasurable fire again.

"Why did you do that?" she protested angrily, although her voice wavered, taking out most of the sting.

"Because I like to," Barrett replied with barely concealed amusement.

"Well, don't do it anymore."

"Why? Don't you like it?"

Barrett was obviously teasing her now and Dani found it was very difficult to stay angry, a discovery that endeared him to her.

"No, I don't think I do," was her prim answer as she sought to put him in his place.

The warmth of his hands left her shoulders and her skin shivered at the unexpected removal. The fact that she enjoyed his touch she dismissed as ridiculous.

"You think . . . but you're not sure. Then there's hope," he murmured.

"Marshall must be wondering where I am," Dani remarked, prepared to argue if Barrett suggested that they remain longer in the study. The atmosphere in the room had become too intimate for her peace of mind.

But Barrett only waved her ahead to the door. Determined not to reveal how anxious she was to escape his presence, Dani held her head high as she walked at his side. As they returned to the chattering noise of the party, she felt his gaze straying to her and sensed the glimmer of amusement in the clear depths of his eyes. Her chin tilted higher.

"I suppose you'd be annoyed if I asked to see you again," Barrett said blandly. His offhand manner irritated her.

"Probably," Dani agreed, sending him a cool glance to show the last thing she was interested in was his company.

"Well, I'm asking." There was that deep smile that managed to be irritating and devastatingly attractive at the same time.

"You're right—I am annoyed." Dani averted her gaze, letting it flit over the crowd as if she was looking for Marshall. In truth, the only person she was actually aware of was at her side.

"Is that a yes or a no?" he asked with maddening persistence.

She stopped and faced him squarely. Her pulse quickened as she met his steady gaze. "Why would you want to see me? You've already made it clear that you object to the way I am now."

"I like the real Dani who always manages to surface when I'm around. I don't want her to disappear completely," Barrett replied, then shrugged. "Of course, if you think Marshall will object to my seeing you—"

Breathing in deeply, Dani remembered Marshall's hint that he and Barrett might be enemies. Some of Barrett's remarks tonight had seemed to confirm that. She didn't think to remind herself that she had considered Barrett an enemy, too. At the moment he represented a connection to her past. She only had to close her eyes to visualize him standing in front of the racing stables talking to a jockey or a trainer while examining a thoroughbred. Despite her promise to her father, she was reluctant to sever this last link with the world she had loved.

"I doubt Marshall would approve," she admitted hesitantly.

"Well, don't disobey his orders." His solemn expression didn't convey the mockery she thought she had detected in his voice.

"Marshall is helping me." She emphasized the word "helping." "He doesn't control my life. What I do with my free time is my business," she asserted, her independent nature resisting any implication that someone else could tell her what to do.

"Okay. How about spending some of your free time with me?" Barrett prompted.

"I'll think about it," Dani conceded. Her heart leaped with gladness and she turned quickly away in case her inner excitement showed in her face.

"Where are you staying?" His hand was touching her elbow, prompting her to get through the crowd.

"The Kingswood Arms." Her voice was calm and controlled. "It's an apartment complex—"

"I know where it is," Barrett assured her.

"There's Marshall. He doesn't look too happy. I must have kept you too long."

Dani saw the other man glowering at them, not far away. Suddenly she realized that she didn't want an argument springing up between the two men. She would have to take Marshall's side, and she didn't want to align herself with him against Barrett. That knowledge came as a surprise—one she didn't want to examine too closely.

With a nervous smile, she turned to Barrett. "Thank you for the dance. I . . . I enjoyed it." Her smooth statement faltered a little toward the end.

"Oh, you want to say your goodbyes now and avoid a confrontation, is that it?" He nodded, a little ruefully.

Her mouth opened for a split second in surprise at his astuteness. "A confrontation?" she said lamely, wondering if he could read her mind.

"Never mind," Barrett grinned. "I'm going to find our hosts to say goodbye, then I'll leave. But I'll be seeing you"—a finger traced the delicate line of her jaw to her chin and lightly touched her lips—"soon."

After sketching a mocking salute in Marshall's direction, Barrett winked at Dani and walked away. She watched him go and crossed the room to Marshall's side.

"You took your time about coming back!" he nearly snarled.

"I didn't know there was a time limit on how long I was supposed to be gone," Dani retorted, holding her head high again.

"I never dreamed you would find Barrett King's company so enjoyable," Marshall jeered.

"Oh, please!" Fire flashed in her hazel eyes. "You knew all along that Barrett was coming to this party and you didn't even tell me."

"I wasn't absolutely positive he'd be here," he hedged, glancing around as if he expected someone to be listening. "I suppose he filled your head with dire warnings about me."

"As a matter of fact, he didn't," she answered sharply—a half-truth, since Barrett had only implied that Marshall was not to be trusted.

There was open disbelief on his face as he studied her expression. Then a complacent smile turned up the corners of his mouth and the blackness of his eyes took on a triumphant glitter.

"Guess he was too busy gloating over the latest victory of that horse he owns—the one your horse beat the other day."

"Easy Doesit?" Dani murmured, pain flicking over her at the memory of the chestnut galloping down the straightaway and the even more poignant memory of The Rogue.

"I guess that's the one," Marshall shrugged, as if it didn't matter to him.

"No." Her head moved slowly from side to side, a puzzled frown creasing her forehead. "No, he didn't mention it to me."

"All that's behind you, anyway," he said with a consoling smile, tucking her hand beneath his arm. "Come on, there are some people I want you to meet."

Meekly Dani submitted to his guidance. The news of the thoroughbred's victory came as a surprise—more so because Marshall had been the one to tell her, as if he wanted to open up old wounds.

But she didn't begrudge the chestnut its victory. In a way, she was almost glad. After all, The Rogue had beaten him soundly.

It was difficult to concentrate on the people Marshall introduced to her because her mind kept wandering back to Barrett. Why hadn't he told her?

CHAPTER SIX

The sun had been up a long time before Dani drowsily blinked her eyes open. She rolled over wearily and glanced at the clock on the bedside table. Ten o'clock. Stifling a yawn, she slid from beneath the covers and shrugged into a light cotton robe before making her way to the small kitchen in her apartment.

After switching on the coffeemaker, she padded into the bathroom where she splashed cold water on her sleepy face. The makeup bottles and tubes were in an orderly row in front of her.

"Ugh!" Dani shuddered as she glared at them.

She hadn't returned from the party until the early morning hours. No wonder she had slept so late. With a sigh of resignation, she touched some mascara to her lashes and applied a little pink lipstick after brushing her teeth. She ignored all the bases and blushers and coversticks.

"Marshall told me to relax today," she murmured to herself, and stuck out her tongue at the bottles. "I don't feel like being a glamor girl today!"

Going through the clothes in her closet, she settled for jeans and a sweater. Running a brush through her hair, she did take the time to fluff and curl the ends the way Giorgio had taught her. She walked into the kitchen just as the coffeemaker emitted its last dying gurgle.

Before she could pour herself a cup, there was a knock at the door. Muttering a few choice insults at Marshall for arriving before she'd had her morning coffee, Dani stalked to the door, annoyed because he hadn't called to let her know he was coming. With an irritated expression on her face, she flung open the door and stared into green eyes that seemed to be laughing.

"What are you doing here?" Dani stepped back, her heart skipping a beat in surprise.

"I came to see you." Barrett made a point of examining the number on the door. "This is Danielle Williams' apartment, isn't it? Or did I inadvertently knock on the door of the Wicked Witch of the West?"

An unwilling smile edged the corners of her mouth, but she refused to submit to his teasing completely. "I haven't had my coffee."

"In that case, I'll have a cup." He smiled down at her lazily.

"All right. Come on in." Dani grinned, turning to lead the way into the kitchen.

"Did you just get up?" he asked lightly. "That party must have lasted half the night."

"I think it did," she sighed, and poured two cups to the brim. "I hope you don't take cream, because there isn't any."

"My father taught me to drink it black. Said it puts hair on your chest." Barrett straddled a chair and took one of the cups from her hand.

"What are you doing here this morning?" she asked between sips.

"Like I said, I came to see you," he retorted with the slightest hint of a smile.

"That's not what I mean."

"I didn't think Marshall would have anything planned for you today, since it's Sunday. I could take you out for a tour of the town."

"I've seen enough museums and galleries and concert halls to last me for one week. Thanks, but no, thanks," Dani replied firmly.

"Oh, I was thinking of something more in the line of a steamboat trip down the Ohio River, or maybe just a stroll along the banks. I promise not to improve your mind."

It sounded like fun but Dani hesitated. "We'll end up arguing. We always do," she sighed.

Barrett shrugged, concealing a smile. "I'll take my chances."

"I'd like to spend some time outdoors," she said with a decisive nod.

"So it's not me you want, but an opportunity to be outside," he mocked.

Dani refused to be tricked into admitting anything. But her attitude toward Barrett King had undergone a change almost as startling as her appearance. Not that she trusted him, because she was certain there was a hidden reason for his attention that she didn't know about.

"I really don't like being inside most of the time," she said instead. "It's an adjustment."

"And have you? Adjusted?" His gaze moved casually over her face, but Dani knew her answer was important to him.

She made a pretense of draining the coffee in her cup. "Of course," she declared airily.

"That's good," Barrett said, still studying her thoughtfully. "I'd hate to think you were unhappy in your new life."

"Why would you think that?" Dani countered.

"A few minutes ago you were ready to turn me down when you thought I was going to take you to museums and art galleries. You must be getting tired of all that culture Marshall's making you experience."

"Just because you can take the finer things in life for granted is no reason for you to make fun of me because I want to learn about them!"

"I'm not making fun of you, Dani," he replied patiently to her defiant outburst. "In fact, I admire what you're doing. But Marshall is teaching you not to trust your own responses. Don't lose sight of the fact that there's as much beauty in a child's crayon drawing as there is in a Renaissance masterpiece, if you know how to look at both of them."

His profound statement left Dani momentarily speechless. She stared unblinkingly as he, in effect, dismounted from his chair and walked past her to refill his cup from the pot. She felt a flash of irritation at the way he was making himself at home before she sprang to her feet to face him.

"I don't believe you!" Her hands clenched into tight fists. "You aren't the kind of man who cares about things like that!"

The sideways look he gave her was half cold, half puzzled. "Why not?"

"Oh, you always say all the right things, but it's only an act with you!" she declared. "It's kind of sickening the way people look up to you. It always made me hopping mad the way Lew would rush to answer any patronizing question you asked!"

The kitchen was small and there was no distance between them. In an instant, Barrett reached out with a long arm and took hold of her wrist. She was jerked forward within inches of his ruthlessly cold face and the taut line of his mouth.

"I never patronized your father!" he snapped. There was fire in his eyes. "If I ever asked for his opinion it was because I valued his judgment. Lew is an excellent horseman and a fine trainer. I admire him. Got a problem with that?"

"That didn't stop you from trying to buy the finest horse he ever owned!" Dani shot back, refusing to believe that Barrett was sincere.

"There were other offers for The Rogue besides mine, weren't there?" As her mouth clamped shut, he gave her a shake. "Weren't there?" he demanded again.

"Yes!" Dani had to be honest.

"But my offer to buy him somehow sticks in your craw. Only mine! And it never occurred to you that you might be treating me unfairly." The initial explosion of fire was gone, leaving a cold anger in its place. "I oughta put you over my knee and paddle you the way your father should have done a long time ago."

Barrett released her wrist in disgust while the humiliating truth of his words sunk in. She hadn't treated him fairly. She might even have misjudged him, but that didn't begin to explain why she was on her guard whenever he was around.

She stared at his averted head, proudly arrogant, and the deep lines around his mouth. Her conscience demanded that she make some concession to the truth, but she refused to let it be at the cost of her pride.

"You . . . you might be right," she said hesitantly. "But not about everything."

Barrett looked directly at her, a cynical smile on his lips. Then, slowly, it changed into a rueful smile. "I lost my temper, didn't I?" he sighed, the light returning to his green eyes. "I'll accept your apology if you accept mine."

"Okay," Dani agreed, feeling somehow the blame was equal.

"What now?" he asked quietly.

"I don't know." A little frown wrinkled her forehead as she took his question seriously. "Guess we cleared the air, didn't we?"

"Hope so," Barrett conceded. He held out his hand to her. "Friends again?"

Dani smiled and placed her hand in his.

"Come on, I'll buy you breakfast before we take a ride on the _Belle of Louisville,_" he offered.

After they'd eaten breakfast at a homey little restaurant, Barrett and Dani strolled around the riverfront taking in the futuristic architecture in the seven-acre park called Riverfront Belvedere. Sometimes they talked. Sometimes they walked in silence, gazing at the flowers and shrubs or the many fountains and reflecting pools. Barrett told her they were used for ice skating in the winter.

The park was guarded by a statue of George Rogers Clark, the founder of Louisville. But the main attraction was the Ohio River, broad and somnolent, flowing ever onward.

Then came the trip on the *Belle of Louisville*, an authentic old paddleboat. After touring the first two decks, including the grand ballroom, Barrett took Dani to the open-air deck on top where a calliope was all steamed up, its brass whistles blowing a lively tune. As the *Belle* maneuvered away from the dock into the river channel, the couple moved to a vantage point at the railings.

"Has she always been here?" Dani asked, watching other tourists and sightseers waving to the boat from the shore.

"No, the *Belle* started out as a ferryboat and packet on the Mississippi River out of Memphis, Tennessee, but her home is here in Kentucky now," Barrett replied. "Kentucky could be technically considered one of the thirteen colonies, since most of the state was once a part of Virginia."

"I thought this afternoon wasn't supposed to improve my mind," she teased with an impish grin.

"It isn't. Sorry about that," he chuckled.

As they watched the slowly changing scenery, there was no real need for conversation. The silence was as comfortable and reassuring as the hand that rested lightly on her shoulder. But Marshall's remark about Barrett's horse drifted into her mind and it seemed like as good a time as any to ask him about it.

Switching her gaze from the water being churned up by the paddlewheel to the strong features of the man beside her, Dani asked, "Why didn't you tell me about Easy Doesit winning the race yesterday?"

"How could I? I didn't want to stir up painful memories for you." His level gaze held hers, stating a fact without offering any sympathy.

"That's true," she admitted, looking toward the distant banks. "I'm not . . . I mean, I don't mind your horse winning."

"I'm glad to hear that," was his reply, then he tactfully steered the conversation away from horses to point out a landmark that was coming up.

As far as Dani was concerned, the trip ended all too soon. She was enjoying the breeze that ruffled her hair and the sun beating down on her face, and she was enjoying the company of the man beside her. Her footsteps dragged a little from the dock to the parking lot where Barrett had left his sports car.

"Are you hungry?" he asked as he slid behind the wheel.

"Yes." A hopeful light shone in her eyes. Maybe he wouldn't take her back to that empty apartment right away.

"Good. Let's get something to eat," Barrett nodded briskly as he put the car in gear and reversed into the traffic.

Ruefully Dani glanced down at her jeans and sweater. "I'm not dressed for it, I'm afraid." A wistful sigh slipped from her lips.

"You look fine to me, and for the place I have in mind, it doesn't matter how you're dressed. Marshall can take you to the fancy restaurants." There was a mocking glint in the look he gave her. "I'd like you to sample some of our local fare."

The moment Dani stepped inside the restaurant, the cheery atmosphere seemed to say welcome. The decor was homespun and bright with an abundance of yellow and greens. It was nothing like the elegant establishments that she went to with Marshall, places where she was always terrified she was going to use the wrong silverware.

"This is nice," she murmured as she sat in the chair Barrett held for her.

"Don't sound so surprised," he laughed softly, taking a chair on the opposite side of the table. "Didn't you think there were any other decent restaurants other than the ones Marshall picks?"

"Of course, it's just—"

"I know, you like it." His teasing grin took her off the defensive and drew an answering smile. "The specialities of the house are burgoo and hot brown."

"What are those?" Her eyes widened at the strange-sounding names.

"Hot brown is a sandwich of turkey, bacon and cheese topped with a white sauce. It's delicious and a local specialty," Barrett explained. "Burgoo was probably invented by the first settlers in Kentucky. It's a peppery hot chowder of beef, ham, chicken, and vegetables."

"I like anything hot," she said. "I'll have the burgoo."

"Good choice. I'll have the same." He gave the

waitress their order when she arrived, then turned to Dani. "Well? Did you enjoy the trip?"

"Oh, yes," she responded eagerly. "And the walk along the riverfront, too."

Her happiness subsided when she saw Barrett glance at his watch. Was there someplace else he had to be?

"Six hours without an argument. That must be a record." She let out an almost visible sigh of relief at the teasing expression on his face. "Why do you suppose that is?" he asked.

"Maybe because you've stopped treating me like a child," she returned lightly.

"I don't see you as a child anymore."

The husky, enigmatic tone of his voice melted her, as did the caressing look in his eyes. A tingling sensation raced down the back of her neck, this time from something that Dani couldn't put her finger on. It somehow made her conscious of him as a man, a compellingly handsome and sexy man, and not just a tenuous link with the world she missed.

Fortunately their food arrived just then and she was able to ignore her wandering thoughts to concentrate on the peppery stew. During the meal, there was no need to talk, and afterward they were too full.

Later, as Barrett stopped the car in front of her apartment, Dani turned to thank him for the day, only to find he was already out of the car and walking around to her side. Some of her surprise must have registered in her eyes as she stepped out of the car under his guiding hand. Marshall seldom bothered being a gentleman.

"I'll see you safely to your door," was his explanation.

In the hallway in front of her door, Dani removed her key from the slender clutch purse she carried. Barrett slipped it from her hand and put it in the lock before she realized what was happening. She stood hesitantly in front of the now opened door, wondering if she should invite him in.

"I . . . I had a wonderful time today," she offered uncertainly.

"So did I." An indefinable gentleness was in his voice, as if he were attempting to soothe a skittish colt.

"Would you like to come in for coffee?" she suggested, trying to steady the sudden increase in her heartbeat.

"I'm afraid I can't." Barrett handed back her keys.

"Of course." Her clipped reply was sharp as she realized how silly it was to think that Barrett might want to spend more time with her. "Thanks again for taking me out."

She took a hurried step into the doorway, only to have his hands close over her upper arms.

"Not so fast," he said softly, drawing her a step backward at an angle that brought her closer to him. A finger tipped her chin upwards. "I prefer a more demonstrative thanks."

This time when his mouth touched hers, it lingered, tenderly probing the softness of her trembling lips. The warm, persuasive kiss was sensual, totally unlike the furtive and unpracticed ones Dani had received from others in the past. When he slowly drew away, the feeling remained on her mouth. Dani resisted the impulse to put a finger to her lips as she gazed at him with rounded eyes.

"Be seeing you," Barrett winked, and gently pushed her into the apartment and closed the door.

That indefinite promise made the evening alone seem not so long, although Dani would have vigorously denied that her thoughts ever turned to Barrett King, except for that kiss . . .

Monday morning brought the return of her hectic schedule, throwing her into the tedious routine of a model. She didn't mention her afternoon with Barrett to Marshall because she didn't think it was important. It certainly wasn't because she thought Marshall would object.

Monday stretched into Tuesday and Tuesday into Wednesday. The time that wasn't spent with the photographer, Marshall claimed, prodding her to see this or read that, or attend this party or that concert.

When he dropped her off at her apartment Thursday evening loaded with more books and CDs as well as a detailed description and video review of the latest creations from Paris and Milan, Dani had to stifle the desire to dump it all back on his lap. She felt too exhausted to care about her ignorance. She was so busy juggling the bundle in her arms trying to extract the key from her purse that she didn't notice the man leaning against the wall of the corridor opposite her door.

"It's about time you got home," a low voice commented.

Dani turned so fast that two of the books slid out of her arms to the carpeted floor. Barrett stepped forward as she bent to retrieve them.

"I didn't mean to startle you," he apologized.

"Well, you did," Dani said crossly. "You shouldn't pop out at people from the dark."

"I thought this hallway was pretty well lit," Barrett commented blandly, a smile flitting across his strong mouth.

His accurate observation earned him an annoyed look. "What do you want?" As she straightened to her feet, the articles once again stacked in her arms and the door key in her hand, Dani noticed the big white box, flat and square, in one of his hands and the paper bag in the other. A tantalizing aroma drifted by her nose.

"I thought you might not feel like going out to eat tonight, so I brought the meal to you," he said, his straight face giving way to a sexy smile. "Hope you like pizza, because this is too big for me to eat by myself."

Whether it was the appeal of his smile or the appetizing aroma coming from the box, Dani's initial irritation began to fade.

"I like pizza," she admitted, putting the key in the lock and turning it. "But how do you know that I'm not going out to dinner?"

"I checked my sister's calendar for local events. I didn't see anything on it that would catch Marshall's interest, so I took the chance that you'd be free," Barrett replied as he followed her in, a somewhat sardonic gleam in his eyes. "From the looks of you, you need a night off."

Setting the books and CDs on the coffee table

in the living room, Dani sighed a little dispiritedly. "I don't have the strength or energy to argue about it," she explained, turning around to follow Barrett, who was already taking over the kitchen table. "Let me do that," she said as he began unloading the groceries from the bag.

Instead of stepping aside, Barrett took her by the shoulders, turned her around and pointed her in the opposite direction.

"You can go take a shower and relax. I'll put the pizza in the oven to keep it warm and toss a salad."

"You?" Dani said in disbelief, looking over her shoulder, his hands preventing her from turning around. Barrett simply didn't seem like the domestic type.

"Who did you expect? My chef and valet have the night off, so that only leaves me," he mocked, giving her a little push to send her on her way. "And hurry up, because I'm hungry!"

The spray of the shower was therapeutic, rinsing away the tension that had knotted her muscles. If it hadn't been for Barrett telling her to hurry, Dani would have stayed longer under the stinging spray. But she turned off the water and briskly rubbed herself dry, then slipped into a long terry robe.

As Dani stepped into the small hallway to her bedroom, Barrett called out to her, "About time! I was beginning to think you'd gone down the drain." Then he added, "The food is on the table."

"I'll be there in a minute," she said cheerfully. "I still have to get dressed."

He stepped into the archway of the hall, the overhead light making his expression seem almost fierce. "You look dressed to me. Come on, let's eat!"

Dani glanced down at the white wraparound robe. It covered everything there was to cover from her ankles to her neck, with only a small vee that exposed the hollow of her throat. With a shrug, she changed her direction and walked down the hallway to the kitchen.

Two small bowls of salad were on the table, romaine lettuce mixed with cherry tomatoes, carrot shreds, green peppers, onions and topped with Italian dressing. Dani slid into the chair Barrett held for her, feeling suddenly ravenous. The salad was soon eaten and Barrett placed the pizza that had been kept warm in the oven on the table.

"And I was going to settle for a bowl of soup tonight," she sighed, appreciatively inhaling the fragrance of the spicy tomato sauce mixed with pepperoni and sausage and cheese.

"All food tastes better when you share it with someone," he commented as he handed her a wedge.

"Providing the company is right," Dani added before she bit into the pizza.

"Say it is," he smiled. "Tell me I'm wonderful."

"I wouldn't dream of insulting the chef," she teased. "He might poison me the next time!"

Their banter continued through the meal, remarkably free of any edginess or tension. If Dani had been amazed when Barrett shooed her out of the kitchen to cook, she was doubly amazed when he helped with the clearing up. She couldn't resist commenting on it as they made their way into the living room.

"Don't you think a man should help in the kitchen?" he countered.

"Well, sure, of course," she said. "But the average man usually doesn't."

"I'm not the average man," he shrugged, and walked over to the sound system to look through the CDs and tapes, leaving Dani to agree wholeheartedly, though silently, that he was not at all like the men she knew. "You have some pretty heavy music here," Barrett interrupted her thoughts.

"That's Marshall's," she explained self-consciously, "he thinks I should to listen to it when I'm not doing anything."

"When is that?" he mocked with a wry grin.

"Not often," Dani admitted, sitting on the couch and tucking her feet beneath her.

Barrett selected a CD and slid it into the player, then walked over to occupy the opposite end of the couch. Leaning back against the cushions, he started to prop his feet on the coffee table, then stopped.

"Is that allowed?" he asked with an arched brow.

"I do it all the time." Dani grinned.

"I like to stretch out." And he slid a magazine over so his shoes would not mar the table.

Dani snuggled deeper in her corner into a more comfortable position and listened to the softly lilting song, a little surprised that Barrett had chosen one of her favorite bands until she reminded herself that he seemed to know instinctively what she liked.

She had barely settled in when the phone rang. Unfortunately, it was on the end table on the opposite side of the couch, where Barrett was seated.

Reluctantly Dani untwined her legs and got up. As she reached the spot where Barrett's legs were sprawled in her path, she watched him reach over and pick up the receiver to hand it to her.

"Hello?" She perched on the edge of the couch beside Barrett, the spiral cord of the receiver crossing over him.

"Yes, Danielle. Marshall here."

Unconsciously she made a face at the telephone. "Hi, Marshall." A hesitant glance at Barrett caught him looking at her with undisguised interest and amusement.

"Just calling to let you know our lunch date tomorrow's at twelve-thirty. That'll give you plenty of time to change at John's before I pick you up."

"That's good," she nodded unnecessarily. "Is there anything else?"

"No, no, that's all." There was a slight pause before he continued, "Is anything wrong, Danielle?"

"What do you mean?" Dani nibbled at her lower lip, anxious for the conversation to end.

"You sound preoccupied. You feeling okay?"

"I'm fine. I was . . . er . . . reading one of the books you gave me," she lied, avoiding the mocking expression in the green eyes watching her. She shifted uncomfortably to escape the suddenly burning warmth of Barrett's thigh against hers and nearly pulled the telephone off the table. The firm touch of Barrett's hand guided her back.

"I see," Marshall replied, obviously pleased by her statement. "I'll see you tomorrow."

"Yes, tomorrow. Goodbye." After his answering goodbye, there was a click on the opposite end and Dani breathed deeply in relief before reaching across Barrett to put back the receiver. "Marshall was calling about my schedule tomorrow," she said, wondering why she felt a need to explain why he'd called.

"That's nice." Barrett's mouth turned down a little. "Why didn't you mention that I was here?"

"It didn't seem necessary," Dani hedged, not entirely sure of the reason herself.

"What would you have said if he'd asked you what you were reading?"

Fire flashed in her eyes for a moment before she giggled. "I have no idea!"

When the laughter died, she found she was leaning against the back of the couch within the circle of Barrett's arms. Her smiling face was turned up to him when she tried to move away.

"Stay here," Barrett ordered gently, holding her tighter.

For a moment she resisted, then allowed her head to rest against his shoulder. With a small murmur of acquiescence, she relaxed, the soothing music washing over her while she was held in Barrett's strong arms. It felt so right to be this close to him.

CHAPTER SEVEN

"I think it's past your bedtime," Barrett spoke from somewhere near her ear.

Her eyes opened slowly. She was drowsy from the bliss of being held and gave a little sigh of contentment.

"I was only resting my eyes," she claimed in defense, but her voice was soft and whispery.

His quiet chuckle was muffled by the closeness of his mouth to her hair and the warmth of his breath was soothing. Beneath her head she could hear the reassuring, steady beat of his heart.

"You've been doing such a good job of resting your eyes that you haven't heard a word I've said for the last fifteen minutes." His feet were off the coffee table and back on the floor as he began to straighten. "It's time I let you get some sleep."

"Don't go," Dani protested drowsily, not wanting to lose the comfortable pillow beneath her head, or the warmth of his muscular arms.

But her husky plea was to no avail. "You're out on your feet, girl," Barrett said firmly.

She felt an arm slide under her knees and in the next instant she was being carried in his arms like a child. She felt no desire to protest this time as she twined her arms around his neck. Her dream-like state of half-sleep sensed the rightness of his action. Through her lashes, she peered at the powerful line of his jaw and chin and the grooves beside his mouth that lessened the fierceness. As her eyes swung lazily to the thick lashes accenting the brilliant green of his, she found him gazing down at her, something very caring in the look.

"I was eight years old the last time my father carried me to bed," she murmured in a sleep-thickened voice.

He made no reply as he entered the darkened room, but Dani expected none. Tugging back the bedcovers, Barrett settled her gently on the smooth sheet. Her hands remained locked around his neck, holding him above her.

"Good night, Dani," he said again in that firm voice that still sounded gentle.

"I'm still not that tired," she said . . . her final protest.

In the light streaming through the bedroom door, she saw his mouth quirk into a faintly amused grin. "Of course not," Barrett agreed. When he began to lower his head toward her, Dani tilted her chin, anticipating his kiss.

At the light touch of his mouth, a seductive heat flooded through her. Her lips moved in response to his kiss, a womanly instinct telling her what to do. Her hands felt the tightening of the muscles in Barrett's neck and the pressure of his hands at her side as he started to draw away. Under the gentle insistence of her lips, his kiss hardened into something more than a simple caress. Dani felt the stamp of possession in the sensual pressure of his mouth, arousing strange new desires, but the languorous weakness that spread through her body melted any attempt to resist.

Then his fingers were closing over her wrists, dragging her hands away from his neck. If she had been more alert, she would have noticed his uneven breathing. Her body cried for an unknown fulfilment it hadn't received and she murmured an incoherent protest.

"You're half asleep and you don't know what you're doing," Barrett declared huskily, a trace of temper in the steel of his voice.

It was true, Dani still did feel woozy, but whether from the exhaustion of the day or the intoxicating touch of his lips, she couldn't say.

"Go to sleep," he ordered crisply. She felt the light brush of his mouth across the top of her forehead before he pushed himself away and rose to his feet.

Her head turned against the pillow, trying to find the warmth and comfort she had known in his arms. Through heavy lashes, she watched the tall silhouette walking closer to the open door.

"Barrett," she murmured softly, and he stopped in the doorway, the light from the hall illuminating his face as he half turned in answer. Vaguely she realized again how devastatingly attractive he could be to some women. "Why do you suppose I don't like you?" she asked.

There was an upward tilt of one side of his mouth as if he found her question secretly amusing. "You'll have to come up with that answer yourself, kid."

"I'm not a kid," she retorted sleepily.

"Good night, Dani. Sweet dreams."

"Good night," she echoed softly, her eyelids already fluttering down so that she didn't even see the door close.

In the next couple of weeks, Barrett came around several times, his arrival always unexpected and coinciding with her free evenings. Sometimes he brought food to be cooked at her apartment and other times he took her out to eat. There was a friendly rapport between them, even when they argued, and her hazy recollection of their intimacy became something she had imagined.

Dani never told Marshall about Barrett's visits. He would have scoffed at the fragile friendship she had with Barrett. And she knew he wouldn't understand her desire to keep some active link with her past. A man like Marshall would never be able to understand the earthy simplicity and satisfaction she had known. He would hate the smell of horses and hay that clung to skin and clothes. To Dani, it was as delightful as the most expensive perfume.

Which wasn't to say she didn't enjoy her new-found sophistication, or the compliments and admiring looks she received. Her reflection in the mirror no longer surprised her. She knew the giant step she had taken into the feminine world was irreversible. Never again would she not care about her appearance or her clothes.

She was an amazing contradiction, she decided, enjoying her new life while preferring the simpler pleasures of her past to the hectic social whirl Marshall kept her in. Privately she was beginning to agree with Barrett that one party wasn't much different from another.

Marshall was in his element at the parties they attended, handing out false compliments with a sincerity that scared Dani a little.

Maybe, she thought, that was another reason why she enjoyed Barrett's company. Except for an occasional compliment on her clothes, he never buttered her up too much.

Although her earlier antagonism toward him had disappeared, she still recognized a streak of ruthlessness in Barrett, a dogged determination to get what he wanted regardless of who or what was in his way. There were moments when his level gaze would rest on her and she would remember that she still didn't trust him, although she wasn't sure why.

Oh well, she told herself, it didn't really matter. At least they weren't enemies.

"Are you tired?" Barrett asked, taking his eyes from the road illuminated by the car's headlights to glance at Dani.

"Mmm, yes," she admitted, snapping out of her reverie.

"I thought you'd fallen asleep."

"I ate too much," she said. "That always makes me tired. Want to come in for coffee tonight?"

Her question coincided with the turn into the parking lot of her apartment complex. Barrett didn't answer immediately as he maneuvered the car into a vacant spot and shut off the motor.

"Are you sure you don't want to tumble right into bed?" he asked. "I know you've had a full day."

"One cup of coffee and then I'll shoo you out," Dani smiled.

"It's a deal." He was out of the car and walking around to her side. She handed him the key to her apartment as usual, before she lightly placed her hand on his arm to walk by his side.

After opening the door, he passed the key back to her as she flicked on the light switch. "Make yourself comfortable while I start the coffee," she said over her shoulder, taking three steps into the living room en route to the kitchen before she stopped short. "What are you doing here?"

Simultaneously Dani noticed the lamp on in the living room and Marshall sitting with crossed arms in the chair beside it. His expression was far from pleasant as he saw Barrett standing behind her.

"I called and called and when you didn't answer, I came over to see if anything was wrong," he answered sharply, but there was an accusing look in his eyes.

"Nothing's wrong," she said defensively. "Barrett took me out to dinner, that's all."

"Oh, he did, did he?" He glared at Barrett. "Wasn't that nice of him."

"That doesn't explain how you got in here," Dani said sharply.

For all her outward composure, she was trembling inside, wondering what would happen now that Marshall knew she was seeing Barrett and hadn't told him.

"A spare key," he answered sarcastically, dangling it from his fingers. "Guess I forgot to give it to you."

"Well, you can give it to me now!" Angrily she stalked to the chair and snatched the key from his unresisting fingers.

"Did you make another one for Barrett to use?" Marshall asked. Dani didn't answer.

"Dani and I were going to have some coffee. Why don't you stay for a cup, Marshall?" said Barrett, his cold eyes meeting the leashed fury of the other man's gaze.

Dani stared at him in disbelief. Why, if she was trying to think of ways to get rid of Marshall, was Barrett inviting him to stay?

"Great suggestion," Marshall agreed, rising to his feet. "Thanks, pal."

"Dani thinks of you as a friend." Barrett shrugged. "Since she's a friend of mine, then we have something in common."

"Don't I have some say in all this?" Dani demanded angrily. "This is my apartment!"

Barrett's level gaze swung from Marshall to her. "Of course. You can make the coffee," he said smoothly, "while Marshall and I decide which one of us will be the host."

"Oh, please!" She wanted to yell. This standoff

was getting out of hand. "You're both my guests and you'll both behave."

"I guess, Marshall, we can trade insults but not punches," Barrett said, his mouth moving into a humorless smile.

Dani was confused by his strange behavior but she could tell that Marshall was even more bewildered. Barrett seemed to be inviting a confrontation with Marshall. Dani glared at both men, then stalked into the kitchen to fix the coffee.

She was furious and even slamming the cabinet doors wasn't going to calm her down. Yet none of the noise she made was loud enough to drown out the voices of the men in the other room, especially Marshall's, which had grown loud and belligerent.

"How long have you been seeing Danielle?" he demanded.

"Several weeks now." Barrett's voice was quieter and she found herself straining to hear it. "Only on the nights when you weren't showing her off to your friends."

"Is this because you feel guilty? She pitched a fit about that horse of hers," Marshall sneered. "At least it got her some free publicity."

"Is that all you think about? I just thought she might need someone to lean on once in a while."

"Oh, yeah?" Marshall snorted. "I was the one who was there to help her when she needed someone after her father walked out, not you. She flat out rejected your offer of help!"

"That was because she didn't trust me," Barrett replied calmly.

"Does she trust you now?"

"Not yet."

Dani's mouth opened a little, wondering how Barrett could possibly know that.

"She never will," Marshall went on. "You'll always be the one she'll associate with the death of her horse and the one she'll blame for her father's failure. After all, you're Barrett King, the epitome of everything her father wasn't."

"That's to your advantage." There was a tinge of mockery to Barrett's husky voice as if he were implying that Marshall needed all the advantages he could get.

"You bet it is," Marshall snarled. "I made her what she is and she knows it!"

"All you did, Marshall, was dress her up and show her how to order from a fancy menu," Barrett said dryly. "Dani is what she is because of her own individual personality and because of the way she was raised. She spent years with her father on the wrong side of the racetracks but she's still a sweet kid. Her father deserves the credit for that, not you."

"I'm going to fix it so Danielle never sees you again," Marshall threatened.

"And how are you going to do that?"

"Remind her that she's breaking her promise to her father." Dani's heart dipped to her shoes at the unmistakable triumph in Marshall's voice.

"She didn't promise Lew she wouldn't see me." There was open skepticism in Barrett's tone.

With a proud look in her eyes, Dani stepped into the living room. "I can answer that question, Barrett," she said, avoiding his gaze. "If you two will come into the kitchen, the coffee's ready."

There was a smug look in Marshall's eyes as he

took the chair directly opposite Barrett, leaving Dani no choice except to take the chair that placed her in between. Cradling her hands around the cup, she stared into the dark liquid.

"I promised my father," she began slowly, "that I would start over, make a new life for myself—and that I would never have anything to do with horses or racing."

"What does that have to do with you seeing me? I don't believe your father would disapprove." The quiet conviction in Barrett's voice was oddly reassuring.

"Oh, really?" Marshall jeered, "Is that why you appointed yourself as official big brother to Danielle?"

Dani looked up in time to catch the look Barrett flashed across the table and shuddered at the thought of that quelling look ever turning on her.

"I don't intend to let you boss her around forever, Thompsen."

"Are you worried that I'll ask her to 'be nice' to someone?" the darker man said sarcastically.

Barrett leaned back in his chair, subtly taking command as he regarded Marshall through half-closed eyes. "To be truthful, I almost believed that you'd asked Dani to *be nice* to me until she didn't mention that I was here one night when you called."

A flush crept into Dani's cheeks when Marshall darted an angry glance at her. "This whole conversation is pointless," she said crossly, wishing they would stop.

"Not pointless," Marshall scoffed. "Any minute now Barrett is going to tell a sordid tale about an innocent young thing named Melissa and how I nearly led her astray."

"Melissa?" she echoed, glancing hesitatingly from one man to the other.

"The daughter of a friend of mine," Barrett explained.

"Well? Go on," Dani insisted as Barrett made a show of drinking his coffee as though that explanation was enough.

But Marshall wasn't going to leave it at that. "A few years ago, Melissa won a local beauty contest. She was engaged to be married at the time, but the bright lights and big city suddenly seemed tempting. She came to me and persuaded me to help her become a model. Of course, the version she gave her family and fiancé was that I'd approached her with promises of a great future. She was about your age and the apple of her father's eye. Anything his daughter wanted, she got, so of course he said yes. The fiancé was a few years older and he thought his love should have some fun before she settled down to married life. He didn't object."

Out of the corner of her eye, Dani glanced at Barrett, who was calmly listening to all this with studied indifference. But she'd figured out that Barrett had been Melissa's fiancé. The thought was chilling but she didn't know why.

"The girl was beautiful," Marshall went on. "But unfortunately, she was kind of lazy. All she wanted was the prestige and excitement of being a model without the work you know it entails, Danielle. She wanted instant success, push a button and be on the cover of *Vogue*. But Melissa did enjoy the parties and the men that would crowd around her. Somewhere along the line, she took a lover.'' He gave Barrett a derisive glance. "Or more than one. I have no idea whether she did it to help her career the easy way or if it was just for fun. Either way, her fiancé found out. And precious little Melissa told him that I had asked her to 'be nice' to the man. Therefore I became the villain.''

Dani's eyes were clouded with tears for the anguish Barrett must have gone through. Now she understood the animosity that existed between the two men and Marshall's cryptic statement that he wanted to show "some people'' that things were not always what they seemed.

"The engagement was broken, needless to say, because Melissa didn't want to give up her new life. Daddy sent her off to New York because he'd invested in some Broadway shows. So he essentially bought her some minor roles and even wrangled her a few television commercials. I understand she's doing quite well, but then she was always a pretty good actress.''

"You didn't mention the way you used the scandal to your advantage,'' Barrett said tightly. "But you always were good at using people and situations. Like you've used Dani.''

"I'm a survivor,'' Marshall chuckled smugly. "Not everyone is born a King.''

"And not everyone is born with compassion for their fellow humans,'' was Barrett's dry reply.

"Compassion doesn't pay.'' Dani could see Marshall was faltering a little despite his tough talk under the pinning gaze of the man opposite him.

"Look, Thompsen, maybe I misjudged you

regarding Melissa, but I still know what drives you. You're too hungry for power to care about anyone unless they can help you.'' There was something very threatening in his softly spoken words. "Now, if you've finished your coffee, I suggest that you leave.''

Hesitation flickered in Marshall's dark eyes as if he wanted to challenge Barrett's right to tell him to leave, but Dani had no doubt that Barrett would do whatever it took to get his rival out.

"I'll see you to the door, Marshall,'' she said, pushing her chair back to rise and forcing him to accompany her.

She could sense the rage still seething in him as Marshall walked rapidly to the door, his back rigid with anger. His mouth curved into a sneer as he turned to say good night.

"Guess you've decided to go over to King's side.''

"I'm not on anyone's side,'' Dani said firmly. "I didn't want the two of you arguing anymore, and this seemed like the best way to stop it.''

"Don't delude yourself that he thinks you're anything special. But for some weird reason, he feels responsible for you. I don't know why.'' He shrugged. "Let him worry about your moral character and I'll see to it that you become a success.''

"Good night, Marshall.''

There was a bad taste in Dani's mouth as she closed the door on his retreating figure and went back to the kitchen and Barrett.

He was leaning against the counter, a fresh cup of coffee in his hands. He didn't look up when Dani walked in.

"Barrett?" He gave her an aloof look. "I'm sorry."

"About what?" he countered as she came a little closer.

"Melissa," she answered without raising her eyes to meet his. "You were engaged to her, weren't you?"

"Yes." His voice was emotionless, which only made Dani realize how very deeply he had been hurt.

"Well, it sounds like you can't blame Marshall too much for what happened. I mean, she must have been selfish and immature before she met him," she ended lamely.

"Don't defend him. Just don't." His bitterness startled her.

"I wasn't," Dani asserted, finally meeting his level gaze. "I always knew he was going to get something out of helping me. I've never had any illusions about that. But he wasn't to blame for what happened between you and Melissa. It would have happened anyway."

"And?" Barrett prompted with maddening calm. "I have a feeling there's another point you want to make."

Dani breathed in deeply to check her temper. She knew she was hearing the anger he had held back when Marshall was there.

"You told me that you preferred the old Dani to the new me. But I'm basically the same person. I am what I am and the way I am, and nice clothes don't make me any different."

This time she didn't look away from his intimidating glare. For some reason that she couldn't explain, she wanted Barrett to understand that she wasn't like Melissa. It was important to her.

"I'm doing all this because it's what Lew wanted. He's my dad—it's his approval and respect that I want. No one else's!" she added when the heavy silence threatened to stretch indefinitely. "I want him to be happy. And if wearing expensive clothes, going to fancy parties, and mixing with the right people can help make that happen, no matter how much I'd rather be with him, I'll do it." When Barrett still said nothing, Dani stamped her foot with frustration. "And I won't have you arguing anymore with Marshall and wrecking my chances to be what my father wants! Do you hear?"

Her eyes filled with unshed tears and she didn't see the corners of his mouth twitch in a revealing smile.

"Well, I guess you're still the same beautiful brat that you were before," Barrett admitted, a devilish twinkle replacing the coldness in his eyes.

"Of course I am!" Dani snapped, still too angry to realize that Barrett was agreeing with her.

"I'm glad you admitted that."

"Admitted what?" she frowned as she studied the arrogant tilt of his head. The mist of tears clouding her eyes began to diminish.

"That you're a beautiful brat," he answered with an irritating grin.

"I did not say that!"

"No, I said it, and you agreed with me."

Confusion reigned as Dani tried to make the lightning adjustment from anger to teasing that Barrett had made. That intimate gleam in his eyes wasn't helping her to think straight either. She heard his soft laughter and felt his arm wind around her waist and draw her close.

"You aren't angry with me anymore?" There was uncertainty in the look she gave him, her head tipping up so she could see his sternly handsome face.

"I never was angry with you," he said, pulling her around in front of him as he locked his hands behind Dani to keep her there.

"I thought you were," she said, addressing the open collar of his shirt and the dark hair that curled on his tanned chest. "Because of the things I said about Melissa. I probably didn't have any right to say them."

"When has that ever stopped you from speaking your mind?" he mocked. His head was lowered close to her downcast face.

Her hands were resting on his shirt front, her fingers playing with a button while she tried to ignore the sight of his mouth so close to her own.

"I'm sorry," she repeated. "I know you must have been very hurt when you found out about Melissa."

"That's all over now," Barrett said quietly, and something in his voice convinced her that was true. And Dani felt secretly glad. "At the time I did blame Marshall because I didn't want to admit that Melissa was exactly what you just said—selfish. And immature. And that's being kind to her."

"Oh, so I'm right. I love to be right," Dani said.

"So I've noticed. But there's something else we have to talk about, Dani," he went on.

"What's that?"

"The promise you made to your father."

Her mouth drooped. "I've bent it a little, but I haven't ever talked to you about your horses or what's happening at the track," she said defensively.

"Why didn't you tell me about it in the beginning?"

"I didn't think you would come to see me very often. When you did, well—" She gave an expressive shrug, not wanting to put into words how much she had looked forward to his visits.

"You broke your word to Lew because of me?"

"Yes." Dani hung her head like a guilty teenager. "Somehow seeing you helped. It suddenly wasn't so lonely."

"Lonely? With all those parties Marshall takes you to?" His question was gentle.

"They're all strangers to me, the people at those parties. I know all the right things to say, but—I know that world isn't mine, no matter what my father thinks."

"I don't think Lew meant you to take that promise so literally."

"Oh, yes, he did," Dani nodded.

Barrett let go and reached into a pocket. "Read this," he said, and handed her a letter.

The scrawled handwriting was unmistakably her father's. "How did you get this?" she breathed.

"It's a letter your father wrote me," Barrett answered, but Dani was already busy reading it.

The letter was short, but her father had never been one for eloquent correspondence. The first part thanked Barrett for coming to see him and for letting him know how she, Dani, was doing. Her eyes glittered with tears as she read the last line above her father's nearly indecipherable signature. *I'm grateful that Dani is seeing you. I don't like to think of her completely alone without anyone she knows.*

"He doesn't mind," she whispered. "Lew isn't upset because I've been seeing you."

"No, he isn't," Barrett replied solemnly.

"When did you see him?" Dani blinked back the happy tears to gaze earnestly into his face. "Was he all right? Where is he?"

"Slow down! I can only answer one question at a time." His smile softened his stern words. "I saw him in New York. He's at Belmont right now and he's fine."

"When were you there?"

"Last week. He's picked up a great four-year-old gelding and the mare he kept placed in both races he entered her in. I think he's begun to put his life back together."

"Why didn't you tell me?" Dani murmured. "That you'd seen him?"

"He made it clear that he didn't want you to know where he was, although he never told me in so many words that I couldn't," Barrett replied with a twinkle.

"I'm so happy!" she cried, throwing her arms around his neck and hugging him tightly. "I've been so worried about Lew, not knowing where he was or how he was. It was awful."

"I know, kitten."

Her face was buried in his neck. At the caressing sound of his voice, Dani lifted it slightly, glancing at the sensuous line of his mouth now crooked in a smile. As she moved closer, Barrett met her halfway.

CHAPTER EIGHT

Something happened in that kiss. The wild melody of joy in Dani's heart turned into a rising crescendo that pounded in her ears until she couldn't even hear the beat of her own heart. The touch of Barrett's mouth, at first probingly soft as always, became masterfully demanding, expertly forcing her to make an instinctive response.

Her breathing was shallow, softening into sighs when his mouth left hers to explore the pulsating cord in her neck. No one had ever aroused such elemental feelings in her before.

"I believe you're beginning to like me," Barrett murmured next to her ear.

"Oh . . . only beginning," she said shakily as if she needed to deny what was happening to her.

Her hands pushed against his chest. An instant later Dani was sorry he had obligingly let her go.

She hadn't remembered feeling so weak since being thrown from a horse a few years ago. Her legs had trembled so badly when she tried to get back in the saddle that her father had to help her mount.

The long length of his body was leaning against the counter again, his dark head thrown arrogantly back while his eyes studied her face. Dani was overwhelmed with emotions she couldn't control . . . and didn't want him to see.

Hoping to distract him, she said, "The next time you see my father, will you give him my love?"

"Of course," agreed Barrett smoothly. "Oh— before I forget," he straightened up, "I won't be seeing you this weekend. This Sunday is my parents' anniversary. I probably won't be back in town until the end of next week."

"Oh," she said in a very small voice as her heart sank. Dani turned away, trying to assume an air of indifference. "Well, have a nice time."

"I'm sure I will," he said with an amused lilt in his voice. "Okay. Time to go. Walk me to the door?"

"Of course." She kept a safe distance between them.

Without Barrett's visits, the following days and nights seemed unbearably monotonous. Dani kept telling herself that she only missed his easy friendship. The powerful sensuality of his kiss wasn't worth getting all worked up about. She refused to consider that she might be physically attracted to Barrett. His fierce good looks didn't affect her at all, she kept saying, and she was immune to the devastating smile.

She was feeling blue simply because she would rather be outdoors in the sunlight instead of under the bright photographer's lights, or in the fresh evening air instead of some crowded party. But that explanation didn't apply to the evenings when she was free and still stayed cooped up in her apartment, feeling lost and lonely.

Marshall never mentioned what had happened, which surprised Dani, who had expected him to grill her about her relationship with Barrett. But he seemed more attentive than he had been before and more confident. Her listless agreement to his suggestions only brought a shrewdly satisfied gleam to his dark eyes.

That same gleam had been there this afternoon when he abruptly informed her that he was changing their plans for this evening. His announcement that they would be attending a private party instead of an exclusive supper club hadn't gotten any reaction from Dani.

As usual, she and Marshall were among the last guests to arrive. She had long since ceased to be wowed by the beautiful furnishings of the various mansions she had been in or the sparkling jewelry and expensive clothes shown off by the people who attended these affairs.

Through her racetrack experience, Dani was able to separate the real guests from the gate-crashers and the social climbers. And Marshall was always a welcome and much sought-after guest. Every group of people they approached stepped back to admit him into their circle.

The last group they stopped at made him the center of their attention, something that Marshall's ego enjoyed and Dani was grateful for, since she wasn't in the mood for chitchat.

Pretending a polite interest in the conversation—or more accurately, Marshall's monologue—she let her gaze wander idly over the room, silently wishing she was out beneath the stars. At the opposite end of the room, she caught sight of a tall, well-dressed man. Shifting her position slightly, she looked for him again.

Her heart fluttered, skipped a beat, then hammered wildly. She only knew one person who wore black tie with quite that casual elegance, and that was Barrett. Unconsciously she must have stiffened, communicating her tenseness to the hand that rested possessively on her shoulders. As she became aware of Marshall turning toward her, the man in the distance turned, enabling her to see the powerful profile that was unmistakably Barrett's.

"Is something wrong, Danielle?" murmured Marshall.

"No, no, nothing," she protested too quickly as Marshall's dark eyes followed the direction of hers.

At that moment the couple who had been in front of Barrett stepped aside. Before, Dani had only been able to see him because of his height. Now she saw the gorgeous blonde clinging to his arm and a numb pain took hold of her chest.

"You seem surprised to see him here," Marshall was saying. "Why is that?"

"I thought he was out of town." The truth came out before she could stop it.

"He's been back for several days," was the mocking reply. "Didn't you know that?"

Her pride was suffering as she shrugged. "No, why should I?" But she couldn't keep her gaze from straying back to the blonde who so obviously had Barrett's complete attention. Even at this distance, Dani could recognize that warm smile and that disconcerting way he had of looking at a woman as though none other existed.

"Wondering who the blonde is?" Marshall whispered sarcastically.

"I don't remember seeing her before." The casually worded admission came out in a tightly choked voice.

"That's Nicole Carstairs—of Carstairs Steel, the current front-runner in the race to become Mrs. Barrett King." The unmistakable pleasure he took in revealing that startling information to Dani drained the color from her face.

Information like that was Marshall's specialty. There was no doubt in her mind that he knew what he was talking about. "You didn't actually think you were the only girl he was seeing, did you?" he jeered softly. "I tried to tell you the other night that all he felt was this weird sense of responsibility for you, but you didn't want to believe me."

She felt sick to her stomach, torn in two by some vague feeling that Barrett had betrayed her, wanting only to cover her ears and shut out Marshall's voice.

"I understand she even spent the weekend at the farm. Just one of the many family friends who gathered to celebrate the Kings' anniversary," Marshall said snidely. His implication was clear enough.

"Please," Dani protested, "stop talking about it. Barrett and I are friends, that's all."

"I know that." His smug smile was infuriating. She wanted to smack it off his face.

Dani quickly spun away from his touch, hating him for telling her something she should have guessed herself. Hadn't she always known Barrett could have—did have—any woman he wanted?

"You'd like to leave, wouldn't you, Danielle?" he said quietly.

"Yes." Her brimming eyes turned back to him, filled with pain she didn't want him to see.

Marshall chuckled as if his triumph was complete. "No." He arched an eyebrow. "Not until we've welcomed Barrett back to Louisville."

She searched the dark face for some sign that this was only a mean-spirited joke. Then Dani realized it wasn't. In that same instant she also realized that Marshall had known Barrett would be at this party tonight and Nicole Carstairs would be with him. This was Marshall's revenge . . . because Dani hadn't told him that she'd been seeing Barrett.

Short of fleeing the room, there was no hope of escape. Marshall was already taking her arm, turning her back around and facing her in Barrett's direction.

Her mind raced ahead, trying to figure out what Marshall hoped to gain by embarrassing her in this way, even as she took the first faltering step to cross the room. Then, with vivid clarity, she knew. He wanted a scene. He wanted to see her publicly attack Barrett as she had done when The Rogue was destroyed. Not to humiliate her, but Barrett.

Her pride gave her strength. The smile she

forced looked so natural that only someone who had known her for years could see the strain in her face. She braced herself to meet Barrett's gaze as she and Marshall came closer.

The brightness in his eyes faded when he saw her. Her heart cried for her to turn away, to escape, but Dani kept moving steadfastly forward.

"Barrett, I didn't know you were back!" She wondered if the delight in her voice sounded as hollow to him as it did to her. Marshall let go of her arm, obviously surprised by her friendly greeting. Fooling him gave her the courage to continue. "I could hardly believe it when I saw you across the room."

"I told Danielle that you'd been back for several days," Marshall said spitefully.

"Did you now?" There was a challenging hardness in Barrett's eyes when he turned them to Marshall, but they were warm when they rested on Dani. "It's good to see you again, Dani." The blonde at his side moved closer, her clear blue eyes openly inspecting Dani as she tried to make it obvious that she was with Barrett. "Nicole, I'd like you to meet a friend of mine, Dani Williams," Barrett said. "Dani, this is Nicole Carstairs."

Dani smiled politely at the attractive blonde even though she didn't want to.

"Nice to meet you, Nicole," Dani murmured. "I love your dress. What a beautiful blue."

A statement that was much too true, as she noticed how perfectly it matched the woman's cornflower blue eyes. The blonde murmured her thanks, quickly turning her attention to Marshall as he was introduced.

"Well, did you enjoy your weekend at home, Barrett?" Dani found herself asking.

"Oh, we had a wonderful party," Nicole assured her, casting an adoring look at Barrett. "Of course it was family only."

Dani flinched. If she had needed proof of Marshall's statement, she didn't now. And Barrett's silence seemed to confirm his relationship with Nicole. The expression on his face was thoughtful and curious. Dani's heart wept a little as she watched it change into a warm smile when he looked down at Nicole.

"Excuse us for a moment, would you?" said Barrett. "I want to talk to Dani."

Nicole pouted slightly before she wrinkled her adorable nose and smiled. "Don't be long."

"I won't," Barrett promised, glancing sharply at Dani when she caught her breath in surprise, then he turned to Marshall. "Keep Nicole company, will you?"

Already Barrett was reaching for Dani's hand and she wondered if he saw the flash of anger in Marshall's eyes. But his attention was on the couple he was leading her to, and Dani eyed them hesitantly.

"Dani," Barrett was saying, "I want you to meet my sister Stephanie and her fiancé, Travis Blackman."

"Dani?" His sister, a very pretty girl with long brown hair, cocked her head, then burst into a wide smile. "Dani—of course, you're the one Barrett has been talking about. She's just as beautiful as you said she was, Barrett."

Dani was taken aback. But, despite her confusion,

she managed to thank Stephanie for the unexpected compliment.

"Your father is Lew Williams, isn't he?" Travis Blackman asked, drawing Dani's bewildered glance to him. She immediately liked what she saw, a pleasant face with brown eyes and brown hair.

"Yes, that's right," she nodded.

"He worked for my father several years ago," he explained, "before we sold our horses."

"Of course, Daddy and I are trying to persuade Travis to buy some more," Stephanie laughed. "From the King stables, naturally," she added with a wink to Dani.

"You'd better be careful that Dad doesn't sell you some high-strung filly," Barrett mocked, "like the one you're about to get hitched to. There's no taming a King, Travis."

Almost automatically, Dani joined in the friendly banter, even though she was mostly paying attention to Barrett, standing next to her and the burning touch of the hand that held hers. She fought the feeling that she would never again be able to look on him as a friend. A subtle change had taken place in their relationship tonight, too subtle for her to grasp immediately.

The smile, the forced laughter were becoming harder and harder to maintain. Any second she felt she would dissolve into tears. In an effort to keep calm, her hand unconsciously tightened on Barrett's.

His head bent slightly toward her, curious, his eyes searching her face as he smiled at her. With the force of a physical blow, his look took her breath away.

"I have to get back to Marshall." The desperation in her voice was clear.

"I think he'll survive a few more minutes without your company," Barrett remarked cynically.

But would she? Dani's heart pounded with dread. She wouldn't be able to keep up this pretense much longer. She managed a wide but trembling smile at the other couple.

"It was so nice meeting both of you." The brightness of her voice was transparently brittle, but luckily neither his sister nor her fiancé seemed to notice. When Dani turned away, she was able to free her hand from Barrett's hold and look wildly around for Marshall.

"What's wrong, Dani?" Barrett's voice was low, but unmistakably demanding.

"Wrong? Nothing's wrong." She flashed him an innocent look that was edged with fear. "I like your sister. She seems very nice."

There was no comment from Barrett and his mouth was set in an uncompromising line. His determined look only made her hurry to Marshall's side.

The arm that Marshall slipped around her waist provided much needed support, and Dani was even grateful for his cold kiss on her cheek. As Marshall said goodbye to Barrett and Nicole, Dani thought how strange it was that Barrett had never really told her the truth, but Marshall had. In his own way, Marshall was a more honest man. At that moment, his questionable motives for bringing her to this party didn't matter. She was too busy clinging to Marshall to notice the fire in Barrett's eyes as she was guided away.

Minutes later they were out on the entrance portico of the huge house, waiting for the attendant to bring Marshall's car. The fresh air revived Dani's numbed senses a little as she leaned heavily against him.

"Now will you cut him out of your life, Danielle?" Marshall demanded softly, drawing her closer.

"Yes," she whispered.

His hand cupped her chin and raised it. The shadows concealed the expression on his darkly handsome face, but Dani was too hurt to care about anything except the comfort of his arms.

"I know what I did tonight must have seemed wrong to you at first," he murmured. "But sometimes you have to be cruel to be kind."

Dani didn't attempt to avoid the lips that moved to cover hers. In fact, she needed someone's kiss to erase the memory of Barrett's. The fleeting warmth she felt seemed to do just that.

Through her pain, Dani decided she understood Marshall's reasons for forcing her to meet Barrett. He must have been determined to keep her from making a fool of herself over a man who belonged to someone else.

The following day Marshall was nearly always at her side, never allowing her to be alone, silently reassuring her in a thousand ways that he was the only one who truly cared. Somewhere, somehow, Dani had misjudged him. Of course, Marshall was shrewd and his actions were somewhat calculated, but to be a success in his field, he had to be. She had never entirely trusted Barrett anyway.

Dani didn't really want to go out to dinner and the theatre that night, but Marshall insisted. And as the evening progressed, she realized he was right. Alone in the apartment she would have brooded over Barrett. She realized now that most of Barrett's attention had been to counteract Marshall's influence, to get back at Marshall for whatever part he had played in Barrett's broken engagement years before.

Later, in front of her building, Marshall parked and switched off the ignition, but it was Dani who made the move that brought her into his arms. He kept her there once she was captured in his embrace. His hands and his kisses excited her a little, though he had none of Barrett's skill, until finally he drew back to trace her features gently in the dark.

"This is all my fault," he said softly. "You were so cynical and doubting at first that I thought I had to give you time to trust me. I never dreamed that Barrett would show up or that you would go to him for what I wanted to give you."

A heavy sigh shuddered through her. "I just needed a link with the past. That's the only reason I ever saw him."

That had been true—at first. With a twinge of pain, Dani knew it had developed into something more. If only she had told Marshall about Barrett's visits, she never would have suffered the torment she was going through now, this piercing hurt of betrayal.

"Are you going to be all right?" Marshall asked gently, brushing her lips lightly.

"Thanks to you, yes." She smiled, giving him

back the kiss and feeling his arms tighten so her mouth would linger against his for a few seconds more.

"I'll come in for a while if you want me to," he offered.

"I'll be fine," Dani assured him, moving reluctantly out of his arms to her own side of the car. "I'll see you tomorrow."

"Not until the afternoon, though," he said with a regretful sigh. "I have some work I have to do. Sleep late in the morning. I'll call John and tell him to postpone your session until next week."

"Fine with me. I could sleep until Christmas." She realized how true that was as a delayed exhaustion seemed to sweep over her—undoubtedly a reaction to the sleepless hours of the night before.

After exchanging goodnights, Dani walked to the entrance of her apartment building and turned to wave to Marshall as he drove away. As she walked down the hall to her door, the carpet muffled her footsteps so that the only sound she heard was the rustling of her long gown.

She unlocked the door and went in, closing it behind her, only to feel a violent force pushing it open. Barrett was right behind her.

"What are you doing here?" Dani breathed, intimidated by the anger in his green eyes.

"I wanted to talk to you," Barrett replied in a dangerously low voice. "But I had a feeling you wouldn't want to talk to me."

A muscle was jumping in his jaw and his stance reminded her of a jungle cat about to spring. His face was set in lines of uncompromising harshness.

Her heart was beating at a frantic pace as she backed away from him.

She attempted to sidetrack him with the first thing that came to mind. "I . . . I didn't s—see you outside."

"I know," he jeered softly. "You were much too busy with . . . other things."

She fought her rising fear as she realized he must have seen her in the car with Marshall. "Th—that's none of your business," she protested, her voice growing stronger. Out of the corner of her eye, she saw the telephone beside the couch. With quick steps she reached it and picked up the receiver with a threatening look. "If you don't leave, I'll call the police and have you thrown out!"

With a swiftness that she hadn't expected in a man Barrett's size, he was at her side and taking it from her hand. Dani didn't want to fight him for it, knowing the strength of his muscular chest and arms. Hadn't he picked her up and carried her like a child more than once?

"You can call anyone you want," he told her, his head arrogantly tilted back, "after I find out what the hell is going on!"

"I don't owe you any explanations." Her tight voice threatened to break under the strain.

"I thought you knew what kind of a man Marshall is." There was no escaping his penetrating gaze.

"I've always been a pretty good judge of people, which is probably why I never completely trusted you," Dani retorted.

"What's happened to you this week?" Barrett demanded. "Last night at the party, you chattered nonstop but you looked at me like I had the plague.

I did try to call you to let you know I was back in town, but I couldn't reach you and I was too busy to get away."

Silently Dani agreed that he probably had been too busy. Nicole had acted as if she commanded every minute of his time, but she wasn't about to tell him that.

"I wouldn't have cared if you never saw me again," she said scathingly.

"I thought we'd agreed to be friends." His voice was tense, the muscle still working along his jaw.

"Well, now I prefer Marshall's company to yours. He's much more fun," she said defiantly.

CHAPTER NINE

"Damn you, Dani!"

With a lightning move that frightened her, Barrett pulled her to him. It was like coming in contact with a high-voltage wire, jolting her to the tips of her toes. Beneath her hands she felt the uneven rise and fall of his chest, not much different from her own ragged breathing.

"What do you know about love? Or sex, for that matter?" Barrett asked, searching her eyes as if he would find his answers there.

"More than you think," she said weakly. She was uncomfortably aware of the ruthless line of his mouth. "I know it takes two willing people."

A mirthless laugh came from his throat. "The first time I kissed you I doubted you'd ever been kissed before, no matter what you claimed."

"Well, I had. You're not the only man on earth,"

Dani asserted. She tried to push herself away from his chest, only to have him hold her closer to his body. She was disturbingly aware that he enjoyed the pressure of the rounded swell of her breasts and that it was arousing him.

A wicked light entered his eyes.

"Let me go!" Dani cried, suddenly frightened by that look.

As her hands reached up to scratch at his face, her wrists were imprisoned behind her back. Before she could kick out with her foot at his vulnerable shins, Barrett was bending her backwards so she was off balance, and any attempt to defend herself with her feet would send her sprawling on the floor.

With one hand, he held both her wrists as she suddenly surrendered to his passionate kiss. A searing fire was coursing through her, making her defenseless, ready to give in to the power of his sensual assault.

When Barrett moved from her mouth to the sensitive areas around her neck and ears, Dani gasped for breath, feeling the betraying shudder of her body beneath his expert lovemaking. "No," she moaned in a plaintive protest. Her mouth opened to repeat the cry again, only to have it die in her throat as his mouth closed over hers, taking full advantage of her parted lips.

Her tense muscles began to relax, allowing Barrett to mold her against his masculine hardness. Slowly he straightened, to see her head still bent back so he could take her lips. And she wanted him to. Nothing in her experience had prepared her for the erotic bliss of his touch.

"Do you see how easy it could be?" Barrett muttered against her mouth.

In an instant she found herself lying on the couch with Barrett above her, holding her there easily, his eyes on fire with desire. Never in her life had Dani been so aware of the difference between a man and a woman than she was at that moment, with his hard, muscular body over hers.

"Are you going to insist that I prove it?" The softness of his voice didn't hide the steel beneath the surface.

But Barrett didn't allow her time to answer as he lowered his head again to ravish her mouth, this time with a sweet seductiveness that disarmed her completely, compelling her to remember the comfort she had first experienced in his arms, knowing instinctively that this was where she belonged.

Lost in the labyrinth of her emotions, Dani blinked in confusion when he moved away. There were a thousand unanswered questions in her eyes as she stared at the erect figure standing beside her.

"Well?" Barrett challenged, his hands on his hips, that unrelenting hardness still in his expression.

"I hate you!" Her voice trembled as she tried to find the strength to move from her prone position on the couch.

He only shrugged. "I've been hated before," Barrett mocked, turning away from her.

Released from his gaze, Dani struggled upright on the cushions, stung by his indifference.

"I hate better than most people!" she retorted, giving in to a surge of childish temper.

"Is that what you felt a moment ago? Hate?" There was something very intimate in the look that swept over her, stripping her of her protective anger and revealing the need that she was trying so hard to deny.

"Go! Get out of here!" she demanded hoarsely, hot waves of shame washing over her. "I don't want anything from you. Not your friendship or your kisses! And save the caveman routine for Nicole. She probably loves it but I don't!"

"Nicole?" A slow smile spread across Barrett's face and he began to laugh.

"I don't see what's so funny," she said crossly.

The laughter stopped, but the devastating smile remained. "So that's what all this is about," he murmured.

"I don't know what you're talking about." Dani turned away from his much too perceptive gaze, wishing she hadn't mentioned Nicole's name. It was unthinkable that she could possibly be jealous of the woman.

He reached down, opening her tightly clenched hands and drawing her to her feet. When she attempted to pull free, he let her go.

"I made a mistake the other night and I owe you an apology," he told her. The mutinous expression on her face changed to one of bewilderment. "I assumed that you knew that Nicole and Travis Blackman, my sister's fiancé, are half-brother and sister."

For a moment, she was afraid to believe the implication of his statement. So Nicole was the half-sister of his future brother-in-law. So what? They still could be lovers.

"Have you been listening to Marshall's gossip?" he asked gently when she remained silent.

"I have eyes. I can see," Dani murmured instead, afraid now to acknowledge the wild beat of her heart. "And last night you were—"

"Last night I was doing my future brother-in-law a favor nothing more," Barrett finished the sentence for her, thoughtfully watching the betraying emotion on her face.

He reached out to caress her, but she turned away. Dani just wanted to cry, because she couldn't understand what was happening to her, but she fought back the tears and struggled for composure.

"Now do you understand?" Barrett asked softly.

"No," she answered weakly, closing her eyes briefly against the magnetic attraction. "No, I don't understand anything."

His smile was gentle, but it didn't relieve the ache in her heart. "Sleep on it. I'll pick you up around eight in the morning."

"Why?" There was confusion on her face.

"Because I'm free tomorrow and I want to spend the day with you."

"But—"

"Eight o'clock," he said firmly, releasing her wrists and touching a finger to her lips. Then he was walking away from her and seconds later, Dani heard the door close.

She was still upset—even queasy. So Barrett claimed he wasn't serious about Nicole Carstairs. Why that should be of such importance to her, Dani didn't know. She and Barrett were simply friends. That thought brought a sickening rush of pain.

A little voice inside her said, *You aren't sick. You're in love.*

And Dani laughed aloud, a shaky laugh that soon caught in her throat. Love was a fantasy that might never happen to her. And certainly not here and not now. Not with Barrett King.

"Marshall. Why can't I be in love with Marshall?" she demanded, not realizing she had spoken her thoughts aloud.

But she wasn't. Tonight she had turned to Marshall to try to erase Barrett from her memory. Marshall's kisses had excited her, but it was Barrett's passionate embrace that had awakened a desire that consumed her, body and soul.

Did Barrett simply feel responsible for her, as Marshall claimed? Dani remembered again the control Barrett had exhibited during that embrace. Yet he had gone to great lengths to make her understand that Nicole meant nothing to him.

All those crazy questions went unanswered as Dani asked them over and over, until exhaustion got the better of her again, and she slept at last.

The morning sunlight brought all her uncertainty back. One moment her heart was leaping with the hope that Barrett might care and the next moment sinking to the deepest depths of despair at her mental argument that he did not. By the time he arrived promptly at eight, Dani was as tense as a coiled spring, her brilliant gaze bouncing away from the levelness of his. In an effort to appear casual and uncaring, she chattered on and on while Barrett patiently sipped the coffee she had poured.

"Aren't you interested in where we're going today?" he asked, stopping her talk with a single question.

"Yes," she swallowed, trying to sound casual and failing.

"Good. Let's take a drive through the country and I'll show you what else Kentucky has to offer besides Churchill Downs."

"Would you like to leave now?" Dani asked nervously.

The slight reluctance in her voice earned her a quizzically amused look from Barrett. "The sooner we leave, the more we'll see."

She nodded agreement as she hurried to clear the table, holding back her tears. Somehow she'd hoped for some indication of Barrett's feelings, especially after the way he had kissed her last night. Yet he was acting no differently from any of the other times he had taken her out. His friendly aloofness hurt.

Loving him didn't seem to change anything. Had it been so very long ago that she'd asserted that they were no different? It was even more true now that her clothes and appearance were impeccable. She had taken her place among Kentucky society, but never had she felt so strongly that she wasn't good enough for a man like Barrett King.

"Dani?" His hand touched her arm when he spoke.

Her first instinct was to turn into his arms, accept the masculine comfort of that broad chest. The impulse was so strong she had to jerk away from his touch to resist it, an embarrassed blush rising in her face when she looked at him. His eyes narrowed and the line of his mouth was grim.

"You don't sound very excited about today." There was an edge to his voice that cut right through Dani. "Is it because of last night?"

Her tone immediately became defensive. "What are you talking about?"

She felt rather than saw his exasperated sigh. "Calm down, okay? I'm not inviting you out today to seduce you. If I wanted to do that, I would've done it last night." His intense green gaze was boring into the back of her neck. "So forget about it."

"That's not easy to do," Dani admitted, knowing she would never forget and dying a little that he would ask her to do so. "I don't know if we can be friends anymore, Barrett."

"It's always difficult for a man and a woman to be friends," he said cryptically. "But all we have to worry about today is enjoying ourselves."

"Yes. Yes, of course," she nodded, forcing a determined smile.

"That's my girl," Barrett said lightly, flashing her a quick smile before he turned away. It was a bittersweet phrase that Dani desperately wished were true.

She could read between the lines. Although Barrett obviously knew it was impossible for them to go back to the easy relationship they had before, asking her to forget his passionate lovemaking meant he didn't want to become seriously involved. If he cared for her at all, it was because he felt obligated.

Proudly raising her chin, Dani vowed silently that Barrett would never guess the change in her feelings toward him. So she played along with his light-hearted teasing and allowed him to believe that last night was already forgotten. What did it matter if her senses were all too aware of him now? The tantalizing nearness of him behind the wheel of the car, close enough to touch, was almost too much to bear.

His tour through the Kentucky countryside around Louisville took them first to Bardstown. Dani was grateful for the many sights to see—anything to sidetrack her attention from Barrett. Tree-lined residential streets were crowned with stately mansions, including the Federal Hill house that inspired Stephen Foster to write "My Old Kentucky Home" while visiting Bardstown more than a century ago.

Dani discovered she was even capable of laughter when they toured the Museum of Whisky History and saw an original bottle of whisky distilled by E. C. Booz in 1854, an old brand name that had become slang for liquor.

The time passed swiftly. When Barrett suggested a Lexington restaurant for dinner, she could hardly believe that so much time had gone by since lunch. The service was fast, leaving little time for small talk as she concentrated on the meal. There had been very little personal conversation the entire day, she realized. Both of them had talked mostly about their sightseeing.

"We should be able to make it home before dark," she said after Barrett had paid the bill and they were on the way to his car.

"We aren't going back yet," he said smoothly.

The thought of being with him in the soft Kentucky twilight seemed so intimate that Dani shivered. "Where are we going?"

"To the auction, of course. You haven't been to it before, have you?" He opened the car door for her.

"Auction?"

"Don't tell me you haven't heard of the yearling sale at Keeneland racetrack," he said mockingly.

The July sale of year-old thoroughbreds, Dani knew, was the biggest and the best in the world. Horse breeders paid to have their colts and fillies considered for sale, but out of the thousand or so entries, only those yearlings with the bluest blood and the most desirable conformation were accepted.

And the buyers were an equally select group. Tickets for seats in the sales pavilion were given only to those who could prove they had the millions that the best yearlings would fetch.

A shiver of excitement raced through Dani. She had always wanted to attend the auction of these untried and unnamed thoroughbreds, whose ancestry went back to a handful of seventeenth and eighteenth-century horses.

"I know all about the sale," she murmured, the excitement dying. "But I can't go, Barrett. You know that."

"Because of your promise to your father," he stated rather than asked.

"Yes," she whispered. There was a lump in her throat and she had to look away from his solemn face.

"I don't see what the problem is." Barrett

shrugged. "You can't possibly break your promise by looking at a horse, unless you intend to buy one."

His mocking tone didn't succeed in raising a smile. "Please take me home."

"Dani, what are you going to do? Lock yourself in a room?" he asked with a gentle kind of exasperation. "Horses are everywhere. You can't spend the rest of your life pretending they don't exist."

"I know that's true," Dani admitted, staring at her tightly clenched hands. "But—Keeneland." she sighed helplessly.

"Answer me honestly," Barrett said. "Do you want to go?"

"That's beside the point," she sighed again.

"It *is* the point," he corrected. "If you want to go, I'll take you. If you don't want to go, I'll take you home."

"It isn't fair," Dani protested. "I want to go, but I won't break my promise to Lew."

"Then I'm taking you to the sale." His mouth closed in a grim line, ending any further discussion as he started the car and reversed out of the lot.

Secretly Dani was glad the decision had been made for her. Attending the Keeneland sale was a dream come true. She soothed her guilty conscience with Barrett's argument that just looking at horses really wasn't breaking her promise.

She and Barrett were whisked through the crowds of tourists outside the sales pavilion and into the select semi-circle of green seats. The noise, the scattered conversation on the merits of one yearling over another, the rustling pages in the catalogue, the raised dais of the auctioneer, his spotters stationed strategically around the arena, the electric excitement that crackled through the air—Dani took in all these things instantly.

Minutes later, the auction began. The first colt was led into the roped enclosure beneath the auctioneer's stand, identified only by the number on its sleek hindquarters. For the first horses, Dani listened attentively to the singsong chant exhorting the bidders to go higher, and strained to see their almost imperceptible signs, a flick of a finger, a bob of the head, the momentary wave of an auction program.

Slowly her mind began to shut out the murmurs of the crowd, the chant of the auctioneer, and the cries of the spotters. Not even the pressure of Barrett's shoulder against hers distracted her as she studied the yearlings being led in, sold, and led out.

It was impossible not to admire the perfection of these prize horses, bred for speed and beauty, the long, gracefully curved necks that swung up and down in cadence with the stride propelling the horse forward. Her father had taught Dani to look for the straight walk, the wide throat, muscular shoulders and haunches, and flat knees. As the hammer fell with the sale of the last horse, she leaned back against the green cushion, watching the milling crowds of buyers slowly exiting the arena.

"Are you sorry you came?" Barrett spoke for the first time since they had entered the sales pavilion.

She swallowed the tight lump in her throat. "Yes, I am." Her cinnamon-colored eyes were misted over when she turned her gaze to him. The expression on his strong features showed no surprise at her answer.

"Why?" he asked, showing no inclination to move from his seat as his gaze swept over the taut lines of her face.

But Dani refused to answer, hunching a little deeper in her seat, a cold misery closing around her. Visions of those magnificent specimens of young thoroughbreds danced in her head, bringing back memories of the time when racehorses had been such a vital part of her life.

"Have you finally realized that you have to live your own life?" he demanded. "Not the one your father wants you to live? Or Marshall?"

"There's nothing wrong with being a model," she said.

"Absolutely not, as long as that's what you want to be."

"Why wouldn't I want to be a model?" she demanded with a defiant ring.

"That's something you'll have to decide for yourself," Barrett replied calmly, rising to his feet and drawing her with him. "Come on, I'll take you home."

But Dani wasn't ready to drop the subject. "Guess you still think I looked better when I ran around dressed like a boy with my hair cropped short and didn't talk about anything except horses!"

His fingers gripped her upper arm tightly as he spun her around to face him. "There was nothing wrong with you. You were a tomboy. So what? You were still one of the prettiest girls I'd ever seen."

"What are you saying?" Dani remembered that she'd had mixed feelings about the way she dressed long before her father had told her it was time to grow up. But there had never been any reason to change. "Are you saying I should go back to the track? Back to being a glorified groom?"

"I want you to do what you want to do, not what someone else tells you." He released her arm and turned away.

"Why?" Dani asked beseechingly, almost in a whisper.

"Why what?" He looked at her quizzically.

"Why do you care?"

"Because I don't want to see you make a mistake and end up unhappy," Barrett said quietly.

"Is that why you've been seeing me? All those times," she murmured, "you were trying to protect me. Thanks, big brother."

There was an almost imperceptible backward movement of his head and a cool look in his eyes. "That's about right. You needed an anchor, some connection with your past. I tried to give you that."

"I think your little sister has grown up now," Dani said numbly, knowing he couldn't have made the way he thought about her any plainer.

"Have you?" returned Barrett, studying her thoroughly.

"Well, I see things more clearly," she stated, turning away so he couldn't see the disappointment in her eyes.

They drove back to Louisville in silence. Dani didn't give Barrett a chance to walk her to her apartment door as she quickly got out of the car, thanked him for the day and told him not to bother to come in. At the building entrance she didn't even turn around to wave.

The shrill ringing of the phone greeted her as she entered her apartment. Wearily rubbing her aching head, she slumped on the couch and answered it.

"Danielle! Where the hell have you been?" Marshall's angry voice sounded in the receiver.

Not until that moment did Dani remember that Marshall had planned to come over this afternoon. "I'm sorry, Marshall," she answered insincerely. "I should've let you know I would be gone."

"I've been calling all over town trying to find out where you were. So where were you?" he demanded.

She ignored the outraged tone of his voice and the question. "Are you busy right now?" she asked instead. "I'd like you to come over."

"Now?" Her request had obviously caught him by surprise. "Is something wrong?"

"I'm not ill or hurt, if that's what you're thinking," Dani laughed bitterly. "I want to talk to you, and I'd prefer to do it tonight." By morning her resolve might weaken.

"I'll be there in five minutes."

CHAPTER TEN

"You've got to be crazy!" Marshall exclaimed when Dani broke the news to him. "You're just beginning to achieve some success. You can't quit now!"

"I can and I am," she said emphatically.

"But why, for heaven's sake?"

"That doesn't concern you." She sat down at the table and opened her checkbook, glad she'd saved the money she had earned. Combined with the nest egg her father had given her, she had more than enough to pay back the money Marshall had spent. "How much do I owe you?"

"Damn it, Dani! You owe me a lot more than money!" His face reddened with anger.

"No, I don't. That's all our relationship was about, anyway—a point you made yourself," Dani reminded him firmly.

"At least tell me why you've suddenly decided to throw away everything I've given you!"

"My decision isn't sudden, Marshall, although maybe it seems that way." A heavy sigh punctuated her statement. "I've been doing some thinking. And I finally realized this wasn't the way I wanted to live for the rest of my life."

Dani did realize that it was Barrett King who had inspired her to be herself—not a wannabe model. Not Marshall's decorative date.

"I'm grateful for the help and support you gave me, Marshall," she went on quietly.

"Oh, Danielle," he groaned, his anger evaporating as he stared intently into her eyes, "I can't let you go just like that. I want to marry you. You and I are a team. We'll succeed together."

"You make it sound like a business merger." A sad smile curved her mouth.

"I love you," he hurried to assure her of that. "We have a fabulous future ahead of us. Everyone thinks we're a perfect couple. Can't you see us in *People?* Like Christie Brinkley and that guy she married . . . whats-his-name."

She could tell he believed his dreams of glory and she felt a little sorry for him. "What you don't understand, Marshall, is that I don't want that kind of marriage—and I'm not going to be a supermodel. What I want is . . . a home and babies." Barrett's, she realized at that moment. She wanted bouncing green-eyed babies with Barrett. "You don't want children."

There was a frown of hesitation before Marshall answered. "Well, I would if that was what you wanted." He nodded.

"You always have a fast answer," she sighed, "but it wouldn't work. I'm still a country girl, in spite of all the clothes and jewelry and makeup."

Instinctively Dani knew that Marshall's feelings for her were only superficial. He was too interested in himself and his career to ever really fall in love. But he continued to argue the point, finally accepting the check from Dani when she put it in his hand.

When she eventually persuaded him to leave, his last words to her were, "I'm still going to get you to change your mind. John has a shoot coming up for a fashion layout in a national magazine. You'll be in it."

Dani smiled. "Goodbye, Marshall." She closed the door. What he didn't know—and she purposely hadn't told him—was that she wouldn't be here tomorrow to listen to him, or any other day. First she was going to fly to New York where her father was. If he still didn't want her with him, then she would find somewhere else to go and something else to do.

Yet she owed it to Lew to let him know that she didn't intend to keep the promise anymore. Horses were a part of her life and they always would be. Barrett had managed to make her understand that she couldn't keep an impossible promise.

The next morning, Dani bought suitcases and an airline ticket, and closed out her bank account. It didn't matter that she might never have an opportunity to wear such beautiful clothes again. Never once did she allow herself to cry. Her movements were silent and unhurried as she packed. She ignored the ringing of the phone and the doorbell. There was no chance that Marshall could change her mind. She simply couldn't see any point in continuing the argument.

Hours later she stepped from the taxi that had taken her from the airport in New York to the Belmont racetrack. Smoothing the wrinkles from her dress, Dani asked the driver to help her stash her luggage in one of the public lockers, paid his fare and went in search of a restroom to redo her makeup and hair. She wanted her father to know that she had transformed herself from a tomboy into a young woman, if that was so important to him.

Lew had to be somewhere around here. Her gaze eagerly searched the rows of stalls, the sounds and scents welcoming her back. She saw several familiar faces, people she had met at other racetracks. When she waved to them, they all waved back, but she could tell they didn't recognize her, a discovery that brought a wry smile to her face.

At the far end of a row of stalls, a small, mouse-gray horse stretched its neck toward her and whickered softly. Dani quickened her steps, her smile now one of pure gladness.

"Nappy!" she crooned softly as the stable pony affectionately butted his head against her shoulder. "You didn't forget me, did you, old boy?" Her arms wrapped themselves around the pony's neck, hugging him quickly before she remembered her beautiful dress. She stepped back to stroke the horse's velvety nose.

"Is there something I can help you with, miss?" a voice asked behind her.

She turned slowly, her misty gaze tenderly wandering over the stocky man who'd spoken to her. "Hello, Lew," she said softly. His bewildered expression was almost funny. "Don't you recognize me?"

"Dani?" he asked, his confused look giving way to glad amazement. "Is it really you?"

"Yes," she nodded eagerly.

"What are you doing here in New York?" Her father took one step forward, reaching out to embrace her. Then he stopped, brushing a hand in front of his eyes as if he just remembered something. The happiness disappeared from his voice when he spoke, replaced by a controlled interest. "You look wonderful! Just as lovely as I knew you would be."

Dani knew what was wrong. The promise. For a moment her head tilted down, her eyes studying the ground near her father's feet. Then she proudly met his gaze.

"I made myself over like you wanted me to, Lew," she said with quiet determination. "I've worn designer clothes, got invited to the best parties, been wined and dined in four-star restaurants. But that's not really me. Guess I finally grew up." She paused, unwilling to say anything about falling in love with Barrett. "And I can't keep that promise, Lew. Horses and racing are in my blood just as they are in yours. And if you don't want me to be with you, then I'll find some other trainer to hire me."

He blinked once, then twice, a tight smile curving

his mouth. "Welcome home, Dani," he said gruffly, and held out his arms to her. Some minutes later he spoke again, still holding her tightly. "I missed you so much, girl."

Self-consciously Dani wiped the tears from her face. "I missed you, too," she sighed. "And you never were a failure at anything."

"How did you know where I was?" His hand affectionately ruffled her hair before he reluctantly held her away from him.

Her gaze met the warmth of his. "Barrett King mentioned that he'd seen you here a couple of weeks ago," she replied, wondering if the quiver in her voice when she spoke his name had betrayed her.

"He kept in touch," Lew explained. "Sent me clippings sometimes about you at this party or that fashion show. I kept telling myself you were happy and I'd done the right thing, but it bothered me, you being out there alone. I was feeling pretty sorry for myself when I sent you away. It took me a while to realize I had either to give up and die, or fight back. Eventually I fought back. If Barrett hadn't been keeping an eye on you, I think I would've come and got you."

"He . . . He was very kind." Dani swallowed back the bitterness. It wasn't Barrett's fault that she had fallen in love with him. He'd never given her any encouragement. "I wish you'd come for me, Lew." *Before I fell in love with a man who thinks of me as a little sister,* she added to herself, all the while knowing that it was probably inevitable anyway.

"Are you sure you want this, Dani?" he asked hesitantly, lifting her chin to gaze anxiously into her eyes. "I've been doing better, but I'm still one step away from the poorhouse. I mean, you're used to better things and a better way of life now."

"But I wasn't happy." She smiled lightly.

He stared at her for a long moment. "Well then," he breathed deeply, a twinkle in his brown eyes, "if you intend to feed those nags tonight, you have to change your clothes. Ready to get dirty?"

"Yes, sir," she said happily, snapping him a mock salute.

Returning to the routine of the racing stables was like putting on a comfortable old coat. There were moments when Dani could almost believe that nothing had changed ... except her. True, she had gone back to wearing jeans and T-shirts, but working with Giorgio and Marshall had taught her to choose colors and styles that did something for her face and figure. And she always used a little makeup now.

She was quieter, not nearly as outspoken as she once had been—partly because of her own private heartache over Barrett, something she still wasn't able to confide to her father. Yet being back with horses, in on the excitement of race days, lavishing care and attention on these beautiful animals, Dani was almost able to convince herself that someday she would forget Barrett. Not soon, but in time.

Yet she dreaded the day when she would meet him again. And it was inevitable that she would, since his life was linked with horses and the track. She didn't try to convince herself that it would be easy. Even the casual mention of his name by her father made her heart skip a beat and her mind conjure up visions of his tanned face and the thick hair that captured the fire of the sun. But it was his level green gaze, looking at her in that very personal way that she found the hardest to forget.

With a dispirited sigh, Dani leaned the pitchfork against the stall door, picked up the wheelbarrow partially filled with used straw and wheeled it down to the next stall. It was a hot, muggy morning with no breeze. She unlatched the door and walked into the empty stall. Cleaning stables had always been one of her least favorite chores.

"You'll need the pitchfork," a voice said from the open door.

Dani couldn't move or turn around. She'd heard that voice in her sleep a hundred times. There was no time to conceal the pain in her eyes as she slowly turned toward Barrett. The sunlight streamed around him, making him seem even taller.

"I should have guessed I would find you here," Barrett said grimly. "There wasn't anywhere else you could run to."

"I didn't run," Dani answered defensively. "I flew . . . in a plane."

"Without telling anyone or leaving a message," he snapped. "Very dramatic. Didn't it occur to you that someone might be concerned?"

"The only one with any right to worry is Lew." She had to hide behind her sarcasm. It was the only defense she had. "I don't know what you're so upset about. I took your advice."

"I didn't tell you to return to your father." The

controlled tone of his voice told her she was provoking him. "And certainly not without telling
someone."

"Marshall knew," she taunted him.

"He only knew that you were quitting. He had
no idea where you'd gone," Barrett said grimly.

"It wasn't his business, or yours." Dani deliberately made her voice cold and uncaring, a miracle
considering her emotional state. "I'm back with
my father now, so you can drop the big brother
routine. Lew is all the family I want. I don't need
you."

The knot in her chest was getting tighter and
tighter. Each beat of her heart increased the pain
until she wanted to die rather than face the rest
of her life without Barrett.

"And I'm supposed to accept that?" he challenged.

"I don't care what you accept." She wanted to
cry but breathed in deeply instead to regain her
self-control. "Just give me the pitchfork and get
out of here." Her voice cracked. "I have work to
do."

She could see his hesitation and held her breath
in fear that he would continue the conversation.
Then, with a savage movement, Barrett tossed the
pitchfork to her. She caught it in midair, thankful
he hadn't made her walk across the stall to get it
because she was positive her legs wouldn't have
supported her.

Her eyes were already blurring with tears as she
watched him walk away with impatient, angry
strides. She leaned weakly against the pitchfork,

racked with sobs. The unbroken sunlight lay in a large rectangular square of gold at her feet.

This wasn't the time to give in to her heartbreak. Not here in the stables where anyone could walk by and ask why she was crying. Resolutely Dani wiped her tears away, telling herself the worst was over. She had confronted him and hadn't lost control. One battle had been won, but the first victory was always the hardest.

Work was the answer. She had to immerse herself in whatever she was doing, block out all but her subconscious thoughts of Barrett. Those she had no control over. With a vengeance she attacked the straw covering the stable floor, stabbing it with the pitchfork as if hoping to kill her love—a pointless hope, but the physical effort served to release the frustration and anguish that twisted her insides.

With a pitchfork full of used straw and manure, Dani walked to the stall door to toss it into the wheelbarrow. There, leaning against the post supporting the wide overhang, stood Barrett, grim determination in his handsome face.

"What are you doing here?" Dani swallowed, summoning up the sarcastic tone that had been her salvation before. "I thought I told you to leave."

In the clear sunlight with none of the shadows from the darkened stall, the power of his attraction struck her all over again. The ruggedness of his powerful features, the dangerous glint in his eyes, that aura of confidence—he always got what he wanted. But not this time.

"We have other things to talk about, Dani," he stated. "I was waiting until you'd finished your work."

She looked away from his compelling gaze. "When I'm finished with this, I have plenty more to do."

Her hands and arms were trembling like her legs, making her attempt to shake the straw from the pitchfork awkward and unsuccessful. She wanted to scream from sheer frustration.

"Then I'll wait."

"There's nothing left to discuss." Her voice was very low, forced through the lump in her throat.

"Yes, there is," Barrett answered, unmoved by her attempt to get rid of him. "I want to take you to dinner tonight."

"I thought I'd made it clear that it isn't necessary for you to see me anymore," Dani muttered. Her eyes were stinging again with tears that she refused to let flow as she concentrated her attention on the pitchfork. "I'm back with Lew and your responsibility for me is over."

"What time do you want me to pick you up?"

"Look—" she began, turning toward him and immediately regretting it. His gaze was cool, but it melted her resolve. She took a deep breath and began again. "I'm . . . I'm just a stable hand now. Not worthy of the attention of the great Mr. Barrett King."

"Skip the sarcasm. It isn't going to change my mind," he said calmly.

"Something has to change it," Dani answered desperately, "because I'm not going anywhere with you."

A frown creased his forehead. "Just because you're back with your father doesn't mean our friendship is over."

"We aren't friends!" she retorted.

He smiled gently and chucked her under the chin. "Are you sure?"

The tender gesture evoked happy memories of more carefree times before she had fallen in love with him. She had to turn away.

"I'm sure," Dani answered in a voice raw with pain.

Barrett sighed heavily and pushed himself away from the post he had been leaning against. "Then come to dinner with me as my enemy."

"No!" She spun around, dropping the pitchfork in the wheelbarrow and raising her hands in a beseeching plea. "I want you to go away and leave me alone!"

"I can't. And I won't." Barrett shook his head. "If we have to go back to square one and start all over again, then that's what we will do."

"Why?" Dani sighed despairingly. "What's the point?"

"Maybe I'll be able to make you trust me again." The flash of anger in his voice seemed to be meant for himself.

"Please. Please." She was begging now and she didn't care about her pride. "Just leave things as they are—and leave me alone."

"I could tell the next morning that I'd frightened you the night I burst into your apartment after seeing you with Marshall," Barrett continued, taking a step closer to her as if he wanted to will her to understand. "The only excuse I have is that I lost my temper."

Dani gasped, swallowing back hysterical laughter. It was ironic that Barrett should be apologizing for his actions that night. That night she had discovered she loved him as only an adult woman can love a man.

"I don't blame you for hating me after the way I treated you," he went on, stopping inches in front of her, "but I swear I'll never give you a reason to be frightened of me again."

His broad chest was even with her head. His strong arms were at his side. Dani held herself rigid, fighting the temptation to find comfort in his caress, the heart-stopping sensation of his body against hers. Clenching her hands into tight fists, she closed her eyes against his provocative nearness.

"Go away," she pleaded, feeling the tears squeeze through her lashes. "I don't want to see you anymore."

"I'm only asking for a chance," Barrett persisted.

His hands closed lightly over her shoulders, the gentle touch snapping the thread of self-control that had held her motionless. A convulsive sob rose in her throat and this time Dani wasn't able to hold it back.

"No!" Her protest was almost inaudible as her fists came up to hammer at his chest. The memory of that other time when she had tried to batter down the steel wall was completely forgotten. This time she only wanted to hit out at the man she loved so helplessly. But strong hands stopped her and drew her against his chest, comforting her.

Dani was torn by the desire to remain in his arms and to break free. While her head refused to nestle against the msucular warmth of his chest, her arms slid around his waist to cling to him tightly. The strength she found in his embrace was irresistible.

"Please leave me alone, Barrett," she moaned softly, her voice muffled by his shirt. "Haven't you hurt me enough? I couldn't help falling in love with you. I'll get over it in time, but only if you stay—"

Strong fingers lifted her chin. She had a fleeting glimpse of his mouth descending before he kissed her lips, wholly possessing and hungrily eager. Dani's mind was reeling under shock waves of sensation and she welcomed his mastery, giving herself up to the passion of the moment. Then, when she realized what she was doing, she tore herself free of his embrace.

Her eyes were wide and pleading as she gazed into his face, begging him not to take advantage of the power he had over her.

"Go away, please," she whispered feverishly, feeling like a wounded animal, wanting only to slink away.

"No," Barrett answered softly, his gaze sweeping possessively over her as he reached out once more to hold her. Dani didn't have the strength to resist. "I'm not going anywhere until you say that again."

"Say what?" she breathed desperately, searching her mind for the words he wanted to hear that would set her free.

"Unless my mind is playing tricks on me, you just told me you loved me, didn't you?" His fingers unconsciously tightened as though to force her to admit it.

"Oh, Barrett, I didn't mean to," she sobbed, unable to hide the anguish the admission caused.

"I know you never encouraged me. It's not your fault that I made such a fool of myself."

"You're crazy!" he laughed. His hands slipped down to her waist and he raised her in the air lightly and easily. "Don't you understand?" He smiled when he set her back on the ground and was gazing into her amazed face.

Dani felt she should hold her breath. It was impossible that Barrett actually meant what he was implying. "No!" She was terrified of his reply.

He kissed her gently on the side of her face. "I love you, Dani," he murmured against her cheek.

"Please don't tease me, Barrett," Dani murmured, letting her fingers curl into the thick hair at the back of his neck.

"What I feel for you is nothing to joke about," he growled, but she wasn't intimidated at all.

She kissed him gently, somewhere around his ear. "I thought you only felt responsible for me—like a brother."

"Those were Marshall's words, not mine. But that was probably true," he admitted, "at first, anyway. That night when I carried you into bed and I kissed you, I knew I was kissing a woman and not an innocent young girl. But you hadn't realized that. I was afraid that if I showed you how much I cared I would frighten you. God," he moaned, burying his head in the curve of her neck, "that's what I thought I'd done."

"You didn't," Dani reassured him, cradling his face in her hands. "That night you saw me in the car with Marshall was the night I realized I loved you. I probably had for a while—I always thought you were hot. I never knew exactly why I didn't trust you . . . maybe it was because I knew you could steal my heart.''

"Well, you've stolen mine.'' Barrett looked down at her and sighed, a happy sigh, one that her own heart echoed. "I've wanted you to meet my parents for so long. I wanted to take you that weekend of their anniversary party, but I knew they'd guess why I brought you. My father never could keep a secret, so I couldn't risk him letting something slip. I'll take you to the farm this weekend after we've spent some time alone.''

"Barrett?'' Her tone was hesitant, an old fear rushing back to haunt her. "About Melissa? You don't really think I'm like her, do you?''

"No.'' He shook his head. "I did wonder if you'd be dazzled by the glamor and all that. I wanted to protect you, but I knew you had to figure out what you wanted. Lew was right about that.''

"What do you suppose he'll say?'' Dani asked, her eyes sparkling brightly as she gazed into Barrett's eyes.

"I don't think he'll be surprised,'' Barrett grinned, locking his arms about her waist. "I had a talk with him before I found you here at the stables. I hope he won't object to losing his only daughter when she's just come back.''

"Lew wants me to be happy,'' she said, nestling against his chest. "I don't know which of us will be prouder, Lew, getting you for a son-in-law or me, about to become your wife.''

"Are you?'' Barrett teased. "Hey, give me a chance to propose, will you?''

"Beat you to it. You always said I was a brat.'' She smiled demurely.

"Mmm," he said, nibbling her ear. "Well, the answer's yes. Let's get hitched. The sooner the better." His arms tightened around her.

"I love you so much," she whispered, and brought her lips to his.

SONORA
SUNDOWN

CHAPTER ONE

A whisper of gold danced over the sage, the first promise of sundown. The tufted heads of grass bowed their acceptance as the evening breeze rustled through them.

A roadrunner darted along, on a parallel course with the gray Arabian gelding as it stepped lightly over the sand and gravel. The roadrunner swerved abruptly to the cover of some mesquite and disappeared. A touch of the rein against the side of the sleek gray neck changed the horse's direction to the right, where a broad rock slope had kept the desert plants from growing.

Metal horseshoes clinked on bare rock. There Brandy Ames checked her mount to a halt and gazed at the unobstructed view. A gray ear swiveled toward her. The horse stretched its neck in protest against the tightened rein and impatiently tossed its head.

Cream yellow had begun to soften the blue of the sky. Fingers of orange spread out from the western horizon, changing the color of the shadows cast by the setting sun. Even Brandy's honey-gold curls had a copper hue.

"I wish I were an artist and could paint a picture as wonderful as this." Absently she petted the sleek neck, speaking aloud to the horse from long habit. "It changes so magically." The horse snorted and Brandy laughed softly. "What do you think, Rashad? Aren't Arizona sunsets something?"

Looping the end of the reins around the horn of her western saddle, Brandy dismounted with springing lightness, moving with unconscious grace to the head of her mount. There she stopped to look at the evening sky once more. The thin clouds were tinted a glorious deep pink.

Her face glowed in the desert light that showed her gentle beauty to advantage. Round, luminous eyes of turquoise-green were accented by the turned-up tip of her nose and the delicately perfect outline of her mouth. Brandy was slight but quite strong, with a deceptive air of shyness about her.

If asked, Brandy would have laughed at the idea, but her natural reserve kept most men at a distance. Now she was alone and there was no need to be reserved. So she cast it aside.

The horse nudged her shoulder as if reminding her of his presence. In answer, she stroked his face without taking her eyes from the sunset.

"Today at the shop Karen was bragging about the Rocky Mountains, all that rugged splendor, blah, blah." A contented sigh accompanied her remark. "Well, she can have them, Rashad. I'll just keep right on falling in love with the Sonora Desert every day at sundown!"

The foothills of the mountains blazed a crimson-orange, set afire by the ball of flame dipping near the earth. The vast expanse of blue sky to the east was turning deep purple as the western horizon lit up with an intense red-orange. The vibrant display of color made her almost breathless for a moment. Her hand trailed away from the horse's face, down to the velvet softness of his nose, then to her side.

The gray nuzzled her shoulder again, impatiently blowing through his nose as his hooves shifted restlessly on the barren, sand-smoothed rock.

"Stop thinking about your stomach, Rashad." Brandy tapped his nose smartly when the horse displayed an inclination to nibble the sleeve of her white blouse. "Your oats and hay will still be at the stable when we get back. No one else is going to eat them. Just look at this sunset!" She waved at the horizon. "You're going to have to learn to enjoy this the way Star did. She loved our sunset rides."

As always, the memory of the pinto mare brought a wistful sadness to her eyes. For as long as she could remember, Brandy had wanted a horse as a child, but not until she was ten years old did her parents give in and present her with an eight-year-old pinto mare. They had been an inseparable pair until age finally claimed the mare last summer, a week after Brandy's twentieth birthday.

Rashad, the spirited Arabian gelding beside her, hadn't really replaced the old mare in her heart.

Brandy still found it difficult not to make comparisons between the two, though the horses were totally different in personality.

Star had been such an important part of her childhood, a friend, a playmate, a confidante for all her secrets. Not that Brandy hadn't had school friends, because she had. But living here in the country west of Tucson, without any neighbors near enough to count, and being an only child, Brandy had come to rely on the companionship of her horse.

As she grew up, she had been alone a lot but had never considered herself lonely. Her parents' love and affection was constant, even if they sometimes marveled that Brandy was actually their child. Both Lenora and Stewart Ames had doctorates in their fields and were full professors at the University of Tucson. Career-minded, they were initially surprised by Brandy's lack of ambition.

Yet their love and wisdom meant that they never tried to force her to follow any particular path. If she preferred puttering around the house and working with her hands, then they were happy for her. If they were ever disappointed because she had postponed going to college after graduating high school, they didn't show it.

Never once had Brandy felt less than equal to them because she held an undemanding position as a clerk in an arts and crafts shop and handled most of the household duties. It was true that at twenty—nearly twenty-one—she was a little slow to leave the nest. But she *liked* the nest—a lot.

Karen, her closest friend and the girl she worked with at the shop, had urged Brandy to move into

Tucson and share an apartment with her. But that would mean giving up Rashad and the freedom of stepping out of the house into the serenity of the desert, miles from anywhere, with nothing to see but the awesome stretch of sand and sage and sky.

And the sunsets—she would miss the sunsets if she lived in the city. Brandy sighed. Sometimes she was content to view them from the shelter of the patio behind her ranch-style home. Other times, like now, she felt compelled to ride several miles into the desert to witness the silent harmony of nature.

Wandering to the edge of the flat rock as if to move closer to the blazing red-orange that claimed the sky, she breathed in deeply. The air around her was cool and still. Soon she would have to slip on the denim jacket tied to the back of her saddle, but right now she welcomed the refreshing change from the afternoon's warmth.

"Spectacular," she murmured. "No sunset is exactly like any other. It's like a magic kaleidoscope in the sky."

Behind her, there was a pawing of horseshoe against stone, rasping and metallic. Brandy glanced over her shoulder, turquoise eyes on the impatient gray.

"Now if Dad was here, he would give you a very scientific explanation as to why we have such great sunsets," she grinned. "Take notes, Rashad. This will be on the midterm. It all has to do with the earth's atmosphere and the way it filters light. The sun seems intensely bright at noontime when there's not so much filtering by the atmosphere, because it's directly overhead. However, at sunrise and sunset, the sunlight has to travel through more of the atmosphere and the violet, blue and green colors are filtered out, which lets the reds and yellows and oranges come through. And," Brandy continued her mock lecture, "the sunsets are more brilliant in Arizona because of the desert dust suspended in the atmosphere during the daylight hours. Got that, horsie?"

The overall hue of the western horizon deepened to a crimson shade. Brandy hooked her thumbs through the belt loops of her jeans and sighed.

"But it does take away some of the magic when you start describing a sunset with words like light rays and filters and atmosphere." She tipped her head to one side in contemplation, feathery curls of honey gold framing her face. "It's much more enjoyable when there's mystery in the wonder of it."

The hush that followed her thoughtful words was broken by a rifle report. Some rancher shooting at a coyote, Brandy thought, ready to shrug it off, knowing how far sound carried in the desert. But the cracking explosion wasn't dismissed by the high-strung Arabian.

Seconds after the rifle shot came the clattering of hooves on stone, and Brandy whirled around to see Rashad bolt toward home. Her first reaction was instinctive. She put two fingers to her mouth and whistled shrilly. Star would have responded to the call immediately, but to the Arabian it meant nothing.

"Rashad!" Brandy started racing after the galloping horse, the graveled earth hampering her attempt to run. "Rashad! Come back here."

But, she knew she didn't stand a chance of catching the horse. Even at a distance she could see the arched neck and the ears pricked forward. He was heading home to the stable, and oats and hay. She doubted if he would slow to less than a canter the whole way back.

"You just wait," Brandy muttered, cursing beneath her breath at the animal's disobedience. "You dumb, stupid—"

There was no need to blame the horse. She ran her fingers wearily through her hair. The fault was hers for not ground-hitching the reins. She deserved the long walk home for being so careless. It was time she recognized that Rashad was not the dependable Star.

At least her parents had gone out for the evening and wouldn't be worried when Rashad returned without her. But the ever-lengthening shadows and the increasing coolness of the air were something to reckon with.

On horseback, the five or more miles she had traveled would seem like nothing, but in this terrain, it was going to be a very long and cold walk. And a hungry one, too, Brandy thought regretfully, as she remembered the sandwiches tucked in the saddlebags.

She turned for one last look at the sunset. The sun had dipped below the horizon, and the first star glittered faintly in the twilight sky. Now darkness would fall with alarming suddenness. The thought of traveling the miles home on foot, totally alone and in the dark, was sobering.

Squaring her shoulders, Brandy started in the direction of home. It was strange how different the land looked when not viewed from the top of a horse. The mesquite and sage seemed thicker and the sloping hill steeper. There was a momentary qualm as she wondered how it would look hours from now, then she thrust the vague fear away.

Briskly she increased her pace, reassuring herself that after a couple of miles, or three at the most, she would be able to see the light on the stable roof. It would be a beacon to guide her the last miles home.

So she walked. One minute she was aware of long shadows and the next there was blackness. The moon was only a sliver in the night sky, its glow next to nothing. Stars shimmered dimly, fairy lights that were pretty but not illuminating.

The only sound seemed to be her footsteps crunching through the combination of sand and gravel and her jeans brushing against the sage and mesquite. It was difficult to avoid the patches of prickly pear cactus. Often she walked into them, discovering too late that the dark mound was not sagebrush. Then she would be forced to backtrack a few steps and go around the thorny desert plant.

Of necessity, she focused her attention on the ground ahead of her, using points of reference to find her way. Whenever she stopped to catch her breath, she would quickly scan ahead to locate them before she started walking again.

It was too dark to read the hands on her watch, but Brandy was positive she'd see the stable light at the top of the third hill. She studied the beautiful night sky and the brightening stars.

Could it possibly get much darker? A wry smile curved her mouth. It was a pity she hadn't listened more attentively when her father had explained the position of the stars and constellations. She might have been able to use that knowledge to orient herself now.

"Maybe that tall clump of mesquite is blocking the light," she murmured aloud, and trudged forward.

She had no idea how far she'd walked already. It seemed like miles, but it probably wasn't. She was beginning to get tired. The temperature had dropped several degrees and she shivered in the cold.

Her head throbbed dully. Brandy blamed it on her increasing hunger. When she got home, she intended to heat up a big bowl of the beef stew in the refrigerator. The tantalizing picture that formed in her mind didn't lessen the gnawing emptiness within.

About a thousand steps later, she stopped kidding herself. Nothing around her looked even vaguely familiar. Somewhere, somehow, she had gotten turned around. Exhausted and feeling slightly weak, she sank to her knees, not feeling the sharp pebbles that bit into her flesh. She was lost.

The next question was how lost. Should she continue on in the hope of sighting some landmark that would help her find her way home? This wasn't the first time she'd been lost in the desert. The difference was that Star could always find the way home when Brandy didn't have a clue.

She couldn't possibly have wandered too far in the wrong direction, she told herself firmly. She rubbed her hands briskly over the gooseflesh on her bare arms. If she continued straight ahead, sooner or later she would either see the lights of her home or run into the graveled road that led to the neighboring ranch.

Time to move on, she decided. Walking was definitely better than sitting in one place freezing to death. A slight exaggeration, she knew, since it was unlikely it would get that cold. She knew that, in general, a lost person should stay in one place. But it wasn't as if she was aimlessly wandering around. She was going forward in a straight line that should get her within sight of her home or the graveled road that would eventually bring her to it.

Brandy hadn't traveled very far when she developed a stitch in her side. Pausing, she pressed a hand against the pain and looked around. Off to her left, she thought she saw the flicker of a light, though she was positive her home was either straight ahead or to the right.

Looking all around, trying to pierce the darkness and the shadowy desert growth, she suddenly saw it again, wavering and fading.

With new purpose, Brandy set out toward it. This time she paid less attention to where she was putting her feet. A light in the desert had to mean people, although she doubted it was her home.

As she drew closer, fighting the sage and cactus that whipped at her legs, her thick leather boots taking the brunt of the punishment, the light became more defined, then took shape. It was a campfire sheltered in the notch of a hill, probably only visible from her direction. Brandy wanted to laugh at the luck that had smiled on her, but she was too weary to do more than grin breathlessly.

"Hello!" She ran toward the fire, an inner relief bringing a happy note into her voice.

At the edge of the circle of light, a dark form moved at her call. This was undoubtedly the builder of the fire and her rescuer. The shape stayed in the curtain of shadows as Brandy burst into the ring of light opposite him.

"Boy, am I glad to see you!" she declared with laughing relief. "Somehow or other I got lost on my way home. I was beginning to think I was going to spend a night in the desert alone."

"Really?" The male voice was low and husky, edged with a quiet kind of anger.

Brandy wondered why. She hadn't expected an open-armed welcome, but she'd thought the man would show some concern when she explained that she was lost.

"I . . . I was out riding." she said and added, "My horse bolted. I was walking home when it got dark. That's when I got turned around."

There was a second of silence before the man in the shadows responded. "And you just stumbled into my camp by chance, is that it?" Again, there was a trace of mockery in the low voice.

"I saw the light from your campfire," she spoke hesitantly, trying to peer through the darkness to see more. A horse stamped in the darkness, and Brandy could feel perspiration gathering in the palms of her hands. "It was a welcome sight, believe me."

Unconsciously she used the past tense. All of a sudden, she didn't feel so very lucky. Who was this man, and what was he doing out here in the middle of the desert?

The fire burned through a thick branch, sending the two parts crumbling into the center. The flames blazed higher, suddenly illuminating the man—and the knife in his hand. Fear welled in Brandy's throat.

Her gaze ricocheted to his face. The wide brim of his Stetson was pulled low, hiding all but the glitter of his eyes. A dark, shaggy growth of hair covered his jaw, cheek, and chin. It was too long to be unshaven stubble, yet not quite a beard either.

A lined suede vest covered the dark shirt he wore and emphasized the broadness of his shoulders. Faded jeans fitted snugly over his hips and thighs. In the flickering firelight, he seemed much taller than Brandy had realized, larger and somehow frightening.

His disreputable appearance did nothing to reassure her. He sure as hell didn't care that she was lost. His only concern seemed to be that she had stumbled into his camp.

He seemed angry that she'd found him. That could only mean he wasn't supposed to be here. Brandy swallowed tightly. Was the man a cattle rustler? That was a logical guess, since these days they were more of a plague than they had been in the Old West. The more she considered the possibility, the more sure she was that she was right.

He wasn't a cowboy from the neighboring ranch; she had a nodding acquaintance with most of them. In the day and age of trailering horses and four-wheel-drive vehicles, it was rare that a working cowboy ever camped out on the range. Whatever this man was up to, Brandy was certain it was no good.

What kind of a position did that put her in? She had seen him. She knew he was camped here. What's more, she could identify him.

A cold shiver of fear ran down her spine as her gaze fixed on the knife in the hand at his side. She could identify him only if she got out of this alive, she realized with chilling terror.

"Look, I don't want to be any trouble." Her voice quavered. "If you could just give me directions to the Ames house, I'll be on my way."

"Is that right?" he asked, not very politely. White teeth flashed in the dark beard growth as his upper lip curled over the words. "You could get lost again." The glittering light in his eyes seemed to indicate that he found that possibility amusing.

But Brandy knew what he really meant. He had no intention of letting her leave. Panic began to engulf her. When the man took a step forward, she knew she had only one chance.

With a gasping cry of fear, she pivoted and raced back into the desert, not caring which way she ran, only that it was away from the fire and the man. There was no sound of pursuit, but she made so much noise she doubted if she could hear him chasing her.

Her blind flight carried her on a path through thickets of chaparral. Thorny bushes and cactus tore at her clothes and skin, and the thick growth and uneven ground slowed her to a stumbling run.

Then she tripped. A startled cry tore from her throat as she fell headlong, hitting the ground with enough force to knock the wind out of her. Gasping for air, she rolled onto her back, unmindful of the prickly brush beneath her. Her eyes blinked open to focus on the tall man looming above her. For a full second she couldn't move.

"That was a stupid thing to do," he said with a sigh that was tinged with exasperation.

He started to bend toward her and Brandy cringed closer to the ground. "Don't touch me!" For all her inner fear, her voice rang defiantly clear.

"Shut up!" He shook his head and reached down to haul her unceremoniously to her feet.

Immediately she began twisting and kicking to be free of the iron grip of his fingers. She struggled furiously, and her boot finally connected with his shinbone.

"You little bitch!" he muttered beneath his breath. "What the hell are you trying to prove?"

With unbelievable swiftness, he captured her wrists in one hand and lifted her off the ground, tucked her beneath one arm and balanced her on his hip. Her feet continued to kick the air, but he carried her as effortlessly as a sack of potatoes, back toward the fire.

"Let me down or I'll scream!" Brandy demanded in a throbbing voice.

"By all means, scream if you want," the man countered smoothly. "Maybe all the rattlesnakes and scorpions will come charging to your rescue."

The realization that no one would hear her cries for help only made her struggle more vigorously, to no avail. By the time they reached the circle of the campfire he hadn't lessened his grip one inch. There he set her roughly on her feet.

The instant he released her, she started to run

back to the safety of the desert, only to be brought up short by hard fingers that dug into the soft flesh of her shoulders and pulled her back against the solid wall of his chest.

"Let me go!" she hissed violently.

"Lost, huh?" he mocked harshly against her ear. "Or do you have some friends on the other side of the hill?"

"No," Brandy protested with genuine confusion, "I told you I was lost. No one's with me, I swear."

Too late she realized her mistake. If he thought someone was waiting for her nearby, he might not harm her. Now he had no reason to hold back.

Terror gave her a fresh surge of strength. Using her elbows and heels, she struck out at him. At the same time, she twisted and writhed to break the bruising grip of his hands. Her breath came in panting sobs of desperation.

"I'm not going to put up with these hysterics much longer," he growled.

Somehow she managed to hook her foot behind his leg and knock him off balance. His hold lessened but he still managed to drag her to the ground with him. Before she could roll free, he was on top of her, the crushing weight of his body holding her down. With a muffled cry, Brandy tried to gouge at his glittering dark eyes with her fingernails, but never even got close.

In a flash both arms were stretched out on the ground above her head, her wrists pinned by his hands. Helplessly trapped, she continued trying to twist from beneath the male length of him. He was too heavy and too strong.

"Are you going to stop this?" he snapped.

She paused to catch her breath. Her head was twisted as far to the side as it could go, her eyes tightly closed. Yet she could feel the burning warmth of his breath against her cheek. Her entire body was held captive by the muscled power of his. Each gasping breath she took carried his potent male scent until she felt suffocated by it.

"Get away from me!" The words rushed in a desperate whisper through her clenched teeth. "I don't want you to touch me!"

"No?" His low voice laughed at her. "I ought to make love to you. It's what a hellcat like you deserves."

Her mind cried out in alarm, although not a sound escaped her lips. She had been so afraid for her life that she hadn't even considered the possibility that he might assault her. Lashes opening, her turquoise eyes rounded with fear as she turned her head to plead openly for him not to hurt her.

The sudden action brought her lips against his mouth, warm and firm and as motionless as her own. Paralyzed by the unexpected contact, she could only lie there beneath him, unmoving and not daring to breathe. Any second she expected to feel the brutal possession of his kiss, and the thought burned like a fire through her veins.

"Please," she whispered when nothing happened. "Please let me go. I swear, I swear I won't tell the police."

The movement of her lips against his seemed to break the spell, but Brandy didn't know what he would do next. A coiled tension seemed to possess him as his dark eyes raked her face.

In the struggle, his hat had come off. Brandy's eyes were drawn almost unwillingly to his dark, nearly black hair, unkempt like the rest of him. A charged second went by before he replied.

"What won't you tell the police?" There was a watchful narrowing of his dark eyes as he moved a fraction of an inch away from her mouth.

"I . . . I won't tell them I saw you," she promised shakily. "I mean . . . I didn't actually see you stealing any cattle, so that would be the truth. I promise I won't say anything about meeting you."

His mouth thinned into a smile. "So you guessed why I'm out here?"

Hesitantly she nodded, wondering if she should have mentioned rustling cattle. Maybe it would only make him more determined to keep her from getting away.

With unbelievable swiftness for a man so large, he rolled away from her and to his feet in one fluid movement. He towered above her, his hands on his hips.

"And you promise to keep it a secret?" he asked with a definite undertone of mocking amusement.

"If you let me go," Brandy qualified the promise hastily.

Slowly she inched into a sitting position, afraid to take her eyes off the man watching her so intently. For the first time she noticed the rips in her blouse, the white material showing dots of red blood where the thorns had scratched her. She tried her discreet best to make sure she was still decently covered.

"If . . . if you could give me directions . . ." her voice faltered nervously.

"Where do you live?"

"At the Ames house—my father is Stewart Ames. It's only about fifteen miles east of Saguaro Ranch headquarters, up on the ridge," Brandy explained as quietly as she could, as the fear slowly lessened its grip on her throat.

He stood for a minute, then shook his head. "I'm afraid I'm not familiar with the place. I vaguely remember a house on that road, but just where it is from here I couldn't tell you. And I sure as hell couldn't give good enough directions for you to make it in the dark."

Brandy believed him. She didn't know why exactly, but something in his tone of voice said he was telling the truth. She scrambled to her feet, clutching the opening of her blouse together in one hand. Even standing in front of him, she still had to look up into his face.

"All I need is a general direction from here," she assured him quickly. "Once I'm in more familiar territory, I can find my own way home."

"Will your parents be looking for you?" The man refused to let her pleading blue-green eyes escape his piercing gaze.

This time she debated silently whether to lie or tell him the truth. The truth had kept her safe thus far, she decided.

"I don't know for sure if they are," she answered honestly, "they went out this evening. It all depends on whether they check to see if I'm home or not when they come back."

"In other words, they may not miss you until morning." He insisted on making her meaning clearer.

Brandy looked down at her feet. "That's right."

He seemed to consider her answer very thoroughly. "Much as I'd like to be rid of you," he said finally, "I can't send you back into the desert to stumble around in the dark. Maybe you'd make it home and maybe not. With my luck, you'd fall and break a leg, then someone would track you back to my camp and I'd get blamed." He turned away from her toward the fire, rubbing the rough beard on his chin with his hand. "I don't need that kind of trouble!"

"But—" Brandy started to protest.

"No arguments." He raised a hand. "You'll stay here for the night. Tomorrow I'll take you back."

"But I can't stay here with you." The words were out before she could think.

He glanced over his shoulder, a wolfish gleam in his eyes. "What's the matter? Are you afraid to trust a cattle rustler?"

Brandy swallowed and clutched her blouse even tighter. "Should I trust you?" she asked with false boldness.

"The only thing we'll be sharing tonight is the warmth from this fire," he told her in no uncertain terms. "Of course, standing clear over there, you're not going to get much benefit from it."

Fear and her subsequent struggles had made Brandy unaware of the cool desert night, but at his words, it hit her with shivering intensity. Suppressing her trembling, she walked to the warmth of the fire, keeping a couple of steps between herself and the man. Still unsure whether she could trust him, she watched him with wary eyes.

The radiating heat from the small fire was blessedly welcome, and her lashes started to flutter down in silent gratitude when she saw the movement of the man's hand to his side. She stiffened at the sight of the leather sheath attached to his belt and the knife that he removed from it. Again the firelight flashed menacingly off the steel blade and the fear came racing back.

The man didn't seem to notice the hasty step Brandy took backward. "Are you hungry?" He moved to the opposite side of the fire, and knelt beside some sticks propped and tied together into an improvised roasting spit.

"Yes," she admitted in a low voice as she saw the cooked small game skewered on the stick. Cutting off a portion of the meat, he handed it to her. Her fingers closed gingerly around the bone that jutted out of the roasted meat. "What is it?" she asked, lowering herself to a cross-legged position beside the fire.

"Jackrabbit." He didn't glance up as he sliced off another leg. "It'll probably be a little tough, but it's food."

Biting into it, Brandy discovered that the meat was a little stringy, but she was too hungry to care. The bone was nearly clean before a thought occurred to her.

"Did you shoot this?" she asked.

"Yes," he nodded.

"One shot?"

Her persistence brought his curious gaze to her face. "Yes. Why?"

A faint smile curved her lips. "I heard a rifle-shot around sundown. That's what made my horse bolt and leave me out here."

"So I'm to blame after all, is that what you're saying?" he said with challenging softness.

"No." She shook her head, honey-gold curls dancing briefly. "I was so busy watching the sunset that I didn't bother to ground-tie him. What a mistake."

"Yes," he agreed dryly.

Tearing off another chunk of rabbit meat, Brandy chewed it quietly and wished the man hadn't been so quick to agree. It wasn't as if she blamed him for spooking her horse, although he had. Anyway, she had a right to be out riding wherever she wanted . . . unlike this outlaw.

CHAPTER TWO

When the rabbit was eaten, he offered her some prickly pear cactus fruit for dessert. Her hunger satisfied, Brandy sat beside the fire sipping hot, strong coffee from a tin cup. She wanted to linger over the coffee, but since there was only one cup, she was sipping it fast so the man could drink his.

"That was good," she murmured when she had drank the last of it and handed the cup back to him. "The whole meal was good. Of course, I was so hungry it didn't really matter what I ate."

The man simply nodded and filled the tin cup with more coffee.

Brandy looked at him curiously. "Do you eat this way often? I mean, taking food from the land?"

"Whenever I'm out on the desert," he admitted with a shrug. "I don't like to be slowed up carrying supplies on a packhorse."

Yes, Brandy thought to herself, there were probably times when he had to travel fast to keep from being caught. It made sense to travel light.

"Are you out here often?"

He studied her across the fire for a long second. "Often enough," was his noncommittal reply. He took a large swallow of coffee, not giving any indication that it was as scalding hot as Brandy remembered.

She started to probe further into his answer, then she realized that he had been deliberately vague. The less she knew about his activities, the less she would be able to tell the authorities. Maybe he didn't trust her to keep the promise she'd made, not to say anything about seeing him. Actually, she wasn't positive she would keep it—maybe he'd guessed that.

He took another swallow of coffee, then dumped the dregs on the porous ground. Brandy watched with sudden wariness as he rose to his feet and walked to the western saddle placed several feet away from the fire, barely within its circle of light. A pair of saddlebags were hooked over the saddle horn. Crouching beside it, he opened one flap and removed a white box.

Curiosity got the best of her. "What's that?" she asked when he straightened, box in hand, and started to walk back to the fire.

"A first-aid kit," he answered an instant before she saw the familiar red cross on the top. "Time to disinfect those scratches you got."

Brandy glanced at her forearms and the vivid red marks etched on her flesh by the thorns. She had been conscious of them smarting now and then, but none of them were deep, not even where the blouse was torn. They looked sore, but they really didn't bother her.

"They don't hurt," she murmured. "I hardly feel them at all."

But he was already squatting on his heels beside her, the Stetson pushed back on his head. The box was open and he was pouring antiseptic from a plastic bottle onto a gauze pad.

"You'll feel them if infection sets in," he said firmly.

Brandy knew there was no telling what germs were on those spiky thorns, yet she was uneasy about having him treat her.

"I'll do it," she said to him firmly, and reached out for the gauze.

"It's easier for me." His fingers closed over the hand she had extended and he began cleaning one long welt on that forearm.

The firelight fully illuminated his face; this was the first time that she had been able to study him at close quarters. There was a ruthless strength to his powerfully defined features, reinforcing her first impression that he was dangerous. The dark brown, almost black, of his beard, eyebrows, hair and eyes was intensified by the sun-weathered shade of his skin. The half-grown beard concealed what she guessed would be a strongly defined jaw-line and angular, lean cheeks.

Without the beard, she thought he would look handsome in an intimidating kind of way. She decided that he was growing it for a disguise. There was something vaguely familiar about him, too, which was silly, because she would have remembered anyone who possessed that potent aura of masculinity.

The one thing about him that surprised her was his directness. He wasn't furtive or sly, just self-assured, completely in command, not at all like a man who lived outside the law, somehow. Yet she wondered why, with all that, a man who was probably in his early to mid-thirties would become a cattle rustler. Admittedly, there was an air of mystery about him.

His attention had moved to her other arm where he was ministering to the cuts and scratches there. His hands and fingers were strong and brown, and showed no calluses from hard work. She was surprised to discover they were gentle, too.

With a start, she realized how lucky she had been during their brief struggle. He was obviously muscular and could have easily broken a bone, or bruised her badly. But he hadn't. The knowledge made her feel somewhat safer in his company.

The last scratch on her arm was cleaned and disinfected. He tossed the gauze pad into the fire and reached for the box. The stinging sensation had left her skin.

"Thank you," she said gratefully.

The sideways glance he gave her was disconcerting. "Take off your blouse and I'll clean those scratches on your chest."

Brandy stared wide-eyed at him, noticing the fresh gauze in his hand and the antiseptic bottle. Her hand moved protectively to the collar of her blouse, and his mouth quirked in dry amusement at her action.

"We've been through the hellcat routine," he

said patiently. "Do you really want to waste all that energy fighting again? Either you take the blouse off or I will." It was no idle threat.

Her breathing became shallow. "Give me the pad and I'll take care of it," she said.

"You'd have to be a contortionist to see what you're doing. It'll be faster and more thorough if I do it." A wicked glint of amusement entered his eyes when Brandy mutely shook her head in refusal. "A woman's body doesn't embarrass me. Pretend I'm a doctor."

"But you're not," she muttered in a frustrated protest.

"You're only going to make it more embarrassing for yourself by making a production out of this," he pointed out. "Skip the maidenly modesty, okay?"

Reluctantly, she gave in, but it didn't stop her fingers from trembling as she undid the buttons of her blouse.

There had been a time as a teenager when she had been terrified that her slenderness would mean a flat chest, and she had been delighted when she finally filled out. Now she was unbearably conscious of her curves as she removed the thin blouse and held it nervously on her lap. Her gaze was riveted to the stitching around the collar of his suede vest.

The cool dampness of the gauze pad touched the scratch on her collarbone. Brandy held herself as rigid as a statue, knowing her lacy bra exposed much more than it concealed.

"You said your last name was Ames. What's your first?" he asked quietly, moving to another welt near her shoulder.

For an instant, Brandy was on the verge of refusing to answer his question. Then she realized he was only making conversation to put her at ease.

"Brandy." Her voice broke slightly.

"Brandy?" His gaze moved to her face before it returned to the scratch on her shoulder. "Too bad you don't carry around a sample of that. I think you could do with a shot of it right now."

"Yes," she said with a shaky smile of agreement. "Wh-what's your name?"

He hesitated for a split second. "Jim."

No last name, just Jim. She knew he was concealing the rest of his identity from her. It was certainly possible that Jim wasn't his first name; he might have made it up for her benefit.

"I have to slip your strap down, Brandy, to get at this one scratch," he warned.

His fingers were already sliding it off her shoulder before she could protest. Her quick glance downward saw the red mark that slashed across the swell of her breast. Although prepared for his impersonal touch, she still wasn't able to keep from inhaling sharply as his hand touched her.

His gaze showed his concern. "Did I hurt you?"

"No," she said quickly, and blushed beet-red.

His head bent again to his task, but the heat of embarrassment didn't ease. The sensation of intimacy was simply too strong for Brandy to be casually indifferent.

"How old are you?" the man who had identified himself as Jim asked.

"Twenty." Brandy glanced up at him with a slightly bewildered frown. "Why?"

A corner of his mouth twitched as he slid her

strap back into place, a suggestion of laughter in the dark eyes that met hers. "You blush like a teenager," he murmured, "or a virgin."

Fresh color flamed in her checks. She would have loved to deny his perceptive statement, but she had the uneasy feeling he would know she was lying. Not that she hadn't done her share of preliminary fooling around with various dates—she simply hadn't been aroused enough or tempted enough to go all the way.

"You can put your blouse back on." While she had been mentally defending herself, he had completed cleaning the last scratch and was turning away.

Brandy quickly slipped it on, fumbling momentarily with the buttons. Out of the corner of her eye, she watched Jim rise and walk to replace the first-aid kit in the saddlebag. When he turned back to the fire, she edged closer to the flame.

"Tired?" he asked.

She glanced at her watch, surprised to see it was nearly midnight. "Yes," she admitted uncertainly.

From the shadow of his saddle he picked up a bedroll and untied it, spreading it over the flat ground near the fire. It was small, big enough for only one person, and Brandy swallowed tightly.

"You can sleep here," he said.

"Where are you going to sleep?" she asked quickly as he moved back toward the saddle.

He flashed her a laughing look, his gaze swerving from her face to the thin white blouse. "Since you've put your modesty back on, I don't think you're going to offer to share the blanket with me even if it gets cold." He reached down and picked up a heavy lined jacket. "So I guess I'll have to sleep by the fire."

"You can have the bedroll," Brandy offered, "I can stay here by the fire."

"Get in the bedroll and go to sleep." His thumb jerked toward the blankets spread invitingly on the ground. There wasn't any laughter in this tone, only command.

Reluctantly she obeyed, resenting the fact that if she didn't, he would probably carry her there bodily if necessary. She gave him an angry glare as she walked by, to let him see that she didn't like to be ordered around. But he didn't seem to notice.

While he added more fuel to the fire, Brandy tugged off her boots and slipped beneath the blanket, cradling her head on her arm. She didn't feel at all sleepy. As she gazed at the fire that had begun to crackle brightly, she wondered if her parents had noticed she wasn't in bed. This very minute they might be organizing a search party for her. Somehow she doubted that they would miss her before morning.

Her gaze shifted to Jim. With that bulky jacket on, he looked even bigger and stronger than before. What would her parents think if they met him?

A crazy question, since her own reactions had varied wildly. One minute she was terrified by him, in the next she was admiring the strength and self-assurance that made her feel so safe and secure. Then she was embarrassed by his cynical mockery, or bridling at the way he ordered her around as if she were a child and not an adult. One thing for sure, she wasn't indifferent to him. No one could be for long.

Blinking with exhaustion, she wasn't aware of having fallen asleep. Then her eyes focused blearily on the yellow haze that filled the sky. Where were the stars? It couldn't be morning already. A twist of her head helped her see the golden globe of the sun just peeping over the horizon.

Sighing, she snuggled deeper in the bedroll, stiff all over from the night they had spent on the hard ground. The air was still cold, biting at her nose and cheeks, and she rolled sleepily onto her side to face the campfire.

There were no flames. No heat radiating from the circle of gray-white ashes. And there was no sign of Jim. Stunned, Brandy propped herself up on an elbow and looked at where the saddle had been last night. It was gone, too.

Had he left her? Had he decided not to risk being caught by helping her back home? Or had he sneaked away before dawn to get a head start in case she didn't keep her promise and told the authorities about him?

The wild flurry of questions raced unanswered through her mind, and throwing back the covers, she scrambled from the bedroll. She reached hastily for her boots. As she started to pull on the right one, a horse snorted behind her.

"Better shake those boots out before you put them on." The husky voice came from directly behind her. "Maybe a scorpion decided to use one for a nest during the night."

At the sound of his voice Brandy turned, a faint twinge of relief going through her at the sight of

Jim leading the saddled horse toward the fire. So he hadn't deserted her after all. Meeting the enigmatic darkness of his eyes, she found herself at a loss for words.

Turning back, she shook the boot before putting it on to be sure no creature had crawled inside. "You should have got me up earlier," she said briskly.

"You were sleeping. No point waking you up sooner than was necessary," he replied smoothly. "The coffee should still be warm enough to drink. Prickly pear fruit is the breakfast special."

He tossed her the tin cup which she almost didn't catch. "Coffee is good enough."

The small pot was sitting in the ashes. After pouring herself what was left, Brandy huddled near the campfire. Her thin blouse offered no protection against the cold, so the dying warmth of the ashes would have to do. Out of the corner of her eye she watched Jim tighten the saddle cinch on the sorrel horse.

"Did you sleep well?" His question was unexpected.

"Yes, why?" Brandy scolded herself silently for sounding so defensive.

"Just wondered." He shrugged in an indifferent way as the stirrup hung freely again along the horse's side.

He walked to the fire and dumped the coffee dregs from the pot onto the ashes. With a stick, he stirred the charred coals to make sure there were no live embers.

"Did you think I'd left without you? Is that what's bothering you?"

Her gaze flew to his face, meeting his mocking and all too perceptive dark eyes. "You could have," she pointed out with an airy toss of her head.

"Yes, I could have." He straightened, the empty coffeepot in his hand. "Are you through with the cup?"

Brandy quickly swallowed the last of the now lukewarm liquid and handed him the cup, watching as he stowed the two items in the saddlebags. Only the bedroll remained to be put away. A shiver danced over her skin as she remembered the wished-for warmth of the blanket.

Come on, sun, she thought as she gazed at the yellow disc that had climbed a little higher in the morning sky. Warm me up.

Standing in one place wasn't making her any warmer. She walked over to her bed and picked up the tightly woven top blanket. When she had shaken out the dust, Jim claimed it.

"I'll take it," he said.

Hesitating for a second, she finally released her hold on it. Maybe he didn't think she was capable of rolling it up neatly enough to suit him.

Picking up the thinner groundsheet, she gave it a quick shake, and her side vision caught a metallic gleam. She turned in time to see him make a foot-long slash in the center of the blanket with his knife.

"What are you doing?" she frowned in astonishment.

He replaced the knife in the leather sheath that hung from his belt. "It's going to be an hour or more before it gets anywhere near warm. You'll be half-frozen by then." Without further explanation the blanket, with its slit opening, was drawn over her head. "You can hold it around your waist with your belt."

For disbelieving seconds, Brandy stared at the blanket, now transformed into a poncho. Already she could feel its warmth and the protection it offered against the cold.

Finally she raised her eyes to his face, and studied his expression. "You've ruined your blanket." It was a totally unnecessary observation, but she said it all the same.

"So I have," he agreed with a mocking twist of his mouth.

To close the subject, he picked up the groundsheet Brandy had dropped. With a few expert flips he had it neatly in a compact roll. As he walked to the horse to tie the bundle behind the cantle, Brandy unbuckled her belt and drew it out of the loops of her denim jeans. She wanted to tell him how grateful she was, but she didn't know how to put it into words without sounding all gushy and artificial. And she sensed that he didn't really require any thanks.

Sighing, she secured the belt around the bulky folds of the blanket-poncho at her waist. She finished just as Jim completed smothering the ashen embers of the campfire. After a brief glance to see if she was ready, he mounted his horse. Kicking his boot free of the left stirrup for Brandy to use, he grasped her forearm and helped her swing up behind him.

"I know about where your house should be," he said as she got settled. "We'll probably meet up with a search party before we reach it."

Brandy agreed with him, balancing her hands on her thighs as Jim touched his heels to the horse's flanks. The sorrel started forward briskly, crossing their camp circle to head toward the northeast.

The gray ashes of the fire were covered with sand, and only their footprints gave evidence they had been there. Soon the desert would wipe away even that trace. Brandy found that thought sad—she wasn't exactly certain why.

Fresh and eager, the horse carried them effortlessly over the sandy ground, avoiding the thicker clumps of brush and cactus. The hush of the morning took away any need for conversation. The country around them was new to Brandy, although the far-reaching vistas were basically the same, viewed from a different angle.

Protected by the poncho and warmed by the body heat of the man riding in front of her, she found the ride to be an exhilarating way to start the day. The cool of the morning was when the desert wildlife came out to forage for food. It was a challenge to try to catch a glimpse of a few creatures before they scurried out of sight.

They had traveled a couple of miles before Brandy noticed a change in the horse's gait. For a moment she thought the sorrel might have a rock lodged in his shoe. She studied his stride for a little while, but couldn't see that he was favoring any hoof.

Glancing around Jim's shoulder, she saw the horse's ears pricked forward, his head held unnaturally high, tossing now and then as he champed to get control of the bit in his mouth. His gait remained joltingly stiff-legged.

"What's the matter with your horse?" Brandy looked over Jim's shoulder to see his stern profile. "Has he suddenly decided he doesn't want us to ride double?"

"No," was the abrupt response.

But he must have agreed with Brandy that something was wrong, because at that moment he checked the horse to a halt. The muscular sorrel danced nervously in place, his neck arching higher. Brandy frowned and started to ask again what was wrong.

"Damn!" The softly muttered oath stopped her question.

At almost the same instant, a touch of the reins made the horse pivot sharply. Brandy barely recovered her balance before the horse bounded into a canter and swerved right. She had to clutch Jim's waist to stay on.

They were obviously fleeing from something or someone—Brandy didn't have time to look, but she guessed it was someone. It was either the search party looking for her or the law, perhaps investigating a report of cattle rustling.

Just as Brandy adjusted to the leaping rhythm of the canter, the horse slid to a stop near a rocky outcrop. Her left arm tried to circle Jim's waist for support, but he grabbed it.

"Get down!" he ordered, nearly pushing her off before she could obey the command.

She moved quickly out of the way of the dancing hooves, expecting the horse and rider to gallop away and leave her there. Instead Jim dismounted a split-second after her. She watched in wide-eyed amazement as he held the reins of the agitated horse and unsaddled him at the same time. He dropped the saddle and pads carelessly on the ground as he moved to the horse's head.

"What's wrong?" Thoroughly confused, Brandy raked a hand through her amber-gold hair.

"Sandstorm," Jim answered tersely.

Something, not someone. Looking to the north, Brandy realized the dark haze on the horizon was not a distant mountain range but a rapidly moving sandstorm. Her stomach twisted into knots.

She had witnessed the unbelievable fury of such storms before, but always from the shelter of a sturdy building. Never had she actually been outside in one, exposed and unprotected.

Her gaze darted in alarm to the man wrestling with the plunging, rearing horse. She saw that he was fighting to unbuckle the bridle.

"You aren't turning him loose?" she breathed.

At that moment the jaw strap came free of the buckle and the horse tore its head out of the bridle. Loose, the sorrel bolted away at a flat-out run.

"He's desert born and raised and knows more about surviving out here than we do." The tightly worded explanation was given as Jim moved swiftly to retrieve the saddle and pads. "Get over to the rocks."

The hand between her shoulderblades didn't wait for her to obey and she was pushed roughly toward the outcropping. Once there, he scanned the uninviting expanse of jagged rocks, then handed her the saddle pads.

"Put these pads over there where those rocks come together in a vee," Jim instructed.

She didn't need to be told to hurry. The feeling

of urgency was all around her. Jim hoped the rocks would break the force of the driving wind. While she jammed the thick pads in, he was shaking out the groundsheet.

Casting an anxious look at the approaching storm, Brandy turned to tell Jim that she was done. He was already at her side, wrapping part of the groundsheet around her and pulling her down with him to a half-sitting position against the rock wall.

His arms were around her, cradling her against his solidness of his chest. The groundsheet had been tucked the rest of the way around both of them and drawn over their heads. In the quiet darkness of the protective cocoon, Brandy was aware of his muscular body lying heavily against hers. There was no thought of the intimacy of their position or the closeness that made both heartbeats sound as one. She was only conscious of the way he was shielding her from the coming storm.

With the suddenness of a striking rattler, it was on them. The howling wind seemed to try to suck them away from the shelter of the rock. Brandy's arms instinctively tightened around Jim's waist.

Fine dust penetrated their improvised shelter choking her nose and throat with its tiny grains. The blasting sand seemed to come from every direction, stinging bombardments of a thousand needles, and Brandy knew that Jim was getting the worst of it.

The roar was deafening. The air she breathed was stifling hot and laden with grit. She wanted to tear away the cover and gulp in clean, fresh air even though she knew the raging storm made it impossible.

"I . . . I can't breathe," she murmured with a gasp, her face pressed into the strong column of his throat.

Jim drew her more tightly into his arms. "Hang in there, honey," he whispered forcefully. "We're going to make it. Just hang in."

Brandy closed her mind to everything except the reassuring beat of his heart beneath her head and the indomitable strength that seemed to flow from the male body that enveloped her.

A minute became as long as an hour. And the storm raged, the hammering din never seeming to abate. The heat, the noise, the suffocating dust, all combined to make it an unending nightmare. When Jim tried to turn her face away from the sheepskin collar of his jacket, she resisted and tried to bury her nose deeper.

"Brandy,"—his fingers slid gently through her curling hair—"Brandy, it's all right. You can come out now." His voice was warm and gently mocking.

When she still refused to move, he pulled away and pried her arms loose from around his waist. Then the quietness struck her and she opened her eyes to the sunlight. The groundsheet had been thrown back, its dark color indistinguishable from the sand that covered it.

"I can't believe it," Brandy sighed, sinking back against the saddle pads, slowly breathing in the air.

Tiny particles of dust floated in the air, but there were far fewer now that the storm had passed. Jim leaned against the wall beside her.

"Can't believe what?" He glanced down at her, amusement in his eyes.

"I didn't think it was ever going to end." Brandy looked up at the blue sky.

She rolled her head to the side, giving him a shaky smile. A dark light entered his eyes and a finger reached out to touch the turned-up tip of her nose, then trailed a dusty path down her cheek. Something in his touch made her heart skip crazily.

"Your skin feels like sandpaper." His mouth quirked.

The gritty film was everywhere. "You should see your whiskers!" she told him with a breathless laugh.

He grinned lazily, his hand leaving her cheek as he pushed himself to his feet. Upright, he extended a hand to help her up. Without hesitation, she placed both hands in his and let him pull her easily to her feet.

He didn't let go right away, not that Brandy minded. The chest that she had snuggled against minutes before was only inches away. She tipped her head to one side.

"Do you know," she said in a voice that was partly teasing and partly serious, "I haven't thanked you for all you've done. Last night and now."

"Guess I should claim my reward for rescuing you, shouldn't I?" Jim mocked huskily, looking into her eyes, then at her mouth.

They had been through too much together in less than twenty-four hours for Brandy to feel self-conscious. She raised herself up on tiptoes as Jim's hand cupped the back of her neck. Her fingers spread across his chest to balance herself.

She felt the rough brush of his whiskers first, then the warmth of his mouth closing over hers. The kiss was gently firm, nothing tentative or uncertain about it, just like the man who gave it.

When the kiss came to an end, Brandy wished silently that it hadn't ended so soon. She gazed into his eyes, veiled by sooty lashes, their expression unreadable. The hand at the back of her neck slowly tightened, drawing her to him.

She didn't need the pressure of his hand to tip her head back to receive his kiss. The hard demand of his mouth ignited a wildfire of desire.

Whirling in a mindless world ruled only by sensations, Brandy felt them exploding around her. Her pulse hammered in her ears as her lips parted under the irresistible command of his. The heady male scent of him enveloped her like the drugging scent of burning incense. Nearly every inch of her skin felt the imprint of his masculine body.

Then the passionate kiss was ended, and his mouth moved with reluctant slowness away from hers. Unconsciously Brandy sighed her regret, letting her head rest against his chest while she came back to reality.

There was an impersonal gentleness in the hands that held her shoulders. It was echoed by the distant but affectionate kiss he bestowed on the top of her head.

Puzzled by his obvious withdrawal, she tipped her head back to gaze into his impassive face. He used her motion away from him to release her completely.

"It would have been wiser if I hadn't done that," he murmured wryly as he turned away.

Brandy frowned, then laughed a little. "Why should you be sorry you kissed me? I'm not!"

Without glancing at her, Jim retrieved the saddle pads and laid them over the saddle. "I can't explain," he answered cryptically. "That's my fault. But let's just say it's best if we forget what happened a minute ago."

"Why?" she persisted.

"I don't want you to get the wrong idea." He gave the groundsheet an indifferent shake and draped it across the saddle.

She felt as if she were lost in a maze and all his answers only led her deeper into it.

"People kiss all the time. No big deal, right? So we find each other attractive," she reasoned with a confused shake of her head. "So what? I mean, I may look young, but I'm not a romantic teenager who's going to misinterpret a kiss as a declaration of love."

"You do look young and impressionable," Jim admitted with a faint twinkle in his eyes.

Could he be any more annoying? Brandy doubted it. "Well, thanks for the compliment, if it is a compliment." Immediately she was sorry she'd lashed out at him. "I didn't mean to lose my temper," she apologized, but he seemed unruffled. "It's just that I don't understand what there is to regret in a kiss."

"I like you, Brandy. You've got guts. If I'd known that when you stumbled into my camp last night, all this talk now wouldn't be necessary."

Brandy sighed at the confusing conversation. "What's that supposed to mean, Jim?"

He studied her for a long moment before answering patiently. "There are quite a few things about me that you don't know. Let's leave it at that."

Frustrated by his deliberately obscure answers, she turned away, lifting her hand in a helpless gesture. "I suppose you're married with three kids. Is that supposed to shock me or make me feel like a home-wrecker?"

His throaty chuckle surprised her. "I'm not married," he declared, with no attempt to conceal the amusement in his voice. He reached down and looped the canteen strap over his shoulder. "Come on, Brandy. We've got a long walk ahead."

For a few minutes Brandy had completely forgotten her predicament. She suddenly thought of her parents who were probably waiting anxiously to hear that she was all right. And here she was arguing with a mysterious cattle rustler in the middle of nowhere.

Taking a step forward to fall in beside him, she noticed his saddle and gear sitting on the ground. "Are you leaving your things behind?" she frowned.

"I can pick them up later."

Brandy supposed it would be foolish for him to carry the saddle over the same ground twice, considering how heavy it was. His long strides put Jim in the lead, although he did slacken his pace so that she could keep up.

Gazing over the vast expanse of rolling desert dotted with shrubs and cactus, she was aware all over again that she could see for miles, yet there was nothing to be seen. "How are you ever going to find your horse?" She hurried to walk with Jim as she asked the question.

"He'll probably head for the corral and water now that the storm is over," he replied.

The corral . . . Brandy guessed that was probably where he was holding the cattle he'd stolen until his partners came to ship them out. She wondered if it was near where he'd camped last night. Thinking back, she knew she hadn't heard any cattle lowing close by. There had been only the rustle of the horse.

Covertly she studied his boldly chiseled profile and tried to figure out his confusing answers of a few minutes ago. It was hopeless. Then she began wondering why a man who seemed capable of doing anything he wanted had chosen to be a cattle thief. It seemed such a shame.

"Jim?" Hesitantly she formed her question, the uneven ground beneath her feet demanding part of her attention. "Have you always stolen cattle? I mean, haven't you ever wanted to do something else?"

"I wondered how long it would take." He gave her an amused look.

"What?" she asked with a disgruntled sigh. He had avoided her question again with another ambiguous answer.

"I was talking about the female instinct to reform a man. Yours has finally surfaced." There was a definite sparkle of laughter in the dark eyes as the corners of his mouth deepened with suppressed amusement. "Were you going to give me a lecture on my wicked ways?"

"I was just curious," she retorted defensively.

She waited for him to reply to her question, but he didn't. She didn't bother to ask again.

CHAPTER THREE

Their weaving, twisting trail through the cactus and sage-studded desert had taken them over two miles of ground. As the crow flies, they had only covered about a mile and a half. The sun was well up in the sky and none of the night's coolness remained. Jim removed his jacket and unbuttoned his vest, while Brandy took off the belt so that the poncho hung free and rebuckled it around her denims.

Halfway up the rock-strewn wall of a drywash, Brandy stopped to catch her breath. The honey-gold hair around her forehead had curled into damp ringlets from perspiration. At the top of the wash, Jim reached down to give her a hand up.

"You can rest up here," he insisted when she started to ignore his hand.

With a shrug of resignation she grabbed hold of

his hand and scrambled with his help to the slanted rim of the wash. There she sat down, leaning back on one elbow in the patchy shade of a desert shrub.

"You can tell I'm used to riding and not walking," Brandy murmured with a self-deprecating smile.

"This sun can drain the energy out of anyone." He opened the canteen and handed it to her.

The water was brackish and warm, but it still soothed her dry throat. Taking another long drink, she handed it back to him. There was a whirring sound in her ears that she attributed to the heat and exhaustion of their trek through the desert; then it seemed to grow louder.

"Jim, I think I hear a helicopter." The minute she spoke, Brandy was positive she was right. Shading her eyes against the glare of the sun, she searched the sky where she thought the sound was coming from. Sunlight flashed on something flying comparatively low to the ground. "There it is!" she pointed.

Turning, she saw that Jim was watching it, too, the brim of his dust-covered hat shading out the sun. His gaze had narrowed.

"It's a search party," he said.

The relief left her voice. "I know."

That meant that in a few short minutes she would be rescued and be winging home to the welcoming arms of her parents. But if Jim was seen—Brandy knew she couldn't bear to see him arrested for stealing cattle, not after all he had done for her. He was a criminal, and liking him didn't change that. Regardless of whether it was wrong or not, she knew she had to help him get away.

"They haven't seen us yet." Her anxious eyes scanned his impassive face. "You can hide in that clump of mesquite over there. They'll never even know you were here, Jim, if you hide right now."

"You're not going to turn me in?" He smiled crookedly at her.

"I can't." She glanced over her shoulder at the circling helicopter that was drawing steadily nearer their position on the rim of the drywash. "They're getting closer. Hurry, before they see you!"

As he slowly rose to his feet, she scrambled upright with him. The lazy smile was still there as she gazed up at him. She didn't really want to say goodbye, but there was no other choice.

"Take care of yourself," she whispered tightly.

He hesitated, his expression growing serious. "I'm not going anywhere, Brandy."

"But—" She looked anxiously over her shoulder.

The helicopter was close enough for her to make out the pilot and the man sitting beside him. Even as she realized that, she saw the pilot point toward them. It was too late.

"Damn it!" Bitter tears filled her eyes. "They've seen us. They've seen you!"

Reaching out, he brushed an imaginary lock of hair behind her ear. "Brandy, I'm sorry. I am very sorry," he murmured cryptically.

"I'm the one who's sorry," she insisted with a confused frown.

His hand settled over her shoulder, turning her around. "There's a clearing over there where the helicopter will probably land to pick us up."

With Jim more or less pushing her along ahead

of him, they started toward the clearing. Brandy couldn't believe it was all happening.

"Aren't you going to try to get away?" she said with disbelief. "You still might make it." Jim didn't answer, but kept pushing her toward their destination. "Do you want to get caught, is that it? You'll go to jail." The helicopter was very near and she had to shout the last to make herself heard above the rotors.

Not until they had reached the clearing did he speak, his hand falling away from her shoulder as he suddenly seemed very remote. "I'm not a cattle rustler, Brandy." His voice was controlled and clear.

"But you said—" she started to protest.

"No, *you* said it," he corrected smoothly.

He seemed so completely different somehow. She made a frowning study of him, trying to figure out what it was. She tipped her head warily to one side.

"Who are you, anyway?" she demanded.

Dust swirled around them as the helicopter descended onto the clearing. Its arrival distracted Brandy as she turned to face it, shielding her eyes against the sand kicked up by the still-spinning rotors. The pilot remained at the controls as the second man stepped out and ran in a crouching position toward Brandy and Jim.

A wide grin of relief was splitting the man's face. "Hey, Jim," he exclaimed as he reached them, vigorously shaking Jim's hand, "am I glad to see you're all right! Raymond saw your horse heading for the main house just before the storm hit." Then the man glanced at Brandy. "You must be the Ames girl."

Numbly she moved her head in an affirmative nod as the poncho-blanket flapped roughly against her side in the whirling wind generated by the helicopter. Her confusion was increasing with each ticking second. Her mind raced to separate the true things from the false. The man appeared to know Jim very well, and Jim *was* his name. In her bewilderment, Brandy recognized that he had been more concerned about finding Jim safe than her. Jim wasn't a cattle rustler, he was somebody important—but who?

Then Brandy remembered that initial sensation that there was something familiar about him. With eyes narrowed against the blowing dust, she turned to study his face. His features were obscured by the beard and the wide brim of his hat pulled low on his forehead. His obsidian-dark eyes returned her gaze with cool alertness.

"Are you ready?" he asked. Part of her mind registered the fact that Jim was repeating the other man's question, but she stared without answering, trying desperately to recognize him. "Ms. Ames, are you ready to leave?"

Ms. Ames? Since when? Brandy snapped out of her daze. If he had spoken with gentle mockery instead of such distant politeness, she might not have felt quite so shocked. It had always been just Brandy and Jim.

"Yes." She nodded her head in case her softly-spoken answer was whipped away unheard by the noise of the helicopter.

It was the other man's hand, not Jim's, that took

a guiding hold of her arm and led her in a crouching walk to the open side of the helicopter. The man helped her into the far rear seat, gesturing toward the seat belts to strap herself in.

Feeling strangely betrayed, Brandy wouldn't allow herself to look at Jim as he climbed effortlessly into the seat beside her. While the other man took the seat beside the pilot, she concentrated on buckling her seat belt tightly.

The man leaned sideways to shout above the deafening roar of the motor to the pilot. "Did you radio the sheriff that we found the Ames girl with Corbett?"

The pilot nodded yes and the helicopter began to rise.

Corbett! The name struck Brandy like a blow. The image flashed in her mind of a dark-haired man with bluntly carved cheekbones and jaw, and a strong chin with a faint cleft. Deep grooves were etched on either side of a sensual male mouth. The rest came back to her: the dark eyes that could glitter with cold menace or sparkle with mockery or reveal no emotion at all.

The beard and the circumstances had kept her from guessing his identity. Who would ever have guessed, she reasoned in silent desperation, that a disreputable cowboy camped alone in the desert would turn out to be James Corbett, the actor?

Shock waves of recognition rocked her. So that's who he really was. She felt sick to her stomach. He had probably thought it was hilariously funny that she had mistaken him for a cattle rustler. She could imagine him relating the tale to amuse his friends. She had made a fool of herself.

Flames of embarrassment burned her cheeks. She sank her teeth into her lower lip to hold back the whimper of injured pride that would make her humiliation complete.

Through her lashes, her traitorously bright blue-green eyes darted a look of smoldering resentment at the man seated beside her. His dark eyes met the look without emotion before he turned his attention to the desert scrub the helicopter was flying above.

Brandy riveted her gaze on the pilot. Jim must have realized that she had finally recognized him, and now that his little game was over, he no longer found her amusing. Her breath caught when she realized that she still thought of him as Jim. Starting now, she had better begin thinking of him as James Corbett, celebrity and actor.

The pilot pressed one side of his headset more tightly against his ear, then signaled to the man in the co-pilot's seat to pick up the set of earphones hooked on the lower part of the control panel. Adjusting it over his head, the man spoke into the microphone, then listened.

Grimacing at the pilot, the man turned in his seat toward Jim. "There are reporters at the Ames house," he shouted. "Somehow they heard the search party had been told to look for you, too. Do you want to land at Saguaro instead?"

The swift glance Brandy darted at Jim encountered a measuring look. His mouth was compressed into a grim line. She wanted only to go home and bring this miserable nightmare to an end, but it seemed she was going to have to run through a gauntlet of reporters before she reached sanctuary.

"We'll go to the Ames house," was the terse command.

The man moved his shoulders in a shrug that said Jim was the boss, and relayed the message to the pilot. Within a few minutes, Brandy saw the familiar buildings of her home just ahead. Cars, trucks and horse trailers littered the driveway and the area around the stable.

As the helicopter began its downward descent, using the graveled road in front of her house for its landing pad, a group of people surged forward to meet it. Brandy caught a glimpse of her parents' anxious faces in the crowd before they were lost in the cloud of dust churned up by the rotating blades.

When it settled on the ground, Jim ordered the pilot to turn the motor off. Its sputtering stop left the slowing, centrifugal whirl of the blades to fill the silence. Fumbling with her belt, Brandy finally got it unbuckled and started to crawl out of the helicopter.

Jim waited for her on the ground, but she ignored the large hand that offered to help her and jumped down unassisted. His broad chest blocked her path to the crowd; unwillingly, she let her gaze be drawn to his face. She was more wary of him now than she had ever been before.

"Excuse me, Mr. Corbett." Her voice sounded cool and surprisingly self-possessed. She didn't want to hear whatever it was that he had been on the point of saying. "My folks are waiting for me."

Brushing past him, she hurried to her relieved parents. The smile she gave them was forced and taut as she tried to guess what they thought about their daughter's return in the company of a celebrity.

Lenora, her mother, looked awfully happy. The camel tan trouser suit that she wore was subtly tailored to reveal her slender figure. Her medium-length hair was ash-blond, lightly streaked with silver for sophisticated highlights. Yet she was as motherly as could be and it was in her arms that Brandy sought shelter.

"You gave us such a scare, honey," Lenora Ames scolded as she cupped her daughter's face in her hands and laughed in relief. "You look like a grubby little kid."

Brandy looked down at her dust-encrusted poncho and the grit that clung to her hair, skin, and clothes.

"I *am* a mess," she agreed before turning to her burly father.

She had taken only one step toward him before she was enveloped in a hearty bear hug. His dark, curling hair was peppered with gray, but his sunburned face was still handsome.

"Are you all right, Brandywine?" Stewart Ames whispered in her ear, using his own pet name for her.

"I'm fine, Daddy." She hugged him a little tighter. Over his shoulder, she could see the reporters clustering around Jim Corbett. Cameras were clicking away, and she knew several had been taken of her reunion with her parents.

When her father released her, it seemed to be a signal for the reporters to close in. There were only three, but the questions bombarded her as if there were twice that many.

"How do you feel, Ms. Ames?"

"Fine," she nodded.

"Is it good to be home?"

"Of course."

"How did you get lost?"

"What was it like spending a night on the desert?"

"Tell us about it!"

The questions followed one another in such rapid succession and Brandy was rattled. Bewildered, trying to decide which question to answer first, she didn't notice Jim's approach. Suddenly he was there, smoothly introducing himself to her parents, and Brandy felt very proud of the way they reacted to him. They were respectful without being awed by his fame.

"We heard you were caught in the sandstorm, Mr. Corbett," her father commented.

"Ms. Ames," one of the reporters broke in, "what did you do when the sandstorm came up?"

There was a pause that allowed Brandy to answer. "Actually Ji—Mr. Corbett saw the storm approaching and we were able to find shelter in some rocks until it blew over," she explained, correcting the impulse to use his first name.

"Do you mean you and Mr. Corbett were together when the sandstorm hit?" a second reporter queried.

"I—that is—" Stammering, Brandy realized too late that no one knew she and Jim had been together before their rescue. Her eyes wildly sought assistance from Jim. There was no one else who could help.

"We met last night," he announced calmly to

the now intensely curious reporters. "She had lost her way in the dark, saw the fire from my camp and came in."

He made it sound so matter-of-fact, as if it was the most natural thing in the world, and not something that would cause comment.

"Then the two of you spent the night together on the desert, is that right?"

Jim Corbett smiled coldly. "I guess you could put it that way, yes."

"Where did you get those scratches on your arm, Ms. Ames?"

Brandy glanced almost with surprise at the marks on her arms. She had completely forgotten about them. She wished she had remembered them and kept her arms beneath her poncho. Thank heaven the poncho covered her ripped blouse! That would really raise some eyebrows.

"Cactus and mesquite thorns," she answered. "I ran right into them."

"What were you running from?" one reporter laughed rather snidely.

She flushed crimson, remembering her wild flight into the desert when she had seen the knife in Jim's hand. She couldn't possibly tell them that.

"Are you asking Ms. Ames if I chased her around the campfire?" He glared at the reporter. "I think she was using a figure of speech when she said ran into some cactus and mesquite thorns."

"That's right," she agreed quickly.

"Why don't you describe your night in the desert with James Corbett?" A reporter gave Brandy a suggestive wink.

She waited, half expecting Jim to speak up and

say that she hadn't known who he was. But he said nothing, leaving her to answer the question as best she could.

"To be honest," she said hesitantly, "by the time I saw the fire last night I was so grateful there was another human being around that I didn't care who it was."

"But afterward?" the reporter prompted.

"Afterward—" Brandy faltered again.

Jim picked up the sentence where she left off. "She ate some of the rabbit I cooked. I put some antiseptic on her scratches and she went to sleep beside the fire. It wouldn't make the tabloids, would it? Well, maybe. Corbett the Bunny Killer."

Not the way he put it, Brandy thought to herself as the others laughed a little self-consciously. He had deliberately omitted the humiliating parts, like her thinking he was a cattle thief and the fact that her scratches were not limited to her arms. She sent up a silent prayer of gratitude that he had, because she never would have been able to endure the innuendoes and snickering.

"Mr. Corbett has a reputation as a ladies' man. Were you concerned about spending the night with him, Ms. Ames?"

"I never even thought about his reputation," Brandy answered honestly, since she hadn't known who he was.

Even now she couldn't admit to knowing anything about him personally, but a man as ruggedly masculine and virile as he was, and a celebrity too, probably had had a lot of beautiful women in his life. Something inside her froze a little at that thought, remembering that expert kiss he had given her, and the open way she had responded.

She had been so stupidly naive. No wonder he had felt the need to tell her that the kiss meant nothing! He was a star and she was a nobody, and a not very glamorous nobody at that.

"Lost the way you were, it must have been a thrill to be found by James Corbett," one reporter observed.

Humiliating was the word, Brandy corrected him silently as she glanced at Jim with an upward sweep of her lashes. His dark eyes held the same mocking light as the night before. Then she noticed the cynical twist of his mouth and turned away.

"Yes, it was," she lied calmly.

"Ms. Ames—" The question forming on another reporter's lips was never completed.

"Guys, guys!" The man who had been in the helicopter with them stepped into the circle of people, a good-natured but authoritative expression on his face. "I think that's enough questions. I'm sure this young lady is tired and thirsty and much in need of a relaxing few hours in the comfort of her home after all she's been through. And I know Mr. Corbett is going to want to rest up before we start filming tomorrow morning. You have your stories, so let's break this up."

Although they grumbled, none of the reporters protested too much. As they began to disperse, Brandy realized that she wasn't going to be able to enter her home without saying some form of goodbyes. Emulating the composure of her parents, who had stayed quietly at her side during all the questioning, she turned to Jim.

"Goodbye, Mr. Corbett," she said stiffly. "Thanks for your help."

His mouth tightened for a second as if in irritation. She supposed it was because she hadn't sounded all that impressed with the privilege of spending so much time in his company. He gave her a challenging look as he offered his hand in goodbye, and she had to resist the impulse to slap it away.

"Pleasure meeting you, Ms. Ames," he murmured.

Her hand rested limply in his, not responding to the firm clasp of his fingers.

"I'm sure you found it amusing." Brandy smiled coldly as she made the sweetly cutting comment.

His grip tightened when she tried to slip her hand away. There was a swift narrowing of his dark eyes as he made a thorough study of her face. Then his gaze darted to the reporters still lingering near their cars.

"You'll be explaining that remark." The threatening promise was issued in a soft tone meant only for Brandy to hear. Her hand was released as he nodded politely to her parents and started to the waiting helicopter.

For a few seconds, Brandy watched him striding away before she turned to her parents. Her mother curved a comforting arm around her waist and started toward the house.

"You go on in," Stewart Ames instructed. "I'll be there in a few minutes. I want to thank the men again for all they've done."

Inside the house, the tension that Brandy hadn't been aware of slipped away. The muscles in her legs ached from her long walk over the rocky desert, she was tired from the night spent on the ground, and she felt caked with sweat and grime.

"You must be hungry," her mother smiled, her eyes still bright with relief at Brandy's safe return. "I'll fix you some soup and sandwiches." Then she laughed. "I'd better fix some for all of us. I just realized Stewart and I haven't even had breakfast. I'd just poured the orange juice when he discovered you weren't in your room and your bed hadn't been slept in."

That confirmed what Brandy had suspected. She almost wished they had discovered she was gone the night before; maybe she would have been found before she stumbled into Jim's camp. In all probability, though, she wouldn't have been, and her parents would have spent endless hours imagining the worst.

"I didn't think you'd miss me before morning," she admitted with a tired sigh. She knew her parents would want to know more than she had told the reporters, but at this moment, she didn't feel up to it. "Look, Mom, what I really want right now is a long, hot bath," she said, changing the subject. "Why don't you go ahead and fix us something to eat and it'll be ready when I get out of the tub."

An hour later, she entered the spacious kitchen. The tantalizing smell of hot tomato soup made her stomach growl. Her freshly washed hair curled damply about her head, droplets of water dotting the shoulders of her clean, blue-striped blouse. Revitalized by the bath, she sniffed appreciatively at the soup on the stove and gave her parents a sunny smile.

"What happened to that little girl that looked like a desert rat?" her father teased, rising from the chair at the table to hold one out for Brandy.

"She got washed down the drain," she declared.

With the ordeal over, appetites returned. Not until all had eaten did her parents' curiosity take over and Brandy was faced with relating what really happened.

"A cattle rustler," Stewart Ames chuckled softly when she explained her failure to recognize Jim Corbett. "That really must have been a blow to his ego!"

"Well, he certainly paid me back," retorted Brandy. "He let me go on thinking he was a cattle thief, and never told me who he was. When I think of the way he was laughing at me behind my back—" She chased the crackers in her soup with a spoon, leaving the sentence unfinished. "It's humiliating!"

"You have to admit it's kind of funny, Brandy," her mother said. "And it might've been awkward, even embarrassing, for Mr. Corbett to tell you who he was."

"Nothing could embarrass that man!" she snapped, then realized that it wasn't fair to answer so sharply. None of this had been her parents' fault and she shouldn't take her wounded pride out on them. "Can we change the subject? I don't want to talk about James Corbett anymore."

Those were famous last words, as she learned to her chagrin the next morning when she arrived at the arts and crafts shop to go to work. She had barely stepped inside the rear door when she was accosted by her wide-eyed girlfriend excitedly waving the morning paper.

"Brandy, is this true?" Karen Justin demanded gleefully. "Did James Corbett really find you wandering around in the desert, lost and frightened? James Corbett, the movie star?"

Brandy turned away to hang up her jacket in the employees' closet in the back room, fighting the frustration that swamped her.

"Actually, I found him," she answered in a controlled voice. "Is the coffee ready?" The first one to arrive at the shop in the morning always put the coffeepot on so that there would be time for a shared cup before they unlocked the doors.

"Yes, I think so," Karen shrugged indifferently, and went right back to her original topic. "You've got to tell me everything that happened!"

Brandy's lips thinned with exasperation as she filled a mug with hot coffee from the pot. "It's all in the papers. You can read it for yourself," she said with determined disinterest, turning toward her friend.

Karen's brown eyes twinkled brightly. "Not all of it, I'll bet. Come on, Brandy," she cajoled, " 'fess up. I won't tell a soul, I promise."

"I was out riding, my horse bolted, I started walking home and got lost in the dark. Then I stumbled into his camp, spent the night, started for home in the morning, got caught in the sandstorm, and the helicopter rescued both of us after that. And that's it," Brandy declared with an airy wave.

Karen ran a hand through her flame-colored

hair. "But what did you think when you realized he was James Corbett?"

"I was shocked." Brandy smiled bitterly at the memory of that moment. She sipped at the coffee. "Where's Mrs. Phillips?" she asked, referring to the owner of the shop.

"At the bank, and quit trying to change the subject," was the scolding answer. "Now tell me, what all did you talk about? Did he tell you about the movie he's starring in, the one they're filming out at Old Tucson?"

"No." Brandy picked at the hem of her cream-colored top, the front richly embroidered with orange, yellow and blue intertwining flowers.

"Well, what did you talk about?" Karen prodded after waiting a little too long for an answer.

"Nothing in particular." Frowning, Brandy smoothed the hem down over her blue jeans.

Karen tipped her head to the side, the expression in her brown eyes becoming thoughtful. "There's something you aren't telling me, isn't there?" Her friend was much too perceptive. "You were alone in the desert with him, sitting by a campfire on a starry night. He must have done something . . ."

"Don't be ridiculous!" Brandy said forcefully.

But Karen saw the rosy blush on her cheeks. Breathing in sharply, she gasped, "He *did* kiss you! Oh, Brandy,"—Karen giggled—"James Corbett kissed you!"

Brandy hadn't told her parents that. It was the one thing she really wanted to forget about her weekend episode.

"It wasn't any big deal," she said self-consciously. "It was really quite innocent. Why, at the time I didn't even know who he—'' She closed her mouth abruptly.

Karen stared at her. "You didn't know what?" she asked curiously. "You didn't know who he— was?" She completed the sentence with a question mark in her voice, a red eyebrow arching in disbelief at the only logical verb that could be inserted. "Is that what you meant?"

With an impatient bang, Brandy set her empty cup on the small utility table. "Yes, that's what I meant," she admitted grudgingly. "I didn't recognize him."

"You didn't recognize James Corbett!" Even though she had guessed the fact a second ago, Karen still didn't believe it when she heard Brandy confirm it. She sank onto the seat of a tall stool. "Are you serious?"

The newspaper had slipped from her hands onto her lap, open to the page with the story of Brandy and James Corbett's rescue.

"Look at that picture of him." Brandy pointed defensively to the grainy newspaper photograph taken of the two of them being interviewed by the reporters. "Who would recognize him with that scruffy beard? Besides, since when do movie stars camp out on the desert?"

"What was he doing out there anyway?" her friend asked, momentarily sidetracked.

"I don't know," Brandy shrugged in irritation. "I heard him tell the reporters that he was looking for some peace and quiet."

Karen hugged her arms around her middle. "What was it like to be kissed by James Corbett, Brandy?"

A sharp pain knifed into Brandy's heart. Even now, though she was hurt by the way Jim had dismissed her once they were found, the vivid memory of his kiss was very pleasant. She was vaguely ashamed to admit how much she had enjoyed it.

"Since I didn't know he was James Corbett when he kissed me, I didn't take notes. If I'd known, maybe I could have checked to see if my heart raced or if my temperature rose," she retorted coldly.

"You don't have to bite my head off." Karen recoiled slightly, startled by the sarcasm. Brandy was usually easygoing and good-natured.

"I didn't mean to," she apologized with a tired sigh. "It's just that I'd like to put the whole incident out of my mind. It isn't much fun to remember how he must have secretly laughed at me when I didn't recognize him." She glanced at her wristwatch, adjusting the leather band around her wrist. "It's nearly nine. Did Mrs. Phillips leave the front door key on her desk?"

"I think so," Karen nodded, following as Brandy walked to their employer's office. "Are you going to see him again?"

Brandy stopped and frowned over her shoulder. "See him again? What do you mean?"

"Did he ask you out?"

"Of course not," Brandy laughed, but the sound had a hollow ring. "You watch too many movies, Karen. Life isn't like that."

"Oh, stranger things have happened in real life than in the movies, you know," the redhead declared with a grin.

"Well, he didn't ask me out and I don't think

he will," Brandy stated firmly. "If he did, I wouldn't accept."

"You wouldn't?" Karen repeated incredulously.

"He's already had enough laughs at my expense. Compared to someone like him, I'm just a country girl. Not his type."

"Maybe he wants a change," Karen suggested with an impish smile.

"Then he can find someone else. I don't care to see him again." Or at least that was what she kept telling herself.

CHAPTER FOUR

The sun gleamed through the window on Brandy's honey-bright hair as she bent to sniff the gentle fragrance of the roses. The bouquet of long-stemmed red roses had been waiting for her when she came home from work that day.

Her first inclination had been to throw them away even before she had read the card that came with them. It was a childish reaction, but Brandy had been hounded all day by friends and strangers wanting to hear the inside story about her night on the desert with James Corbett.

Finally she had stopped protesting when they declared what a thrilling adventure it must have been and let them think what they liked. Nothing she said was going to change their minds.

After second thoughts, she decided it would be wrong to throw away such beautiful flowers simply because she felt frustrated and unable to cope with fifteen minutes of undeserved fame.

The message on the card was simple enough, wishing her well, and signed "Jim." She refused to concede that the signature was her main reason for keeping the roses. It was a lot easier to accept a bouquet from Jim, the cattle thief than from handsome James Corbett, the celebrity.

Nibbling at her lower lip, Brandy stepped back to survey the arrangement and nodded in satisfaction at the result. She had chosen the china vase that had been in her mother's family for generations. Its translucent cream finish and delicate design was a perfect foil for the ruby red roses.

Carefully she picked up the vase and carried it into the living room. There she hesitated before deciding that the white wall behind the walnut cabinet would show off the bouquet better than an open display on the coffee table in front of the sofa.

She was just centering the vase on the cabinet when she heard the front door open, followed by the light footsteps of her mother.

"Hello, Brandy." The casual greeting was followed immediately by a delighted, "What beautiful roses! Where did you get them?"

"From Mr. Corbett," Brandy answered in a noncommittal voice.

"How thoughtful of him." Lenora Ames walked over to admire the full blooms.

"Oh, Mom," she shrugged, "I'm sure he was just trying to keep up his image."

"That's a cynical remark, coming from you." She gave her daughter a thoughtful look.

"I'm not cynical. The roses were only a polite gesture. I'm sure Mr. Corbett just told his secretary or assistant to send me some flowers. They're very pretty and I appreciate them, but I'm certainly not bowled over by them," Brandy said coolly.

"I wasn't suggesting that you were," Lenora said dryly.

Moving away from the vase of roses and her mother's questioning look, Brandy walked toward the kitchen. "I'll go start dinner. Where's Dad?"

"Putting the car in the garage. He'll be right in." There was a pause. "Brandy, what happened today?"

Halting in the kitchen archway, Brandy turned slightly. "Nothing happened. I went to work, that's all."

"Stewart and I were besieged with questions about the incident this weekend. You must have been, too. I know you have mixed feelings about the experience and I thought—"

"Yes, I do," she agreed forcefully. "I don't like to be made fun of, and he seemed to think it was unbelievable that I didn't know who he was. Everyone is making a big fuss of it, saying how romantic and thrilling it must have been. I thought it was humiliating." Pride tipped her chin to a more aggressive angle. "Now if you don't mind, I'll go fix dinner."

Her mother made no attempt to stop her—or to bring the conversation back to James Corbett. Her father, when he came in, commented that the roses were lovely, but never asked who had sent them. Brandy assumed that her mother had told him.

The next day, she deliberately omitted mentioning the bouquet to Karen. Her friend's overactive imagination would have been off and running in a heartbeat. Karen undoubtedly would have assigned romantic significance to red roses, and Brandy was tired of her flights of fantasy concerning James Corbett.

The furor caused by her escapade in the desert had finally dwindled down to an odd remark here and there by Thursday. The tension that stretched Brandy's nerves taut had eased. She no longer felt constantly on guard when a customer or acquaintance entered the shop. At last now she could finally believe that, in time, the whole episode would be forgotten.

By Thursday evening, with her parents busily preparing for their next day's classes in the large den, Brandy felt that life was beginning to return to normal. Sighing, she leaned back against the overstuffed cushions of the redwood chair and tucked a hand behind her head.

The sun lingered above the western hills and the enormous Papago Indian reservation that lay beyond them. A scarlet-pink hue was beginning to edge the yellow glow. The spectacular display of sunset colors had started.

From her vantage point on the L-shaped patio that bordered the south side of the house and part of the east, Brandy could view the silent yet colorfully explosive end of the day.

"With a view like this, why did you ride out into the desert?" a low voice inquired behind her.

Sitting upright with a start, she turned toward the voice. She hadn't heard the sliding glass doors

open from the house to the patio. Yet there stood
James Corbett.

This time there was no possibility she could mistake his identity. The only trace of the old Jim that
she saw was the glitter of his dark eyes and the air
of hidden danger. The beard was gone, revealing
his rugged features; and so were the faded denims
and the sheepskin-lined suede vest and dusty shirt.
No stained and dusty Stetson covered the curling
dark hair.

There was nothing unkempt about him now. A
silk shirt in an understated blue molded his wide
shoulders and chest, the long sleeves rolled up to
reveal his tanned, muscular forearms. Faded jeans
hugged his legs and thighs. The force of his magnetism was unmistakable, so compelling that Brandy
was amazed she hadn't guessed his identity at once.

The shock of seeing him again finally receded.
"H—how did you get here?" she asked weakly.

His mouth shifted into a crooked line that wasn't
exactly a smile. "Your mother let me in. She said
you were out here watching the sunset."

"Yes," she murmured as if he needed confirmation that she actually was on the patio. Disconcerted by his unexpected appearance, she averted
her gaze. "I got the flowers. Thank you." That
sounded so abrupt and insincere, she wished she
hadn't mentioned the roses.

"You're welcome." There was a faintly teasing
inclination of his dark head. "Mind if I sit down?"

"Not at all." Her hand gestured nervously for
him to take his pick of the empty patio chairs.

To her dismay, he chose the one closest to hers,
the chair already angled to face her. As he sat down,

she stood up and walked to one of the hardwood pillars that supported the beamed overhang shading most of the patio. The fingers of one hand closed over the rough wood. "This isn't a social visit, Mr. Corbett. Why are you here?" She turned to look at him as she voiced the question, unaware that she was framed by the setting sun. Its golden rays ignited the amber curls of her hair.

"What makes you so sure it isn't a social visit?" He tipped his head to one side, sooty lashes veiling the watchful look in his eyes.

Her mouth tightened as again she glanced away from his powerful features. "If you came to see if I recovered from the ordeal, then the answer is yes, I have."

"Glad to hear it, Brandy," Jim replied diffidently.

His use of her first name grated on her already raw nerves. Mostly, she admitted silently, because when she wasn't looking at him and he spoke, she could almost believe it was Jim sitting there and not James Corbett. It was crazy to keep thinking of him as two different people.

Her fingers were pressed against the wood pillar and she stared out at the sunset. "You don't really need to stay, you know. You don't have to be so polite."

A low chuckle mocked her attempt to get rid of him. "I've never been accused of being a gentleman—because I'm not. So your thinly disguised invitation for me to leave isn't going to work."

Brandy pivoted sharply, an angry glare in her turquoise green eyes. "Listen," she snapped. "I know you're not a gentleman. That's a fact I unfortunately forgot for a few minutes."

The hard, masculine mouth smiled lazily. "Finally we're getting to the point of my visit."

"Which is?" Brandy demanded.

"I know you were hurt and upset when you discovered who I was last Sunday—"

"No one likes to be fooled," she broke in. "I know you were amused that I didn't recognize you. The whole episode must have given you quite a few laughs these past few days. So if you're here to apologize, Mr. Corbett—"

"No such luck," he interrupted coldly, "I don't regret what I did. And if you call me Mr. Corbett one more time, you're going to have to face the consequences!"

Remembering his overpowering strength, Brandy realized that he was prepared to back it up. Although she was somewhat intimidated by his attitude, she refused to let him boss her around quite so casually.

"What would you like me to call you?" she asked with a defiant toss of her head.

His dark eyes narrowed thoughtfully. "You had no problem calling me Jim."

"It was the only name I knew at the time, so what else would I call you?" Brandy asked him haughtily.

"And are there a few other names you could use instead?" he taunted softly.

"I didn't say that," she retorted.

"No, you thought it." He studied her for a long moment. "Haven't you wondered why I didn't tell you who I was?"

"I think I can guess."

"Can you?" He smiled wryly. "Then I hope I don't bore you too much with my explanation."

Brandy had to look away from the coldness of his gaze to conceal her nervousness. "By all means, explain," she insisted in a low voice to keep her voice from trembling. "I'm sure you'll make it interesting."

The air around her crackled with electricity. She knew she was provoking him, but she couldn't seem to stop herself. His deception had hurt, after all, and she had no intention of forgiving him right away.

"When you stumbled into camp that night," Jim spoke with iron self-control that Brandy couldn't help but admire, considering her own rudeness, "my first thought was that you were a crazy fan who'd followed me. One of those obsessive types who want to have sex with celebrities or star athletes. They'll do almost anything to get it. I had no way of knowing whether you were one of them."

That explained the anger that had blazed in his eyes when he saw her, Brandy realized, but his assumption wasn't exactly flattering.

"You must have been disappointed," she commented. "Isn't that one of the side benefits of being a celebrity?"

"No." He bit out the single word. "My personal life is more public than I would like. Which is why I tend to guard the privacy I do have and I don't waste it on the so-called side benefits you referred to. If I want a woman's company, I choose who and when."

Some of the starch went out of her at his forthright explanation. "I understand," Brandy said, and she meant it.

"Then I hope you understand if I admit that I did think it was funny that you mistook me for a cattle thief. It was so ridiculous that I knew it couldn't have been a trick to persuade me to let you stay the night." Brandy glared at him. "You were so absolutely convinced I was a rustler that I didn't know how to tell you the truth. And after a while, I didn't want to tell you."

"Of course not. Why bother?" Brandy declared.

"Take it easy." With an effortless, animal grace, he pushed his long length out of the chair and walked to the wood pillar where Brandy stood. Her head tipped back to gaze into his face, so compelling in its rugged, chiseled lines and sheer maleness. "I liked being with a woman who didn't know I was famous, Brandy. For the first time in a long while, I got to be an ordinary man. It was a pleasant change."

Breathing in shakily, she leaned back against the pillar. His explanation was undoing all the imagined insults and humiliation she thought she had suffered.

"I would've found out who you were eventually."

"Yes, I knew you would," he admitted, his dark gaze not leaving her face. "But in the beginning, I planned to leave you close to your home where the search party could easily find you. The sandstorm changed that."

"Why?" Brandy asked, remembering that he had resisted her attempt to help him escape when they had first seen the helicopter.

"Because I saw that the helicopter was from the

Saguaro Ranch. I knew it might be up there just to search for you, but I doubted that Don Peters, my manager, would've volunteered his services. The fact that he was in the helicopter meant they were looking for me as well. The man has enough problems without me giving him any more."

He was standing in front of her, tall and strong and vitally attractive. A foot and more separated them, yet the sensation remained that he was disturbingly close. Brandy felt herself surrendering and tore her gaze away from his face.

"It wasn't fair of you not to tell me who you were," she protested, but with none of her former belligerence.

"When I saw the helicopter, I realized I had no choice." A hand moved to the pillar, almost touching her golden curls. "It landed before I could explain anything. I hoped I'd be able to speak to you privately after we got you back home, but when we were in the helicopter you finally recognized me, didn't you?"

His arm, tanned and sinewy strong, was only inches from the soft flesh of her cheek. Her honey-colored hair hid her face as she looked down, unable to meet the disconcerting directness of his gaze.

"Yes, I did," she admitted. "I heard the man . . . your manager . . . refer to you as Corbett. That's when I realized who you were."

His expression hardened slightly, making him look withdrawn and aloof.

"If you'd seen the look that came into your eyes when you recognized me,"—one corner of his mouth lifted in a humorless smile—"you would understand why I put off telling you."

"What do you mean?" She raised her head, confused by his comment.

"In your eyes, I suddenly wasn't human anymore. I was some big movie star, not a man," he said. "And for a while, I didn't care why you thought I hadn't told you the truth."

She wanted very much to believe what he was saying—she was only beginning to realize how much. Searching the darkness of his eyes, she tried to find a flaw. "And now you do?" she asked in a wary voice.

"You still don't trust me, do you?" His dark head tipped to the side, studying her hesitant expression with a resigned gentleness.

"Give me a reason to," she said.

"Okay," he replied with a faint smile. "I think I behaved myself during the time we spent together."

"Well . . . yes, you did," she admitted.

"Then have dinner with me on Saturday night." The grooves around his mouth deepened.

"I . . . I beg your pardon?" Brandy was certain Jim didn't mean what he had just said.

"I said, have dinner with me Saturday night."

"But why?"

"Why do you think?" he countered with maddening ease. "Because I want to have dinner with you, of course."

Her forehead smoothed as she nervously moistened her lips. "You don't have to take me to dinner. I understand everything now and there isn't any need for you to make this gesture."

"Brandy, I'm not a gentleman. I don't make gestures," he answered patiently.

That enigmatic light in his dark eyes was making her believe things that he didn't mean. Brandy looked hurriedly away. His sexy charm was going to her head. In another minute, he was going to talk her into accepting his invitation. Her inclination was to accept. Then darting him a sideways glance, she suddenly realized how foolish this was. He was James Corbett. They lived in very different worlds . . . and they always would.

"Stop looking at me that way!" he growled.

Brandy shook her head weakly. "I can't help it."

"Dammit, Brandy!" He sighed with exasperation. "What do I have to do to make you understand?"

"I can't forget who you are," she protested. "And I'm flattered that you want to have dinner with me, but—"

"Flattered!" His tone was sarcastic. "I'm not some god or king bestowing a favor on you."

"Then what do you want me to say?" Brandy snapped. "If you want a simple yes or no, then the answer is no!"

Before she could change her mind, she moved away from the pillar to put a safer distance between them. She kept her back to him to hide the tears that scalded her eyes.

Everything was so crazy. She wanted to turn around and take back her answer, even though logic insisted she had made the right decision. An inner voice argued for her to accept. It was only dinner; she could go, just for the experience of dating a celebrity. It would be something to tell her children someday. But some instinct warned her that time spent with Jim Corbett would mean much more than that.

"The next time, Brandy," his voice was controlled and calm, "things will be different."

Brandy glanced over her shoulder and looked at him with shimmering eyes. "No, they won't," she said firmly.

Holding her gaze for a long moment, he said nothing, then he turned and walked through the sliding glass doors. She didn't feel any relief when he'd gone, because she knew she hadn't seen the last of him.

All weekend Brandy jumped at the sound of every car driving by the house. Each ring of the telephone made her heart skip a beat, but by Monday morning Jim had still not contacted her. As each day of the week dragged by, she couldn't help wondering if he'd decided she wasn't worth it. She realized how irrational she could be. Even though she didn't want to go out with him, she wanted him to keep asking.

Although more than a week had gone by without her hearing from him, that didn't mean she didn't hear about Jim Corbett. Karen, blithely unaware of his visit and his invitation to dinner, had avidly passed on every morsel of gossip she picked up from the papers, TV, and online.

It was from her that Brandy learned of the torrid affair between Jim Corbett and Laura Jones, one of the supporting actresses in the movie being filmed at Old Tucson. One newspaper article

Karen found had included a photograph of the two together, the gorgeous brunette nestled in Jim's arms. A stab of pure envy had pierced Brandy's heart at the sight of it.

The jabbing sensation didn't lessen when she learned—from Karen, of course—that the couple had spent the previous weekend in the border town of Nogales, an hour's drive south of Tucson. Along with sight-seeing in Mexico, they had attended a bullfight. Brandy had cattily decided that the brunette looked bloodthirsty enough to enjoy such a spectacle.

By the the second weekend with no word, Brandy acknowledged that she had seen the last of Jim Corbett. What had she expected, she asked herself as she carried the lightweight stepladder from the back room of the shop. A mere mortal couldn't compete with the stunningly sensuous Laura Jones.

"What are you going to do with that ladder, Brandy?" Karen frowned and jumped forward to move a large ceramic cherub out of Brandy's way.

"I decided it was time to rearrange the wind chimes display." She maneuvered the cumbersome length of the ladder safely by the cherub. Her path to the hanging chimes was now clear of obstacles. "We've had the same things up since April, and people like to see something new. Besides, the sound is beginning to drive me crazy."

"Want some help?"

"I think I can manage," Brandy replied, concentrating on setting up the ladder without hitting any of the chimes.

"I'll take care of the customers and when Mrs. Phillips comes back from lunch, I'll give you a hand so you don't have to keep running up and down the ladder. If she comes back from lunch, that is," Karen added with a roll of her eyes. "If she didn't have hardworking employees like us, I don't know how she'd make a living out of this store. She's never here half the time."

"That's why she hired us, so she wouldn't have to be," Brandy laughed as she climbed the ladder, dodging the chimes that swung about her head.

"Uh-oh," Karen murmured, "Mrs. Goodwin just walked in. She ordered hand-dyed yarn for an afghan she's making. It wasn't in the last shipment and Mrs. Phillips promised her we'd have it by today."

"Good luck," Brandy whispered as her friend moved reluctantly toward the woman.

Sitting precariously on the top step, nearly hidden from view by the hanging chimes, Brandy began taking them down, replacing them with whimsical stuffed toys made by a crafts collective.

Someone else entered the shop, but since she knew Karen would be free in a few minutes to wait on the new customer, she didn't let her attention stray from her task. Her hand froze on a ceiling hook when she heard the man's voice.

"I'd like to look at some of your leather tooling equipment." The deep, husky voice belonged to none other than Jim Corbett.

"Um—of course, Mr. Corbett," Karen stammered her disbelief at the identity of her customer.

Carefully peering through the chimes and toys so as not to draw attention to herself, Brandy saw him remove his sunglasses and turn to follow Karen. She held her breath. Had he found out that she worked here and come to see her? It didn't seem possible, but she knew that she was desperately hoping it was.

Karen was all thumbs when they reached the leather counter, nearly dropping the tray of tools he'd asked to see. Then when he helped her, she nearly swooned—and Brandy didn't blame her. Jim looked much handsomer than she remembered, if that was possible, and so casual and at ease.

Not daring to move, afraid that if he hadn't come to see her, it might prove embarrassing, she waited for him to mention her name. Her perch on the ladder and the hanging objects concealed her from view.

"Do . . . do you work in leather, Mr. Corbett?" Karen asked.

He glanced up from the tool he was inspecting and smiled faintly. "It's a hobby of mine. I like working with my hands."

"Bet it's a good way to relax after filming all day," her friend suggested agreeably. As some of the shock of coming face-to-face with James Corbett receded, Karen's talkative personality began asserting itself. "You don't know what a thrill it is for me to meet you, Mr. Corbett. I've been a fan of yours for a long time. I've seen all of your movies, some of them more than once. My overdue fees at Blockbuster—you wouldn't want to know."

"Thank you. I'm not sure my movies are worth it."

"Oh, I am!" Karen assured him with a rush. "I can hardly wait until the one you're filming here is released, so I can go see it. Being a movie star must be so, so exciting."

"In some ways," he agreed, but Brandy detected a note of dry cynicism. "In others, it's much more tedious than your job."

"I find that hard to believe," Karen laughed, self-consciously flicking her flame-colored hair behind her shoulder. "But then I've never seen a movie being made before."

Selecting the tools he wanted from the array Karen had shown him, Jim handed them to her to ring up. Brandy decided his presence in the store had nothing to do with her and could only hope now that Karen wouldn't mention her name. Perhaps her friend would still be too flustered to remember her.

"Would you like a behind-the-scenes look at a movie being filmed, Ms.—?" he inquired as he paid for the tools.

"It's Justin, Karen Justin," she introduced herself quickly. "Would I ever!"

"I could arrange a pass for you one day next week if you're free," he offered.

"Oh, yes. The shop is closed Thursday afternoons," Karen declared excitedly.

"Great. And if you can persuade Ms. Ames to come down off her perch, she might like to join you." With that Jim turned, his mocking gaze looking directly at the hanging chimes behind which Brandy was hiding.

The unexpected sound of her name startled her so much that she jerked backward, bumping against the chimes and sending them banging into each other. She had to grab hold of the ladder to keep from falling, and swatted a stuffed monkey with button eyes out of the way. But she was spared further embarrassment as she regained her balance and awkwardly descended the ladder. Jim was waiting at the bottom, his dark eyes laughing.

"Did you really think you were hidden up there?" he murmured.

"I wasn't trying to hide," Brandy said self-consciously. "I was rearranging the display."

Glancing warily at Karen, she caught the knowing look in her friend's eyes, and understood exactly what she was thinking.

"I see, you were just working quietly," he smiled crookedly. "Since you were so preoccupied, maybe I should repeat my invitation."

Brandy couldn't admit to eavesdropping. "What invitation was that?"

"I offered to get a pass for you and Ms. Justin to visit the set while the movie is being filmed. Your friend mentioned that the shop would be closed next Thursday afternoon—I'll arrange it for then if that's okay." The challenge in his expression was undeniable.

Brandy remembered his parting statement that the next time things would be different. She wanted to refuse the invitation out of sheer cussedness, while at the same time she wanted to accept with equal intensity. The conflict must have been written on her face.

"Of course it's okay," Karen spoke up, her eyes pleading with Brandy not to throw away this once-in-a-lifetime opportunity.

"Yes," Brandy agreed with a small, reluctant sigh, "Thursday will be fine."

"Good." There was a suggestion of triumph in the smile that curved the masculine mouth. "Just check in at the gate when you arrive and everything will be taken care of for you."

"Thank you very much, Mr. Corbett," Karen smiled angelically. "This is really nice of you."

"My pleasure." But his look at Brandy confirmed what she already knew. Being nice had nothing to do with it. He was proving a point: he always got what he wanted.

As he said goodbye, Brandy realized just how experienced he was at handling women. First he'd kept her in suspense for nearly two weeks without contacting her at all. Then, just about the time when she decided she wouldn't see him again and was regretting she hadn't taken advantage of his invitation, he appeared.

There had been no reason to refuse the invitation he offered the second time; Jim had seen to that. On the contrary, he'd invited her girlfriend to come along, and it was a daytime invitation for a tour of the movie set in Old Tucson. Brandy had no doubt they would never be alone.

He'd changed the rules and she'd accepted without a protest. Well, it was what she had been secretly wanting, regardless of how illogical it was. Karen was probably right. It was the chance of a lifetime and she might as well enjoy it.

If only Thursday afternoon didn't seem so far off, she thought silently. There was too much time to think.

CHAPTER FIVE

"I'm so excited! Look at the way I'm shaking." Karen held out a trembling hand to confirm her statement.

"Relax." Brandy smiled, but the palms of her hands were clammy with nervous perspiration and an army of butterflies was fluttering in her stomach.

Karen parked her car in the lot like the other tourists and they walked to the entrance building that would admit them to Old Tucson, a recreated town of the Old West.

"I hope I don't talk too much," Karen sighed worriedly. "I hope he hasn't forgotten we're coming today."

"He hasn't," Brandy assured her promptly.

"Of course not." She smiled wryly. "Not with you along, he won't forget. Especially when you consider the trouble he went to to get you here.

Every time I think about you turning down a date with James Corbett, I become more convinced that you must have rocks in your head."

After he had left the shop on Monday, Brandy told Karen about his visit to her home, hoping to minimize the second invitation. She got a scolding for keeping it a secret all that time.

"We've been all through this before," Brandy protested in self-defense. "Besides, what could I possibly have in common with a movie star?"

"Who cares?" The chiding exclamation was accompanied by an exasperated sigh. "If you never go out with him, you're never going to know whether you do or not. I only hope you haven't lost him to that Jones hussy."

"I haven't had him, so I can't lose him," Brandy pointed out.

Karen ignored the accuracy of that observation. "Maybe they quarreled and he's turning to you for consolation. That might explain why he waited so long before seeing you again."

"It's possible." But somehow, the idea that a man as confident and self-possessed as Jim might need consoling sounded strange.

As they stepped out of the brilliant midday sun into the comparative darkness of the entryway, they had to pause inside the threshold until their eyes adjusted. An older couple was at the ticket window, so they moved to take their place in line behind them.

A balding man in an old-fashioned starched white shirt with a garter around one sleeve and red suspenders down the front smiled as they approached the ticket window.

"Good afternoon, ladies," he greeted them with professional cheerfulness.

Brandy's throat became parched, a sudden attack of nerves making her incapable of speech, but Karen suffered no such difficulty.

"I believe James Corbett left some passes for us?" she began. "I'm . . ."

The politeness in his expression was immediately replaced by a friendly warmth. "You must be Ms. Justin and Ms. Ames," he identified them before Karen had a chance. The gleam in his light blue eyes lingered on Brandy for a speculative moment. "He told me you'd be coming. If you'll wait a few minutes, I'll get somebody to take you through."

"Thanks, we appreciate that," Karen smiled as they started to move to one side so as not to hold up the other people waiting in line.

"Ms. Ames," the man's voice stopped Brandy, "the picture in the paper didn't do you justice. You're much prettier."

There was only one photograph he could be referring to, the one taken after she and Jim had been rescued in the desert. Brandy had hoped that incident would have been forgotten by now, or at least that no one would remember her name. She wondered what the man might be thinking at this moment, with the special passes Jim left for them.

"Thank you," she responded to his compliment self-consciously, and moved hurriedly away from the window.

While they waited, she and Karen studied the small photographs of the more well-known movies and television series that had been filmed in Old

Tucson. Only a few minutes passed before the ticket clerk was signaling them to come forward.

On the other side of the turnstile a man waited, dressed in cowboy gear with a star pinned to his chest and a gun belt strapped around his hips. The illusion of an Old West town marshal was negated by the dark sunglasses he wore and the walkie-talkie he carried in his left hand. The balding man stepped out of the ticket booth to introduce the girls to their colorful escort.

"This is Rick Murphy. He'll take you through to the movie set. Rick," he turned to the man, a bright twinkle in his eyes, "Ms. Ames and Ms. Justin are guests of Mr. Corbett, so you take real good care of them."

"Ladies." The man called Rick Murphy touched the front brim of his hat in acknowledgment, then motioned them through the turnstile. "Follow me, please."

"We're really getting the VIP treatment, aren't we?" Karen whispered in a giggling voice.

Brandy gave her a silencing look and didn't reply as they started up the path of hard-packed sand to the main street of the town. A tall fence hid the parking lot from view, letting them walk back into time with the ageless Tucson Mountains in the distance forming a backdrop for the scene.

"Since you girls are from Tucson," Rick Murphy said, "I imagine you know most of this was built back in 1939 for the film *Arizona*. Then it was abandoned for quite a few years."

"I had heard that," Karen answered. "Actually, Brandy is from Tucson. I've only been here for a couple of years. I'm originally from Breckenridge, Colorado.''

"That's in the middle of the Rockies; quite a change of scenery and climate," the man observed with a pleasant smile.

"You're telling me!" Karen grinned. Then she glanced around at the tourists wandering along the broad sidewalks. "I've never been out here when they've been filming a movie. How do they keep all the people out of the way?"

"They close off the area from the public when they're shooting a particular scene," he explained.

Brandy looked curiously ahead of her. "Where are they filming today?"

"In the little Mexican village." His head bobbed to indicate its location.

At the next narrow road leading in that direction, Rick Murphy turned, walking around the barricade that blocked the road. A security guard was standing on the other side, dressed much like Rick. The man nodded briefly to the trio as they passed.

Leaving the main street, the buildings changed from wooden western fronts, painted to look antique and weathered, to the dull tan of adobe. Ahead, Brandy could see and hear activity going on. Then, as they drew nearer, the motion and voices stopped. She and Karen didn't need to be told that filming had begun.

Quietly they approached the group gazing intently at the action going on in front of the cameras. The technicians and onlookers blocked their view of the actors. Cranes held cameras and cameramen aloft, while below more equipment was joined in a complex network of wires.

Brandy was only partially aware of what was going on. She was concentrating on finding Jim Corbett. He might be one of the actors in the scene, but it was also possible that he was watching from the sidelines.

At the far end she saw him. His shoulder leaned against a brick building, the powerfully defined chin and jaw cupped thoughtfully in his left hand as he watched the scene unfolding. A thumb was hooked in the waistband of Levi's, one leg slightly bent at the knee in a relaxed pose.

Yet even with the brim of his Stetson pulled low on his forehead to shade his eyes from the glare of the sun, Brandy could sense the piercing watchfulness of his dark eyes. When he was dressed in Western gear that brought to mind the lawless frontier, the dangerous quality he had was heightened.

Although, even without the beard, Jim looked very much like the man she had met in the desert, intimidatingly male and strongly independent, there was gentleness in him, though he had insisted he was no gentleman.

Her heart skipped a beat as she saw him straighten and turn in her direction. A smile of greeting curved her lips in anticipation of the moment when he would see her, but his gaze didn't encounter hers.

He started walking in her general direction, the object of his attention between them. Other people milled about, signaling an end of that take. He stopped behind a man in dark-rimmed glasses with a pen tucked behind one ear, who wore a white shirt that had seen fresher days.

Almost instantly the two men were joined by a

raven-haired woman, the object of Jim's attention. Brandy could understand why when she saw the low-cut peasant blouse and the creamy shoulders it revealed. A full skirt swung about her ankles, made of brilliant red material that set off her dark beauty and revealed the sensuous curve of her hips.

With a sinking heart Brandy recognized the beautiful woman as Laura Jones, whose name had been romantically coupled with Jim's in the past two weeks. Her arm slipped around his waist, and she bestowed a dazzling smile on him before turning her attention to the second man. It was clear that he was the director of the film, judging by the quiet yet brisk way he gave orders.

An animated discussion ensued. Brandy doubted that the actress was ever anything but animated. The woman was a black flame, a blaze that could never appear subdued.

What a pair they made standing together like that, she thought with an envious sigh. Their dark good looks were compelling, almost irresistible. No wonder their names were linked—they made a perfect couple.

Brandy was aware of Rick Murphy explaining to Karen what was happening on the set now, but the activity of the film crew didn't interest Brandy. Her whole attention was centered on Jim as she became conscious of a forlorn feeling in her heart.

What an idiot she'd been to think she might have attracted him! She was about to look away in despair when her gaze was met by his. Unconsciously she held her breath, wondering if it was actually her that he was looking at or perhaps someone else standing behind her. There was a barely perceptible nod of his head in acknowledgment before he glanced at the upturned face of the brunette.

Brandy turned quickly away, hoping he wouldn't realize how much she'd wanted him to notice her. The irregularity of her breathing was matched by the erratic rhythm of her heart. Yet her gaze kept sliding back to him.

Her heart raced crazily when she saw Jim walk away from Laura. She tried frantically to concentrate on what Rick Murphy was telling Karen, but she was only conscious of the tall figure making his way toward them. Although she pretended to be surprised, she knew the exact instant he reached them.

"I see you made it safely here." His concern seemed genuine.

"Yes, we did." Brandy smiled nervously. "Thank you for inviting us. Karen and I think it's fascinating."

"Oh, yes," Karen agreed enthusiastically. "Rick has been explaining everything. I always knew movie-making was complicated, but all these details escaped me."

"I hope you enjoy the rest of your tour, then," Jim said dryly as he noted the faint pink in Brandy's cheeks. Then his attention shifted to their escort. "Thanks for looking after them for me, Rick."

"Anytime, Jim," the man replied, touching his hat brim and walking away.

Brandy cast an apprehensive glance at Jim, realizing that he was to be their guide. When he'd invited them at the shop, she had wondered who would show them around. Later she told herself that he would probably be working. The knowing glint in his eyes said he knew exactly what was going on in her mind.

"He's a hottie, isn't he?" Karen observed with a resigned sigh. Brandy glanced at her girlfriend in alarm, then realized she was referring to Rick Murphy and not the man standing beside her. "Too bad he's wearing a wedding ring," she added, staring after him with a wistful expression on her face. She looked at Brandy, a wry smile pulling up one corner of her mouth. "But then that's just my luck, isn't it?"

"I think you could put Rick on your list," Jim told her quietly. "He lost his wife a year ago in a car accident."

"That's too bad," Karen murmured with genuine sincerity, but a gleam of hope appeared in her brown eyes.

"Aren't you working today?" Brandy fought to maintain her composure.

"Not today." The lines around his mouth deepened. "I thought I would volunteer my expert services to show you around."

"That's nice of you," Brandy said self-consciously.

"Isn't it?" he mocked.

"Hello-oo!" A female voice interrupted them, all husky and warm, vibrating with a sensual undertone. Laura Jones was twining her arm possessively through Jim's, totally ignoring Brandy and Karen as she claimed his attention. "How about joining me in something tall and cold and wet?"

Up close, the actress was absolutely, stunningly beautiful. Dancing eyes of dark velvet offered an entirely different invitation as she gazed at Jim. He didn't attempt to deny her claim of ownership.

"Sorry." An indulgent smile edged his mouth. "Not this time. I have guests." He looked pointedly to Brandy and Karen.

"Guests?" Laura echoed, her rounded brown eyes staring at them with open curiosity, waiting for an introduction.

Jim did the honors. "Laura, this is Karen Justin and Brandy Ames," he introduced. "This talented and beautiful actress is one of my co-stars, Laura Jones."

"And a friend, honey," the brunette laughed throatily as if implying a much closer relationship than that.

Brandy felt sick when she noticed the intimate look the actress gave him. The woman was as subtle as a steamroller.

"Whatever." Jim shrugged, refusing to attach a label to their relationship. There was a faint tightening of the brunette's mouth, as if his noncommittal reply bothered her. It lasted for a fleeting second and was gone.

"Brandy—that's an unusual name." Artificially long lashes swept up as Laura Jones turned her attention to Brandy.

"Yes, it is unusual," Brandy agreed without offering any explanation for her parents' choice. There wasn't one, except that her mother had liked it.

"Of course!" A smile flashed across the brunette's face. "I know why it's so familiar now. You must be the girl who spent the night on the desert with Jim."

The way she said "girl" made Brandy feel that

she had worn her first bra just last week. Obviously Laura was jealous—but why?

"Yes, that's right," Brandy admitted, a hint of suggestive warmth in her voice. She deliberately didn't add any more, guessing that the actress's imagination was vivid enough to paint whatever picture she wanted.

Laura gave Brandy a cold look before she tipped her raven head back to gaze at Jim. "You didn't tell me she was so pretty," she accused, pouting in a very alluring way.

"No, I didn't," he agreed smoothly. "But it's true. Brandy is just plain . . . gorgeous."

Laura's expression soured at the caressing quality in his low voice, but she smiled quickly to conceal her displeasure. "Careful, Jim, or you'll fall in lust."

Brandy noticed she avoided the word *love.* "Will I?" His dark eyes glinted wickedly at Brandy's flushed cheeks. "I hope so," he added calmly. "She is tempting."

"You're impossible!" Laura declared, tempestuous fire blazing in her eyes.

"You're learning," he drawled, glancing with open challenge at her ill-concealed irritation. "You'd better go and get your cold drink while Bill is still inclined to let you have a break."

Red lips were pressed tightly together. "I think I'll do that," she said coldly, releasing his arm and whirling away with a haughty toss of her black hair.

"Whew—for a minute, I thought she was going to explode," Karen whispered to Brandy. "Talk about fireworks!"

Her comment hadn't been meant for Jim to hear,

but he did. "The next segment of the scene they're shooting calls for Laura's character to lose her temper. No problem for her, if you know what I mean," Jim said, an audacious twinkle in his eyes.

Brandy couldn't help smiling in agreement, while Karen added, "It won't be acting as much as it will be reacting."

Jim didn't seem upset that Laura was angry, and Brandy wondered if he had intended to use her to make the actress jealous. If they'd quarreled as Karen had suggested earlier, perhaps it was because the brunette had been taking him too much for granted. He wasn't the type to be dominated by anyone, male or female.

"Since they're still blocking camera angles for the next scene," Jim said, "I'll take you over to the sound stage and show you some of the props and tricks of the trade."

Stepping between them, he guided them back toward the main street, a hand resting with light but firm pressure on Brandy's back. As they passed the barricade, tourists who were aware that a movie was being filmed in the off-limits section of the western town looked curiously at them.

The name James Corbett whispered through the crowd like a breeze rippling through prairie grass. Those who had cameras immediately snapped pictures, regardless of the distance or angle, to prove to the folks back home that they'd really seen a movie star.

Jim ignored the stir he was causing, his purposeful stride neither rushing nor slowing as he escorted Karen and Brandy past the ice-cream parlor. Brandy guessed that he was probably used to it. One young girl rushed toward them, anxiously thrusting a pen and paper at him.

"Could I have your autograph, please, Mr. Corbett?" she breathed, gazing at him through dazed, unbelieving eyes.

Taking the paper and pen, he smiled at the young girl pleasantly, though still with a suggestion of aloofness. Bold, sure strokes spelled his name on the paper, completely legible with no pretentious flourishes.

"Thank you," the girl gushed when he had handed the paper back, holding it almost reverently in her hand.

"That's quite all right." He smiled again. "Excuse me."

He waited for Brandy to catch up; she had drifted a half step behind him. She felt proud, pleased with his courtesy. It was as if he wanted the onlookers to know she was with him. Karen must have noticed it, too, because she caught Brandy's eye and winked knowingly. Self-conscious, Brandy averted her gaze.

An employee of Old Tucson unlocked the door to the sound stage, which was housed in a building whose exterior matched the Old West design of the rest of the town. Inside, high ceilings arched overhead, and lighting equipment hung from the rafters.

There was no dividing wall in the large barnlike room, but it was sectioned by different sets. The one they went to was an old-fashioned saloon with a long wooden bar stretching the length of one wall. Behind the bar was a large mirror flanked by shelves containing liquor bottles and glasses. Above the mirror hung a large painting of a voluptuous woman, barely covered by a diaphanous robe, reclining on a divan.

A second side of the room had swinging doors and large-paned windows. They gave the illusion that the main street of town was directly outside. Actually, it was a realistic painting of the town's street. The third wall of the U-shaped room had a series of doors that seemed to lead to back rooms and a staircase leading to the second-floor hall, with more doors supposedly leading to second-floor rooms. From Brandy's point of view, she could see there was nothing beyond the doors except steps leading down from the second floor on the outside of the set.

The center of the room was cluttered with tables and chairs. All of them looked battered and worn. A deck of cards sat on one table with neat stacks of poker chips, and a roulette wheel was set up at the back of the room.

"This," Jim explained, "is where we shoot the interior scenes. This saloon, for example, has been used countless times for different movies. The public generally doesn't recognize it because the decor is changed or we rearrange the door on another wall or have the stairs leading to the second floor in a different place. It makes it very easy to duplicate the set in Hollywood, if another take is needed after we've left the location."

"It's so small, though," Karen commented.

"A camera makes everything look larger. That, and the fact that the camera only shows you one section of the room at a time, creates the illusion that the room is large. It's convenient because several small sets can be reconstructed and the viewer is rarely aware of how small they are." He paused, a dancing gleam in his dark eyes. "The only drawback to the camera making things larger is for the actresses. The camera adds ten extra pounds whether they want them or not. It's the main reason they constantly diet."

"I don't blame them," Karen laughed. "Nobody needs ten extra pounds except supermodels."

"As for the props, I guess you know all about the fake furniture that gets broken over people's heads. And the breakaway bottles," he added. "They used to be made of candy, but too many of the technicians and acting crew were eating the props, so they use something else now. Iced tea is used in place of hard liquor for drinks, except for beer—no one has come up with a substitute that looks enough like it and can keep a head of foam. As long as the beer is warm, the foam stays. If you've ever tasted warm beer, you know why the beer is only occasionally sipped by the actor." Jim smiled. "Unless, of course, the actor is English."

He gestured to the far end of the building.

"That's the interior of the sheriff's office," Jim identified the stage set they were passing. "This next one,"—their destination—"is used for scenes shot in the interior of a house. Right now, it's a dining room, but by changing the furniture and curtains it can be transformed into any room."

This three-walled interior set was unique in that it continued into an outside desert scene. The floor of the building was covered with realistic-looking sand and shrubs, and a large saguaro cactus stood guard near the outside wall of the room. A scenic backdrop had been painted to continue the desert landscape.

"Isn't there enough desert outdoors to satisfy you?" Brandy asked curiously.

"More than enough, but occasionally the script calls for a night sequence. We usually don't film at night. The cameraman puts a special filter over his lens and the scene becomes night," he explained. "Or if a sunrise or sunset is needed, then the special effects men use a combination of lighting to duplicate it. That way the sunset will last as long as it takes for the actors to do the scene right. And then we splice in real footage from the second unit's film."

"I was sure you were going to say it was used in rainy weather," Karen laughed.

"The heat and blowing sand are the bad things about Arizona weather. The heat you suffer through. The blowing sand does bring us indoors, but rain, almost never. Usually it has to be manufactured out here."

"What do you use for rain? A garden hose and a fan?" Brandy asked, finding it all fascinating.

"Well," one corner of his mouth tilted upwards, "I suppose that sounds logical except for one problem. Falling water doesn't photograph very well on a camera. When you see it raining in a movie, it's generally raining milk. On film, it looks like water."

"You're kidding!" Karen stared at him skeptically.

"I'm not," Jim said with a smile. "I'm afraid Gene Kelly danced and sang in the milk, not the rain."

"You're destroying all my illusions," Karen moaned in mock despair.

Jim laughed, a rich, deep sound that sent shivers of pleasure down Brandy's spine. She joined in, charmed all over again by this compellingly handsome man.

"Okay. On to the wardrobe department, where you'll see some true artists at work," he said.

CHAPTER SIX

At the wardrobe department, an older woman, at Jim's request, gladly showed Karen and Brandy some of the clothes that would be worn in the film. The sketches had all been completed weeks ago, faithful reproductions of period dress for men and women in that era and part of the country. The costumes were all individually sewn and fitted to the person who would be wearing them.

The wardrobe personnel on location mainly kept track of the costumes and made sure they were ready when they were needed. A seamstress took care of any last-minute alterations and repaired any rips or tears that occurred during filming.

From there, Jim took them to the stables where the animals used in the film were kept; mostly they were horses, with an occasional burro or mule. A nearby rancher supplied a herd of cattle when they were needed. All of the mounts were trained stock, accustomed to crowds and the bustle of the camera crew.

One pathetic-looking horse in the corral caught Brandy's eye. He looked utterly out of place with the others. There was no healthy gloss to his coat and his ribs showed.

"Jim, what's the matter with that horse?" Brandy used his first name quite unconsciously. Not even when his gaze focused with warm thoughtfulness on her face did she realize that she had gone back to the first name she'd known for him, without even thinking.

"Nothing is the matter with him anymore. He was never sick, just underfed," he replied.

"You'll have the Humane Society breathing down your necks if they see him," she commented.

"That's where he was found." His tone was thoughtful. "It took a lot of searching before we could find a horse like that."

"Why did you need him?"

"In the film, the character I portray has a grueling ride through the desert. At the end of the ride, my horse was supposed to be on its last legs. I wasn't supposed to look too much better. That's the reason for the beard I'd grown when you met me. Luckily they got those scenes out of the way first." He rubbed his smoothly shaven jaw as if just the memory of the scruffy beard made him itch. "You're looking at the horse—well, a healthier version of him."

"What's going to happen to him now?" Brandy leaned against the corral fence, staring compassionately at the horse.

"He's become something of a pet. Harry, the stock contractor, seems to think he has a chance to make it in the movies when his looks improve. The horse is a glutton for attention—and corn and oats," Jim told her. "If he doesn't fill out, Harry will probably sell him to someone who'll take care of him."

"I hope so," she declared.

"Let's go over in the shade and have a cold drink," he suggested.

The cool shadow cast by the barnlike stable was already being used as a sun shelter by some of the film crew. Jim introduced them as wranglers for the stock or stuntmen and stuntwomen who doubled as extras.

With the promised cold drinks in their hands, Brandy and Karen accepted the bale of hay offered as a seat by one of the men. No such deference was shown to Jim, and he seemed not to expect it as he leaned a shoulder against the building only a foot or two from where Brandy and Karen were sitting.

The conversation continued as everyone swapped stories of other location films they'd worked on and the things that had gone wrong, sometimes hilarious and sometimes dangerous.

The movie people didn't seem to object to being interrupted by questions from Brandy and Karen. In fact, they seemed to enjoy their audience. Brandy knew she could have sat for hours listening to their anecdotes.

One man clapped his hands on his thighs and pushed himself upright from a squatting position.

"Well," he breathed in, "I guess they aren't

going to need me today. They oughta be wrappin' things up about now, I would say, because the light's going."

Brandy glanced at her watch. Nearly six. It seemed impossible that more than four hours could have passed since she and Karen had arrived at the gate, but the lengthening shadows didn't lie. She stood up, brushing off the wisps of hay that stuck to her chinos.

"We should leave, too," she told Karen.

"I guess you're right," Karen sighed, and got up from the bale with obvious reluctance.

The rest of the group started dispersing as Jim stepped forward. Brandy smiled at him, aware of how much she had enjoyed the entire afternoon. He studied her with quiet thoughtfulness.

"Thanks for showing us around." Brandy didn't know what else to do, so she offered him her hand.

The gesture brought a hint of a smile to his mouth as he accepted her hand with mock solemnity. "I hope you enjoyed it. I'm just sorry you have to leave so soon."

"It's late." She was reacting crazily to the firm grip of his hand as he held hers longer than politeness required.

"Yes, it is," Karen said as though she hated to admit that fact, "and by the time I drive Brandy home and get back to my apartment, it's going to be even later. I've enjoyed it all so much, Mr. Corbett. I can't thank you enough for asking us to come."

"My pleasure," he said smoothly. "And please call me Jim."

"Yes . . . all right, Jim." A pleased smile beamed from Karen's face.

His attention shifted to Brandy, who was waiting for Karen. "Didn't you drive your car today?"

"No," she shook her head, "Dad's using it. Mom was going to need their car to go to some meeting or other after classes, so Dad borrowed mine to drive to Phoenix this afternoon."

"Karen, you don't have to drive so far out of your way to take Brandy home. I'll give her a ride," he said.

"Oh, no—" Brandy started to protest, not wanting him to think she had been angling for an invitation.

"Accepted," Karen declared, blithely interrupting.

"But—"

"But what, Brandy?" Jim wouldn't listen her attempts to argue. "Your house isn't out of my way and I'm willing to take you, so why object?"

Brandy struggled for a tactful explanation. "I just don't want you to think—"

"I know what you don't want me to think," he interrupted dryly. "If you're ready to leave, we'll go and get my car. It's in the private lot."

Brandy hesitated an instant longer, then nodded agreement. She couldn't seem to figure out her ambivalence toward him. She wanted his company, his attention, and she wanted to avoid him. She felt like a child who threw away a toy, then wanted it back.

"Okay, that's all settled," Karen said happily. "I'm off for home. See you tomorrow, Brandy, and thanks again for the tour, Jim."

With a cheery wave, she was walking away toward the main gate. Out of the corner of her eye, Brandy glanced at Jim who was studying her silently. She was not going to seem childish or make a fool of herself again by trying to refuse his invitation. She couldn't forget who he was, but if Jim Corbett wanted to give her a ride home, she was going to take it. The decision didn't lessen her nervousness.

"Let's go." Brandy said with a determined lift of her chin.

With a nod, Jim agreed, his hand on her elbow to guide her in the right direction.

Without Karen, Brandy felt awkward and self-conscious. Her lighthearted friend had made conversation easy. Now she couldn't think of a thing to say that wouldn't sound fake.

Various members of the film crew waved to Brandy and Jim as they left. No one seemed to care that Jim was escorting her and not Laura.

Now that Brandy was alone with Jim, she wondered again whether he was using her to keep the obviously possessive Laura Jones in line. All the gossip seemed to indicate that their relationship was on an intimate level. Yet Jim had been cool toward the actress, even antagonistic at times.

It was all too much. She was out of her league. She was used to straightforward relationships with men, yet every time she was with Jim Corbett, she felt pulled in two different directions at the same time. Never before in her life had she felt as confused as she did now.

"Why the frown?" He looked at her carefully as he opened the passenger door of the Jaguar with a flourish.

Immediately the frown smoothed itself away. "Was I frowning?" She shrugged, and then quickly slid into the contoured leather seat. "I was just thinking—about nothing really important."

He made no comment as he closed her door and walked around to the driver's side. The powerful engine sprang immediately to life at the turn of the key. He reversed the car out of the parking stall and turned it toward the parking lot exit.

"Are you still worrying, Brandy?" Jim asked quietly, flicking her a brief glance while he waited for a break in the traffic before pulling onto the road.

"Worrying?" she stalled. "I don't know what you mean."

"Is your inferiority complex kicking in? I mean, the great James Corbett is taking you home." He studied her slyly.

"I don't feel inferior to you, Jim," Brandy corrected softly.

"That was the impression you gave me when you turned down my dinner invitation," he replied, as the car accelerated onto the road.

"I don't feel inferior to you," she repeated, "it's just that we're totally different. And we live in very different worlds."

"You saw a part of my world today and met some of the people I work with. You were pretty friendly to them. Were they that different from the people you know?"

Brandy felt trapped. "No," she admitted.

"Then why don't you reconsider your decision?"

"Which decision?" she countered.

"The one about having dinner with me," he answered smoothly.

Brandy wanted to take back her refusal. She wanted to say yes to Jim this time. But the words of acceptance stuck in her throat. She had been so adamant before. Rather than say anything she stared out the window, hating the wall of pride she had erected.

Jim let the silence stand, not prodding her for any kind of reply. Slowing the car, he turned it into a side road and switched off the motor. Her heart thudded against her ribs as she darted him a wary glance.

"Why are we stopping here?" She looked around to see if there was a reason.

"It's a good quiet place to walk." He opened the door and stepped out. "Are you coming?"

Surprised by the unexpected challenge, Brandy hesitated. "But ... my parents will be expecting me home. I'm usually there to fix dinner in the evenings."

An amused look lit up his dark eyes. "I wasn't suggesting that we spend the night, just go for a short walk. You're a grown woman—I doubt that your parents will worry if you're a couple of hours late. As for dinner, I'm sure your mother can fix it on her own."

Brandy surrendered to the inevitable and stepped out of the car. He waited until she had walked around to join him before starting out.

Heat radiated from the sun-baked desert floor, although the intensity of the sun was on the wane. The scattered forest of giant saguaro cactus rose to dwarf them as they made their way around the sagebrush and prickly pear.

The tops of the rounded ends of the saguaro

and its arms were crowned with a waxlike blossom, the state flower of Arizona. The saguaro and the organ pipe were always the last cactus to bloom, and their smaller cousins were the first signs of spring.

In March, the little hedgehog cactus would open its rose-purple cups, and a month later the spiny ocotillo would release its scarlet-flamed trumpets. But the giants waited until late May, with the first saguaro blossom signaling the beginning of the Papago Indians' New Year.

Walking among these ancient towering plants with their vertical ridges of thorns, Brandy felt her gaze pulled repeatedly to the majestic saguaros. Their trunks stretched upward to the sky, a multitude of arms raised boldly to the sun. Their endurance in a hostile climate was legendary. A saguaro is seventy-five years old before it begins to branch out.

Most of the cacti surrounding Brandy and Jim now were older than the state of Arizona. Some of them were nearer the age of the United States. The timeless strength of them awed her.

"They're magical," Brandy murmured. "I've always loved them."

Jim glanced down, an indulgent gleam in his eyes. "I take it you don't regret coming for a walk."

"I don't regret it." She darted a quick look at his amused expression. "I didn't really object in the first place."

"Didn't you?" He seemed to doubt her.

"Well, only a little bit," she admitted.

A car hummed along the road behind them, an

unwanted reminder of civilization. Brandy much preferred to enjoy the natural beauty around her.

"Let's move on," Jim suggested, taking her arm and walking at a leisurely pace that kept her by his side.

"You know, I'm never able to understand why some people don't like the desert," she commented idly. "Even Karen says it's harsh and ugly and barren."

"It's a case of different tastes, I suppose," Jim answered idly.

"Do you like the desert?" His answer was suddenly important to her. She didn't think she could stand it if he didn't see the beauty in it that she did.

"Yes," was his simple reply.

"I don't think I'd ever want to live anyplace else," Brandy declared, looking over the landscape that had always been part of her home. There was a haze of lavender on the edge of the western horizon.

"Neither would I."

She glanced at him in surprise. "But you don't live here."

"Yes, I do," he smiled. "I have for years, but it's been one of my few well-kept secrets."

"Where?" she demanded in a doubtful voice. "You don't mean around here?"

"If you say I don't, then I don't," he shrugged, taunting her with his smile.

Stopping, she gazed at him, realizing that he was telling her the truth. "You're serious, aren't you?" she said. "You *do* live in Arizona."

"Yes," Jim nodded.

"You don't have to tell me where," Brandy added

hastily. If it wasn't common knowledge, then he obviously wanted his home kept secret. Although eaten up with curiosity, she didn't want to force him to disclose the actual location.

"I don't mind telling you. I don't think you'll spread it around, knowing how much I value my privacy." But he held her expectant look for a while without satisfying her curiosity. "My home is the Saguaro Ranch."

Her turquoise eyes widened. "But that's owned by a corporation in California," she protested. "It has been for years."

"That's right," Jim agreed smoothly. "I simply happen to be the sole stockholder of the corporation."

"I don't know what to say," she laughed, believing him yet finding it incredible.

"How about . . . hi, neighbor?"

A wide smile dimpled her cheeks as she held out her hand. "Hi, neighbor." After a brisk handshake, he still held it, but Brandy was still too surprised to notice. "How do you manage it? I mean, how could you keep it a secret?"

"There's a small airstrip on the ranch. I fly in and out when I want to. No one has to know," he answered.

"But the men on the ranch know, the ones that work for you," she pointed out.

"Yes, but then I pay their salaries, don't I?" Jim pointed out. "Part of what I pay them for is to keep quiet."

"They've done an excellent job." Brandy shook her head.

"Oh, there've been one or two slips," he said, "but everybody denied everything."

"Isn't anyone suspicious about you staying there now?"

"Were you?" Jim countered.

With a smile, she answered her own question. "I assumed that you were invited to stay there while you were filming the movie by whoever owned the ranch."

"That's what everyone believes. And of course, it's true, since I did invite myself to stay there." Laughter danced wickedly in his eyes. "Out here, I'm a rancher and I drive a dusty old Jeep, not a Jaguar."

With a small, amazed shake of her head, Brandy lowered her gaze, absently focusing on the large hand that held hers. "You've been my neighbor all this time," she mused, a half-smile still on her lips.

The pressure of his hand increased slightly, drawing her serene, jewel-colored eyes back to his face. The unfathomable darkness of his eyes seemed to pull her into their depths.

The fluttering in her chest took away her breath as she seemed to float into his arms, always a captive of those compelling eyes. Tilting her head back, Brandy watched them draw nearer, their warmth burning her. Then her gaze slid to his descending mouth.

As it closed possessively over hers, her lashes fluttered down over her cheeks. There was nothing exploratory or tender in his kiss. Its fierceness demanded that she respond.

The moaning sigh that slipped from her throat

released the last of her inhibitions as she wound her arms tightly around his neck. She craved the sensual caress of his hands that sent strange new sensations shooting through her.

The world became a sundown of the senses. The colors in her mind were ten times more brilliant, painted by a heavenly hand in a scattered rainbow of reds and orange, the vivid spectrum ranging from coppery gold to scarlet to magenta, cerise and lavender.

The sensuous touch of Jim's lips along her neck and the hollow of her throat evoked more fiery sensations that rocked her slender body. Then he was withdrawing from her, not loosening the hard embrace that kept her pressed against him. His dark head was drawn back, a challenging look in his eyes.

"Tell me again that you won't have dinner with me," he dared in a husky, threatening tone.

She wondered how he could think she would refuse after the way she had surrendered so completely to him.

She opened her mouth. "I—"

He covered it immediately in a powerfully erotic kiss that robbed the strength from her legs until she was clinging weakly to him for support. Then he rained rough kisses over her eyes, nose, cheeks and ear.

"I'm not going to let you go until you say yes," he warned softly, his mouth moving against the lobe of her ear.

"Then,"—Brandy swallowed to steady the throb of ecstasy in her voice—"I'll wait a while," she whispered, turning her head to find his lips.

"You witch!" He laughed, but gave her the kiss she sought and drew away before she was satisfied. He stared silently at the soft glow on her face, his own reaction to the burning embrace not as transparent as hers. His chest heaved as he took a deep breath. "I think we'd better go back to the car before you start something you might regret."

At this moment, Brandy was positive she wouldn't regret anything that might happen, but she checked the impulse to wind her arms tighter around his neck. When his hands slid to her elbows, she reluctantly let her arms be pulled away.

Brandy was half afraid that he was going to withdraw from her the way he had done that morning on the desert after the sandstorm. She didn't think she could endure it if he asked her to forget about this kiss, too.

But instead of stepping away, leaving her trembling and alone, Jim wrapped an arm around her shoulders and drew her to his side, protectively nestling her against his shoulder. Matching his step to her smaller stride, he started toward the car.

In the car, Jim didn't start the motor. He turned sideways in the seat, his arm resting along the back cushion. His powerfully carved and bronzed features were drawn in lines of serious contemplation.

"Success or fame doesn't change a man, Brandy," he said quietly. "He remains essentially what he always was. But his faults or weaknesses are magnified ten times over, whether it's vanity, selfishness, conceit or cruelty. The same is true of whatever good qualities he possesses. The man doesn't change. The only thing that does change is the way the others, friends and strangers, look at him."

His eyes seemed to look into her innermost soul. "Do you understand what I'm saying?"

A wonderful warmth filled Brandy's heart as she realized what he was telling her. The joy of the knowledge shimmered in her blue-green eyes.

"Yes. You're saying that you are the man I met on the desert. That you were never anything else," she answered quietly. "I changed you into someone else in my mind."

He released his breath in a slow sigh, a devastating smile curving the hard line of his mouth. Her pulse raced at the sight of it, sensuously male and irresistibly warm.

"I, Jim Corbett, would like to hear you say again that you'll have dinner with me on Saturday night." The forthright, caressing voice sent shivers dancing down her spine.

"I would love to have dinner with you on Saturday night." Her voice vibrated with pure emotion.

"I'm not going to let you change your mind, you know that, don't you?" he asked. "I'll kidnap you if I have to." His mouth quirked to make a joke out of what was essentially a threat.

"Promise?" Brandy smiled impishly.

There was a wickedly playful gleam in his eyes as Jim faced the front of the car. "Just try me," he murmured, and turned the key in the ignition.

Brandy leaned back in her seat as the Jaguar moved on to the road. A mixture of blissful contentment and giddy excitement claimed her. She had fallen in love with Jim Corbett, and it didn't frighten her. Not at all.

Silently she gazed at him. His rugged masculine profile was outlined by the crimson-orange rays of

the setting sun. The formidable strength in his
features was reassuring.

With a sideways glance, Jim intercepted her study
of him. Without a word he reached out and took
her hand, holding it gently in his all the way to
her home.

Once in the driveway, he didn't shut off the
motor or release her hand. His dark eyes surveyed
her silently for a minute.

"Seven-thirty on Saturday?"

It seemed like such a long time till then. "Seven-
thirty," Brandy agreed.

Jim hesitated. "I may get held up. We'll be shooting on the weekend, so if I'm not right on time,
don't give up on me." He softened it with a winning
half-smile to make his statement sound like less of
an order.

"I'll wait." For an eternity if I have to, she added
to herself.

"You'd better mean that, Brandy." For a brief
second, the intensity of his low voice made her
think she had spoken the thought aloud. "Because
I'll be here. If I'm going to be very late, I'll try to
phone you."

"Okay," she nodded understandingly.

Reassured, his eyes darkened with an intimate
fire. "Come here."

She didn't need a second invitation to move
toward him, her lips parting willingly under the
hard pressure of his. While her senses were still
whirling from his heady kiss, Jim moved away.

"You'd better go in," he said, "before your parents decide to send out another search party for
you."

"Yes, I'd better." But her shaking hands moved very slowly for the door handle.

As she opened it, Jim repeated, "Saturday at seven-thirty."

As if she could forget.

CHAPTER SEVEN

The headlight beams from a car turning into the driveway flashed onto the living room window.

"He's here. Mom, do I look all right?" Brandy felt more nervous than she had been on her first date or any date since then. She looked from her mother's patiently smiling face to her reflection in the gilt-framed mirror.

Choosing what to wear had been agonizing. She couldn't make up her mind whether to pick something sophisticated or casually elegant. In the end, the outfit she chose was neither.

The cream-white outfit in a thin, clinging knit and wide legs did show off her golden tan and slender curves. The tunic top was simple, the perfect background for the Navajo squash-blossom necklace she wore. The turquoise stones almost matched the blue-green shade of her eyes. Earrings in blossom shape drew attention to the long curve of her neck.

"You look lovely," Lenora Ames assured her.

"I hope so." Brandy started as she heard a car door slam.

"Brandy." There was a hint of caution in her mother's voice.

An affectionate smile touched Brandy's mouth. She knew what her mother wanted to say: Jim was older, more experienced and accustomed to a very different lifestyle. He was a celebrity. She shouldn't become too deeply involved with him. Brandy knew all of that, and it didn't change a thing.

"I know what I'm doing, Mom," she insisted gently.

But her composure went out the window when the doorbell chimed. She opened the front door and smiled tremulously at the tall man dressed in a dark suit and charcoal-gray vest of shimmering silk.

He gave her a slow appraisal, and the darkening glow of admiration in his eyes restored her confidence. She reached for his hand to draw him inside the house.

"You're only a quarter of an hour late," she declared brightly, as if the minutes hadn't dragged.

His attention shifted to the glossy shimmer of her lips, his look almost a physical caress as his hand tightened around hers with unmistakable possessiveness.

"You're beautiful," his deep voice murmured softly.

Inside, with the door closed, the light of intimacy in his eyes held her a silent captive. Brandy wanted to lose herself in the midnight depths of his gaze. She forgot that they weren't alone in the living room until her father coughed. A faint pink tinted her cheeks as she withdrew her hand from Jim's. His features softened into a half-smile.

"I'll get my bag, then we can leave," Brandy murmured.

"No hurry," Jim drawled lazily, moving into the room toward her parents. "Good to see you again." He held out a hand to her father.

There was a friendly exchange of greetings while Brandy collected her bag, then walked with quiet pride to her place at Jim's side.

He glanced down, his eyes moving warmly over her glowing face. "Ready?"

"Yes," she nodded. "Good night, Mom, Dad."

His hand slipped lightly to her elbow. "Good night." Then he added perceptively, "Don't worry, Mrs. Ames. Brandy is quite safe with me."

Her mother smiled in surprise and looked curiously at Brandy, but didn't say anything. In the next instant, he was guiding Brandy toward the door.

Outside, she tipped her head sideways, an earring brushing the side of her neck. "How did you know my mother was concerned about me going out with you?"

"It's normal," Jim smiled down at her. "Among other things, I have a reputation."

"True," she agreed with a jesting light in her eyes to match his. "Some say you love 'em and leave 'em."

"Worried?" He held the car door for her.

"Not yet," she laughed, but it was strangely true.

Before she could slide into the car, his hand caught her arm to hold her motionless. Surprised, she looked at him with questioning eyes. A finger lifted her chin as he smiled and briefly kissed her parted lips.

"Don't worry," he ordered, and settled her into the car.

What did that mean? Brandy watched him walk around the back. Was he telling her that this time it would be different? She was too eager to enjoy every minute spent in his company to use any of the precious time trying to read his mind.

"Are you hungry?" Jim reversed the car out of the driveway and turned onto the road leading to Tucson.

"Starved!" Brandy declared fervently. "Where are we going?"

He named a restaurant that she was familiar with although she hadn't been there. When she didn't comment, he asked, "Is there something wrong?"

"No," she answered quickly. "I thought"—she hesitated—"I thought that we might eat at your ranch. I wasn't sure whether you'd want to go anywhere public."

"Do you think I'm ashamed to be seen with you?" The dark slash of his brows drew together in an exasperated frown.

"No, I thought you'd want privacy," Brandy protested.

The frown was swept away by a quiet chuckle, the rapid transformation from controlled anger to humor confusing her with its swiftness.

"Why is that funny?"

"Because I convinced myself that you'd be reluctant to spend an evening alone with me in my home." Jim darted her a brief look, a gleam in his eyes. "The real truth is that I didn't trust myself to be alone with you."

A hot weakness licked through her limbs at the prospect of Jim making love to her. The heady thought took her breath away.

"No reply?" he said with teasing humor.

Brandy shook her head. "None," she said, not able to make her voice sound calm and unconcerned when her senses were in such turmoil.

His voice immediately became very calm and gentle. "Does the idea frighten you, Brandy?"

"No," she breathed.

There was a surprised silence, then she saw the flash of a rueful smile. "Wish you hadn't said that."

"Why?"

"Because I might take you at your word." His gaze smoldered over her face, stopping her heart, then sending it rocketing off. "And it's too soon for you yet."

He was probably right, Brandy acknowledged silently. She wasn't used to the fact that she loved him. A few days ago she hadn't even wanted to see him again, probably because subconsciously she'd known she would fall in love with him if she did.

They were driving through the mountain pass, the curve in the road giving them their first glimpse of Tucson. The lights of the city glimmered low in the purple haze of sunset. The mountain ranges protecting the city were dark silhouettes against the sky.

"Have you been to this restaurant before?" Jim deftly changed the subject.

"No. Have you?"

"Yes. It's expensive—and discreet so there won't be a stir when we arrive," he assured her.

It was true, Brandy later discovered as they entered the restaurant. Jim was recognized instantly, although she was sure that even if he hadn't been a well-known actor, he still would have commanded attention.

The maître d' stepped forward. "Mr. Corbett, this is indeed an honor," he said with a deferential nod of his head.

Jim acknowledged the comment with a smile. "A quiet table for two, please." He emphasized the word "quiet."

"Of course, sir."

Within a few minutes they were led to a secluded corner of the room. It was impossible for Brandy not to be aware of the heads turning as they walked by the tables of people. It was silent recognition, unlike the camera-clicking, autograph hounds at the movie location in Old Tucson. She realized that their arrival hadn't created that kind of stir in this restaurant, but he was definitely the object of attention.

She wasn't aware of being studied with almost equal interest. Not simply because she was with Jim Corbett or envied because his arm rested so possessively along the back of her waist.

As a couple they made a stunning contrast. Jim was tall and broad-shouldered and utterly masculine, while Brandy was deceptively shorter next to him, slender, curvy and quintessentially feminine. Her simple cream white outfit and her fair coloring were set off by the darkness of his hair and eyes, and the expensively tailored dark suit he wore.

At the table, Jim stepped ahead of Brandy to hold out a chair for her. When she sat down, he leaned forward as if to edge her chair closer to the table. Instead he warmly pressed his mouth against the most sensitive part of her neck, sending a thrill all through her.

Disconcerted by his action, she glanced around the room, catching the knowing looks of those who had seen the intimate caress. She tried to laugh away her emabarassment as Jim sat beside her.

"You shouldn't have done that. You made all your female fans jealous."

"And all the men envious," he countered, lazily surveying her self-conscious expression.

"Don't be silly." Brandy opened the menu to escape his disturbing gaze.

"I'm not," Jim replied smoothly. "I saw the looks you got when we walked through. There isn't a man in the house who wouldn't want to trade places with me. Now they know they have to go through me to get to you."

She gave him a startled glance, but he was studying the menu. She wasn't able to tell by the impassive expression on his face whether he was serious or merely being gallant.

"I guess they thought that since I was with you, I was someone they should recognize and they were trying to place me." She tried to shrug away his compliment, if that was what it was.

"Possibly," Jim admitted, his dark gaze dancing over her, "but that wasn't all they were thinking."

The waiter appeared at their table. "Would you like anything to drink?"

His arrival successfully changed the subject. With that order taken care of, Jim leaned back in his chair, unconsciously flexing a shoulder muscle. The action prompted Brandy to notice the faint lines of tiredness around his mouth.

"Did you have a rough day?" Her softly worded question was gently sympathetic.

"Does it show?" His mouth crooked wryly, then he sighed. "It was a physical day, running up and down stairs, busting down doors, rolling in the dirt, discovering muscles I'd forgotten." He laughed quietly at himself. "Just your average, ordinary day at the office."

"That's what it sounds like," Brandy agreed with a dimpling smile. "It also sounds as if you aren't in very good condition," she teased.

"I'm getting old," Jim shrugged without a note of regret in his low voice.

The waiter returned with their drinks. Brandy waited until he had left before she responded to Jim's statement.

"You must be ancient. What are you—all of thirty-three?"

"You haven't read my *People* profile or you'd know I'm thirty-four," he corrected.

"Jim, honey!" The throaty female voice struck Brandy like a body blow.

Her widened blue-green eyes swerved to the raven-haired Laura Jones gliding toward their table. A stunning gown of black lace left little of the actress's figure to the imagination, the color intensifying the midnight blackness of her hair and eyes, the vivid red of her lips and her ivory complexion. Brandy felt like a pale nothing in comparison.

A quick glance at Jim found him rising to his feet, his expression unrevealing. She couldn't tell if he was surprised, glad, or annoyed by the brunette's appearance.

Without regard for the onlooking customers, or perhaps because of them, Laura moved directly to Jim, spreading ringed fingers on his chest and rising up to kiss his smoothly shaven cheek. A red brand was left on his tanned skin.

"Look what I've done," Laura murmured, her dark eyes sparkling in satisfaction at the scarlet mark. She reached into his pocket and removed his handkerchief, dabbing at the mark with the familiarity of a wife—or a mistress. Brandy's stomach churned at the sight. "There, bad boy," the brunette purred, "it's all gone now."

When she started to replace the white kerchief in his pocket, Jim took it from her hand and put it away himself. "Thank you, Laura," he offered dryly.

There was a sensuously petulant droop of her lower lip. "I'm really angry with you, you know, for running off like that tonight, without a word."

"I was late," Jim answered smoothly. "You remember Ms. Ames, don't you?" forcing Laura to direct her attention to Brandy.

Cool brown eyes looked at Brandy. "Of course, I do," the actress drawled. "Brandy, isn't it? I remember it was such an unusual name."

The comment left the impression that if it hadn't been for the name Laura would have forgotten even having met her.

"That's correct, Ms. Jones," replied Brandy.

"Please call me Laura," she insisted, and looked pointedly at Jim. "After all, we do have so much in common."

Meaning we both want the same man, Brandy thought with a sinking feeling. At this moment, she felt miserably inadequate. She couldn't compete with the likes of Laura Jones for Jim's attention.

"As for you, Jim," Laura smiled bewitchingly, "I'll forgive you for not taking the time to let me know you were coming tonight. I know you like to be punctual when you tell a girl you'll pick her up at a certain time. Since you did come to my party after all, I won't scold you for what I went through, wondering if you'd come or not."

Brandy looked warily at Jim, questions racing through her mind. What was Laura talking about? What was all this about a party? Jim hadn't mentioned anything about it.

"Was your party this evening, Laura?" He kept his distance, aloof and cool. "I remember you mentioning it, but I'm afraid I forgot about it."

"Now you're being cruel," the actress declared. The secret smile on her face seemed to say that she knew why and understood. "You know very well that I told you we all would be meeting here tonight."

The statement caused a painful picture to form in Brandy's mind. If Jim had no intention of joining the party and had brought her here anyway, it could have been for only one reason—he'd wanted Laura to see him with her. She couldn't believe it was all a coincidence.

"The others are in the lounge," Laura continued. "Why don't you bring your drink and come and join us? And you, too, Candy—I mean, Brandy."

"No, thank you," Jim refused smoothly. "I think Brandy and I would prefer to have a quiet dinner alone."

"Nonsense!" A practiced, throaty laugh emitted from the perfectly outlined red mouth. "Every girl loves a party. Isn't that right, Brandy?"

What was she supposed to say? She looked to Jim for an answer, but he seemed to be studying the dark-haired beauty standing so near his side. They were such a perfect pair, but were they a couple? Was she supposed to be persuaded to join the party, or refuse? She didn't want to be drawn into their argument—whatever it was. It hurt to think that Jim was using her this way. It hurt unbearably.

Feeling betrayed by the way he had led her to believe that he'd genuinely wanted only her company tonight, Brandy refused to answer Laura's question in any positive way.

"Not necessarily," she hedged, glancing at Jim.

"Don't be silly." Laura waved aside her response. The slender wing of an eyebrow was lifted in sarcastic mockery as the brunette studied Jim through her long lashes. "I do believe she's afraid of you, honey. She doesn't want to say the wrong thing and make you angry."

A black frown clouded his features as he shot Brandy a stormy look. "Do you want to go to the party?" he demanded.

No, she wanted to scream, *I want to stay here and have dinner with you alone.* But how could she say that? Surely it was already obvious that was what she wanted.

"It doesn't matter to me," she shrugged, and looked away, feeling angry, hurt and confused all at the same time.

"There, you see, she does want to come!" Laura declared triumphantly. "She's simply too shy to tell you so!"

His mouth thinned into an uncompromising line, his jaw clenched tautly. "In that case, we'll join your party, Laura. Lead the way." His hand closed over the back of Brandy's chair. Only she could feel the controlled violence in his seemingly polite assistance.

The look on the brunette's face was one of feline satisfaction as she led them toward the lounge. Jim's hand clasped Brandy's elbow. He paused once to tell the waiter they were joining some friends, forcing Brandy to do the same. The delay put Laura several steps ahead of them.

"There was no need to dither about joining the party," Jim's voice growled near Brandy's ear. "You should have said so instead of hinting."

Brandy retaliated, "If I'd wanted to go, I would have said so. But it was obvious that it was what you wanted!"

"What *I* wanted?" Jim glared.

"It's why we came here, isn't it?" She tossed her head back and stared straight ahead, the silver earrings bouncing against her neck.

He laughed softly, his black mood vanishing as quickly as it had come. "I should have remembered that you speak your mind. Oh, well. We're committed."

She tipped her head back to look at him. "Do you mean you didn't want to?"

"No," he said quite firmly, the grooves around his mouth deepening, "I would have been much happier to have a quiet dinner with you."

They entered the lounge. The bombardment of greetings from the party members prevented Brandy from asking Jim anything else. If his intention in taking her out was to make Laura jealous, he wouldn't be willing to tell her that. Not when he must know that at the very least she was infatuated with him.

There were approximately ten people in the party group, not counting Brandy and Jim. The exact number was hard to say, because some were on the dance floor, floating around changing partners, and one or two were dashing back and forth to the bar to get quick refills of their drinks.

One thing Brandy saw instantly was that there were more men than women. The women who were there were attractive in a plain sort of way— not surprising under the circumstances, Brandy decided. She doubted that Laura would allow any genuine competition around her. The actress's monumental ego was probably also the reason more men were invited, so that she could be sure of lots of attention.

None of the people were among those Brandy had met at the movie location. Those who noticed her now as Laura introduced her regarded her curiously. Their looks were already accompanied by questioning glances from Jim to Laura. Whatever had been going on between the two of them must have been common knowledge.

Brandy felt uncomfortable. The artificial chatter and forced spontaneity was grating. She was glad of the firm grip that kept her at Jim's side, despite Laura's less than subtle attempts to separate them.

Although Brandy was seated beside Jim, Laura occupied the chair to his right, her hand resting casually on his arm. The talk, led by Laura, centered on the day's filming, a subject that Brandy knew nothing about. There was little she could do except listen and pick up enough to join the conversation later.

One of the apparently unattached men sat down in the chair beside her. He was comparatively young, only two or three years older than herself, with sandy hair streaked platinum by the sun—or a skillfull hairdresser.

"Hello there." Despite the friendly smile that accompanied his greeting there was an oddly sulky look in his blue eyes, a pale shade unlike the brilliant color of hers.

"Hello." Brandy knew she had been introduced to him, but his name escaped her.

"Bryce Conover is the name," he replied wryly, interpreting the blank look in her expression. "And you're Brandy."

She smiled an apology, then glanced at Jim to see if he had noticed the man at her side, but his dark head was tilted toward Laura, listening intently to what she was saying.

"I know you don't remember me," Bryce Conover's voice was low, meant only for Brandy's ears, "but I noticed you when you came out to the set the other day with Jim."

"I'm sorry. There were so many people," Brandy shrugged. She felt suddenly cut adrift.

It was true that Jim had kept her by his side as though that was where he wanted her to be, and he had made it clear that he hadn't wanted to join this party. Yet there he was talking to Laura—he was virtually ignoring her now.

"That's all right. I understand," Bryce replied. The trace of bitterness in his voice said he was accustomed to being overlooked, but didn't like it. A slow tune was playing softly in the background. "Would you like to dance?"

A refusal formed on her lips—until she saw long, scarlet fingernails curling possessively on Jim's wrist and the seductive light in Laura's dark eyes as she gazed into his face, the hard mouth curved slightly in an answering smile. Brandy doubted if Jim would even notice she was gone.

"Yes," she said firmly. She bestowed a determined smile on Bryce as she rose to her feet, aware of Jim's sideways glance of frowning surprise.

"I asked Brandy to dance," Bryce informed him. "You don't mind, do you, Jim?" The question was offhand with a suggestion of challenge. His arm curved around Brandy's shoulders.

"Of course he doesn't," Laura answered before Jim had a chance.

Bryce Conover didn't wait for a further answer as he turned Brandy toward the small dance floor. Reluctantly, she moved into her partner's arms, resisting his efforts to hold her close to him. Her gaze strayed to the table and Jim.

"You might as well forget about him." Bryce's

pale blue eyes noticed her guilty start. "Corbett is all staked out. He's Laura's property."

"Really?" Brandy tried to sound coolly indifferent. "Does he know that?"

A mocking smile was her answer. "Everyone knows the two of them are skirmishing now. That's the way it always goes when you have two strong personalities. The outcome is obvious—Corbett will come out on top. But they have to go through this stage. It always happens. It's like a courtship ritual."

Brandy's skin went cold. "I see," she said stiffly. "And what's my role in all this?"

"You're the fair-haired ingénue, a striking contrast to Laura's more earthy attraction. Regardless of what you seen in the movies, the ingénue rarely ends up in the hero's arms in real life." His head bent toward hers. Brandy turned, but not swiftly enough to avoid the caress of his lips against her cheek. "You're being used, honey, to bring Laura Jones up to scratch."

His statement crystallized the doubt that had plagued her since Laura had appeared. She didn't want to believe it, but the ugly facts were staring her in the face. What other conclusion could there be?

The music ended and Brandy pushed herself out of Bryce's arms. His hand snaked out to claim her waist, but she jerked away.

"There's another song starting. Let's dance, honey." His sandy head bobbed toward their table. "They don't want you there."

Her turquoise eyes flashed toward the table. From this angle, Brandy could see Laura leaning sideways in her chair toward Jim. His granite features revealed nothing. If he found her glistening red mouth alluring, he didn't show it.

Laura's half-turned position exposed more cleavage where the plunging neckline gaped open. Brandy wanted to rush over and stuff a dinner napkin down the front of the black lace gown, but it wouldn't have concealed the actress's voluptuous charms, and the impulse died before she was tempted to act—and add a roll from the breadbasket while she was at it.

A wounded anger drove Brandy back to the table. All of her doubts might be true, but she wasn't going to hide in a hole like a whipped animal. Bryce followed, his displeasure obvious.

"You're a fool, Brandy," Bryce muttered as they drew near the table. "She'll tear you apart."

At their approach, Jim's gaze swerved to them, his eyes impenetrably hard, flicking from one to the other with the smarting sting of a whip. Brandy became aware of Bryce's arm curving smoothly around her waist and the admiring expression on his face despite his last cutting remark. Yet Jim seemed not to care about the attention she was getting from her new partner. Maybe he was relieved to have her off his hands.

Before Brandy could reach her chair at Jim's side, another man crossed her path, dark-suited with a smoothly polished appearance. He stopped beside Jim, blocking her from the chair. Brandy paused, waiting for an opportunity to claim her place at the table.

"Hello, Mr. Corbett." The man touched the

back of Jim's shoulder in greeting, then glanced to Laura. "Ms. Jones."

"Spencer, this is a surprise," Jim replied in a voice that made it clear it was not a surprise.

Bryce whispered in Brandy's ear, "He's a newspaper columnist."

The man glanced around the table at the animated gathering. "Quite a celebration. Is someone engaged?" The probing question got him a feline smile of satisfaction from Laura.

"Oh, no, Spence!" Her laughing protest was overdone. "All we have to celebrate is the fact we don't have to work tomorrow."

"Too bad," the columnist shook his head in mock regret. "I thought I might finally hear the two of you were getting serious."

"You have to remember, Spencer," Jim picked up his glass to study the liquor whirling inside, "we're working on the same picture. It's natural for us to be seen together. We're friends. Fellow actors. That's all." He directed a dark, measuring look at the columnist, almost daring him to imply that there was anything more.

"That's right," Laura agreed huskily, a demure smirk on her face. "Jim and I are just good friends."

"I'll quote you on that," the man laughed smugly.

A pain like cold steel plunged into Brandy's heart. She knew that the standard answer of "just good friends" meant the relationship was much more intimate. She watched in sickening anguish as the man walked away from the table. A muscle twitched in repressed anger alongside Jim's power-ful jaw when he met her tortured look.

As best as she could, she tried to conceal her hurt. She wanted to sit anywhere but next to Jim, but Bryce was already holding out the chair for her. With a proud lift of her chin, she sat down.

Without asking the others, Jim signaled the waiter and asked him to prepare a table for them in the dining room. Brandy silently applauded his decision. She wanted the evening over with quickly.

A few offered a token protest, but not Laura. She was much too anxious to be by his side.

CHAPTER EIGHT

Laura had supervised the seating arrangements at the circular dining table, ordering Brandy to sit beside Jim, a move that surprised Brandy until she realized that Laura had saved the coveted seat to his right for herself.

Conversation was again dominated by the flamboyant actress, although twice Jim did try to encourage Brandy to join in. But as the meal progressed she only got quieter, withdrawing into herself.

When everyone was through eating, they lingered at the table over coffee. As the waiter came around to refill their cups a second time, Brandy wondered how much longer the evening could drag on. A tiny sigh escaped her lips.

The sound drew Jim's gaze to her downcast face. He refused more coffee and pushed his chair away from the table. A moment later, he was drawing her up and away from the table.

"It's time we left, Brandy," he answered the unspoken question in her eyes.

"So soon?" Laura protested petulantly, but otherwise unruffled by his announcement. "The night is young."

"The night may be, but I'm not. And it's been a long day," was his smooth reply.

After saying goodnight to the other members of the party, Jim guided Brandy out of the restaurant to his car. He gave no explanation for his tight-lipped silence. Brandy reminded herself that she didn't care, and that she just wanted to get home the fastest way possible.

But it wasn't true. She did care. It didn't matter how crazy it was for her to have fallen in love with Jim Corbett. It wasn't something she could change in one evening, or maybe even a lifetime of evenings.

Soon they were speeding out of Tucson. Pride kept her silent as she stared out the window and tried not to remember how well they had gotten along during the earlier part of the evening. That was before Laura had appeared and Bryce had raised the ugly probability that Brandy was being used.

Without warning, Jim slowed the car onto the shoulder of the road and switched off the motor. Brandy stiffened, self-consciously brushing a feathery gold curl away from her temple.

"Why are we stopping here?" she asked curtly.

He turned slightly, leaning against his door, his arm resting across the steering wheel. The shadows of night concealed his expression, but not his piercing gaze.

"I want to know what's the matter," he stated evenly.

She stared straight ahead. "I don't know what you're talking about."

"Something got your back up, and I want to know what it is."

She glanced at the bag in her lap, gleaming white in the pale moonlight. "You've mistaken," she replied, trying to make her voice sound as cool and even as his.

"Your silence says a lot," he mocked.

"My silence!" she laughed without humor. "You haven't said a word since before we left the restaurant." She hurled an accusing look at him.

"Considering how little you said at dinner, I decided it was a waste of time until I could find out what was really bothering you." The darkness didn't lessen the intensity of his watchful gaze. "I want to know why you're angry."

It was a command. Brandy pressed her lips together, wanting to vent all the anguish inside her, yet unwilling to let Jim know that she had fallen in love with him.

"I'm not angry." The answer came out snappishly defensive.

With a swiftness she should have remembered, he moved her head around to face him. The moonlight softened his features, but not his eyes. His closeness, the controlled anger glittering in his gaze, let her see that he meant exactly what he said.

"I want to know," he repeated with finality.

Part of her wanted to cower, but Brandy wasn't the type to give in without a fight. She let him hold her gaze without faltering, almost without flinching.

"I don't like to be used any more than I like to be laughed at," she replied.

A dark brow shot up. "Used?" Jim asked arrogantly. "Is that what I'm supposed to be doing— using you?"

"Oh, please," she sighed with exasperation. Her fingers closed over the wrist of the hand that held her chin, but she couldn't push it away. "Spare me the fake innocence. I'm not that naive."

"I'm beginning to wonder." His mouth thinned into a grim line. "How am I supposed to be using you?"

"Isn't it obvious?" she protested. Her lashes fluttered down to conceal the pain in her eyes. "I know why you invited me out tonight, so you don't need to go on pretending."

"Do you have to talk in riddles? Just say whatever it is in plain English." His fingers tightened on her chin.

"I'm referring to Laura," Brandy lashed out, "and that ridiculous charade of an evening."

He breathed in deeply, giving her a long, considering look before relaxing his hold. "I see," he drawled sardonically. "You've come to some conclusion about Laura and my motives for asking you out tonight."

She wasn't going to comment on that. "Would you please take me home?"

"I suppose you also think you're entitled to an

explanation. I'm not giving you any," Jim declared coldly.

"I didn't ask for any," she snapped.

He muttered a curse—then his hard mouth closed bruisingly over hers.

Brandy fought his kiss for about five seconds before she let him overpower her resistance. An arm curled around her waist to drag her sideways from the seat and against the rock wall of his chest.

She wound her arms around his shoulders, a hand slipping to the back of his neck to explore the luxuriant thickness of his dark hair. The hard metal of her silver and turquoise necklace was digging into the soft flesh of her breasts.

His lips left hers and she breathed in the intoxicating air, scented with the sweet freshness of the desert and the musky aroma of his maleness. The hard, masculine lips roughly explored the arched curve of her throat.

Black fire blazed in his eyes as he lifted his head to gaze into her face. Her thudding heart raced faster at the unmistakable desire that burned in his look.

Jim moved her the rest of the way around and onto his lap. A hand slid in a sensuous caress along her hip and thigh. Cradled in his arms, she drew his head down to hers, lips parting at the touch of his.

The passionate mastery of his mouth and the arousing touch of his hands over her body carried her to another plateau of erotic sensation. She let Jim's expertise teach her what she didn't know until, with a broken sigh, Jim pulled his mouth away from her pliant lips.

He pressed her honey-gold head against the hollow of his shoulder. The erratic beat of his heart beneath her ear was in tune with the staccato rhythm of hers. The hand cupping her breast gently withdrew from beneath her tunic, tenderly smoothing the rumpled material.

"Jim." Her whispering voice echoed in the darkness.

"Sssh!" His mouth moved against her hair in understanding as he held her closer. "Now do you understand why I didn't dare to be alone with you at the ranch?" he murmured.

Her lashes fluttered down. "Yes," she answered softly, almost with regret.

"In a car, there's time for second thoughts." She felt the movement of his lips against her hair; the corners lifted in a smile.

"Second thoughts?" she repeated warily, wondering if he was sorry he had made love to her.

"Brandy." His soft chuckle moved the air about her face. "Are you always so unsure of yourself?"

"No." She tipped her head back to look at the rugged, compelling face so close to hers. She had never been unsure before. "Only with you," she admitted hesitantly. She was still wary of letting him see how much power he had over her, yet it wasn't her nature to keep everything bottled up inside.

The suggestion of a smile faded from his mouth. His expression became thoughtful as he studied her face.

The grooves around his mouth deepened suddenly into a wry smile. "I'd better take you home."

Before Brandy could protest that she didn't want

to leave yet, Jim was pushing her gently off his lap and settling her again in the passenger seat.

After the car was started and they were back on the road, he took her hand and started talking, mostly about the film he was making and the crew. It was several minutes before Brandy realized he was explaining some of the things that had been discussed at the party that night, things that she hadn't known at the time or understood. A flood of love warmed her heart at his understanding way of including her in his life.

In the driveway of her home, Jim shifted the gears into neutral, but left the motor running. The house was dark except for one light shining through the window near the front door.

"It isn't very late. Would you like to come in for some coffee?" Brandy offered.

"No," he said, "I have a lot to do tomorrow, so I'd better have an early night."

"But you aren't working tomorrow." She frowned, remembering Laura's statement that they had tomorrow off.

"We aren't filming tomorrow," he corrected. "But I have script revisions to go over as well as a business meeting with Don, my manager. It'll be a full day."

"Of course. I wasn't thinking." She smiled weakly, trying to hide her disappointment. For the last couple of miles she had been hoping that Jim would want to spend at least part of tomorrow with her.

"Do you get up early in the morning?"

Brandy looked at him curiously. "Sometimes. Why?"

"I like to take a ride in the desert in the morning before the sun gets too hot. Want to come with me tomorrow?"

"Yes." She couldn't say it fast enough.

"Is five-thirty too early?" he asked, adding, "I'll trailer my horse over here."

"That's fine," she agreed swiftly.

He gave her a faint smile, and Jim leaned over and kissed her lips, his mouth moving warmly over hers. Brandy still felt the sensual pressure after he had moved away.

"In the morning," was his good-night promise.

Shaken slightly, she nodded and stepped from the car. Jim waited in the driveway until she had unlocked the front door and stepped inside. Only when he had driven away did she realize that he had kept his word. He'd said he wouldn't explain about Laura, and he hadn't. She wasn't any more sure about where she stood with him than she had been before. But at the moment nothing bothered her.

Humming merrily, Brandy filled the small glass with orange juice, taking a quick swallow, then turning to put the pitcher back in the refrigerator. There was a shuffle of footsteps in the hall.

"Brandy!" Her father paused in the doorway in the act of tying the sash of his robe. His pepper-gray hair was disheveled from sleep, his expression startled and disbelieving. "Lenora said she heard someone moving around."

He glanced out of the dark windows. "What are you doing up at this hour?"

"Jim's coming over. We're going for an early morning ride." She set the juice pitcher in the refrigerator and walked to the counter. "He should be here anytime now."

Stewart Ames frowned at the clock above the sink. "At five o'clock in the morning?"

"Look again, Dad." Brandy sipped hurriedly at her orange juice. "It's half-past five."

"The sun isn't up." He shrugged as if to add that a few minutes made hardly any difference.

The sound of an engine prompted Brandy to look out of the kitchen window. A pickup truck hauling a horse trailer had stopped in the drive. She reached for the fringed leather jacket she had dropped over a kitchen chair.

"He's here now, Dad." Brandy pulled on her jacket. "The coffee's already made. All you and Mom have to do is plug it in to warm it up."

She started toward the side door, glad that she had already gone out and saddled her horse before fixing a small breakfast. Her father's voice stopped her at the door.

"You know why it's called the crack of dawn, don't you, Brandy?" he asked in an offhand voice as he ran his fingers through his tousled hair.

"Why?" She tried not to sound impatient, but she really wasn't in the mood for any of his scientific explanations—not when Jim was waiting for her. She heard the clank of the trailer tailgate being lowered outside.

"Because you have to be cracked to get up at that hour." Stewart Ames grinned, a bright twinkle in his eyes. "Or else in love."

A beaming smile spread across her face. "Is that

right!" Brandy laughed and blew him a quick kiss, darting out of the door.

The liver-colored sorrel was tied to the outside of the trailer, saddled and bridled, his four white feet clearly visible in the dim morning light. With ears pricked, the horse turned to watch Brandy's approach.

Jim threw the last bolt to refasten the tailgate. "Good morning."

"Good morning," Brandy returned the greeting.

"Are you ready?"

"My horse is saddled and waiting at the stable around the back," she answered. Her heart quickened at the warm way his gaze ran over her. The reins were pulled free of the slipknot that tied them to the trailer and Jim fell into step beside Brandy, leading his horse around to the rear of the house.

Dawn was streaking the eastern horizon when they mounted and rode off toward the empty desert. The comfortable creak of saddle leather filled the sage-scented air. The gray Arabian that Brandy rode pranced a little, tossing his head, showing off in front of his quieter partner.

"It's peaceful, isn't it?" she said as the pale golden sunrise tinted more of the sky.

"Very," Jim agreed.

They rode on in silence, enjoying the quiet birth of a new day. It came softly, the golden light building to orange, the purpling sky lightening to blue, then the golden sun rising slowly above the horizon. It was subtle, nothing like the blaze of glory that was sundown.

At the top of a hill, Jim reined in his horse. As

Brandy glimpsed the panorama spread before her, she did the same.

"I never get tired of this," she said, knowing he felt the same affinity for the desert.

Hooking a leg around the saddle horn, Jim leaned forward in his saddle, his expression relaxed and at ease. His dark gaze didn't pause in its slow survey of the land.

"This land helps me keep the right perspective on life. In the desert, man is just a humble creature. Material possessions become irrelevant. All the money in the world couldn't buy this," he stated, then glanced at Brandy, a wry smile tugging the corners of his hard mouth. "In my work, that's a good thing to remember."

"Then it's more than just a need for privacy that brings you to the desert," she observed.

Jim shrugged lazily. "I suppose there are a lot of reasons if I ever took the time to think of them all." He unhooked his leg. "Let's ride on."

At Brandy's nod, they set off at a trot. "How long will you be filming here in Tucson?" She swerved her horse around a growth of prickly pear cactus, then back alongside the sorrel.

"A month at the most."

"And then?"

"Back to Los Angeles for post-production." His dark eyes squinted toward the sun, as if measuring the hour by its height.

The thought that he might be gone in less than a month didn't sit well. It was inevitable that he had to leave someday, but she didn't really want to think about what it would mean to her.

"When the movie's finished, what are you going to do?" she asked instead.

"I've signed to do another one. Filming starts as soon as this one is in the can. It'll be the end of the year before I have any free time, and not even then if Don has his way." He was silent, the gap filled by the muffled thud of the horses' hooves on the gravelly sand and the creaking of the saddles. With a flash of perception, Jim voiced the answer to the question Brandy was just thinking. "Sorry. No location shots in Arizona."

"Oh." It was a wistful sound. Determinedly she raised her chin. "You travel a lot, don't you? It must be fun to see so many different parts of the world."

"I used to enjoy traveling. But now—" Jim held her gaze for a searching second, then looked ahead. "Well, I never had any reason to hurry back, except for the ranch."

What did that mean? He had accused her of talking in riddles, yet he was doing it.

"And now?" she askd.

"And now I think it's time we headed back to your house." The grooves around his mouth deepened.

He knew he had deliberately misunderstood her question. Brandy guessed it was Jim's way of saying he wasn't prepared to answer it now. Was it because of her or Laura? Confused, and angry about it, she compressed her lips together in a straight line. Without argument, she followed alongside as he made a half-circle to return.

On impulse, Brandy dug her heels into the gray's

flanks. "Race you back!" She hurled the challenge over her shoulder as the Arabian bounded forward.

She was three lengths ahead, the Arabian at a gallop, before his sorrel broke out of a trot, stretching his white legs to catch them. The desert was flat and unbroken before them. The two horses and riders raced unchecked through the sage, jumping or dodging the clumps of cactus.

Brandy's horse held the lead, the air rushing past her face and ears. No matter how eagerly she urged Rashad onward, the sorrel kept gaining ground until they were running neck and neck.

Then the sorrel's nose was in front, then his head and neck. In the next stride, Jim reached out and grabbed Brandy's reins beneath the gray's mouth. With uncanny balance and timing, he slowed both horses to a plunging walk before he released the reins.

"We had you for a while!" Brandy declared, breathless from the exhilarating run that had momentarily banished her anger.

"You would have had us again," Jim replied with a laugh. "Pecos can catch almost anything at a quarter of a mile. After that your Arabian would have left him behind."

"That's not fair!" Both horses were blowing and tossing their heads. "You stopped the race when you were ahead," Brandy accused.

"So I did." He edged his horse closer to hers. "That qualifies me as the winner, doesn't it?"

There was a wicked glint in his look. Brandy shook her head with exasperation and smiled. "Only because you didn't play fair."

"Everything's fair."

His hand curved around her neck, applying pressure to draw her sideways toward him as he leaned out of his saddle. "It's time for the loser to pay up," he said. Then his mouth closed over hers.

The spark he ignited was just flaming to full life when he moved away. For a breathless instant, Brandy gazed at him, her face glowing, her turquoise eyes sparkling. She laughed, a thrilled, happy sound. "If I'd known you were going to do that, I would've lost the race sooner!"

"Better luck next time," Jim chuckled.

Although he nudged his mount into a trot, he didn't suggest a second race. Brandy let Rashad set the pace, a prancing lift to his gait compared to the sedate, reaching stride of the quarter horse.

"Unless something unforeseen happens, I'll have a full schedule this week," Jim said after a time. "I'll be working late every night, so I won't be able to see you until the weekend. I'll try to call, though."

"That's all right, I understand." But Brandy wished he'd said something definite about the weekend instead of leaving her with the feeling that he would have to fit her in.

Wistfully she remembered that Laura would see him every day. Jealousy stabbed at her heart, though she told herself it was irrational.

CHAPTER NINE

"Brandy, phone for you." Karen walked to the counter, smiling politely to the customer Brandy was helping. "I'll take over here." She whispered behind her hand, "It's *him*!"

It took all of Brandy's willpower to walk sedately to the phone, and not race as her heart was doing. After two days, she had almost given up hope that Jim would call.

Taking a deep, calming breath, she picked up the receiver. "Hello."

"Brandy? Jim." He didn't have to identify himself. She always recognized his husky voice. "Hope there's no rule about you getting personal calls at work."

The warmth in his voice sent pleasant chills down her spine. "Nope," Brandy assured him.

"Are you free this evening?"

"Yes." Her heart skipped a beat.

"I know this is short notice, but Tom McWade, one of the stuntmen, and Ginny Baker, the director's assistant, drove down to Mexico last night and got married," he explained. "The cast and crew are giving them a party tonight after the day's shooting is over. Will you come?"

Her first reaction was a definite yes, followed immediately by her wondering why hadn't he asked Laura. Or was she going to be used again to make Laura jealous?

"Brandy?"

"Yes, I'm here." Nervously she twined the spiral telephone cord around her finger. "Perhaps you should ask Laura instead. She knows everyone and would fit in better than I do."

It was Jim's turn to pause. "If wanted to take Laura to the party, I wouldn't ask you," he said firmly and with a trace of grimness. "Do you want to come or not?"

"Yes—"

"Good. I'll leave word at the gate to expect you between six and seven," he interrupted her. "I'm due on the set, so I'll let you get back to work. See you tonight."

Jim didn't wait for her response as he hung up the telephone. Brandy stared at the receiver in her hand, wishing she had refused, no matter how much she wanted to see him again.

A few minutes past six o'clock, she was parked in the lot at Old Tucson. She sat there with the motor off, wishing she had the strength to leave.

But it was no use. She had to take the chance that Jim really meant what he said and did want to take her to the party.

She walked into the entrance building, where the same balding man was on duty. His eyes twinkled brightly when he saw her.

"Hello, Ms. Ames," he greeted her cordially. "I've been expecting you."

She smiled faintly. "Mr. Corbett said he would let you know I was coming."

"He did." The man held up his hand, signaling for Brandy to wait. He stepped out of the door at the rear of the ticket booth and motioned to someone on the other side. Immediately a security guard in cowboy regalia appeared on the other side of the turnstile. "Troy will take you through to the shindig."

Her escort was older than Rick Murphy who'd taken her and Karen through before, but he was just as friendly without being inquisitive. He veered away from the center of the western town, leading her toward an area best described as a back lot. From there, Brandy could hear the sound of voices and laughter.

"Guess the party has started already," she observed with a smile.

"About two hours ago," he agreed, "at least for those who were finished for the day."

"Who's still working?" By that Brandy meant Jim, but she didn't have to explain.

"Mr. Corbett was wrapping up a scene. It should be finished by now," was the reply.

As they neared the small gathering, a familiar figure separated itself from the group to walk jauntily toward them. Pale blue eyes looked Brandy over.

"Well, well, well. Who have we here?" Bryce Conover demanded. "If it isn't the fair-haired little ingénue come to try her luck again!"

"Hello, Mr. Conover." Brandy kept calm, refusing to react to his baiting.

"Call me Bryce," he insisted. He flicked an arrogant glance at the guard. "That'll be all, Smith. I'll look after Ms. Ames."

The man nodded curtly, plainly not liking the autocratic tone. At Brandy's thanks, he touched his hat and walked away.

"You didn't have to dismiss him like that," Brandy accused in a low voice. "You could have been more polite."

He arched a lofty brow at her tone. "What for?"

"Oh, please." Brandy stared at him with astonishment. "It would have been polite. Isn't that enough?"

"If you say so." Bryce took her hand and tucked it under his arm, pasting on a smug smile.

"So why are you being nice to me?" Her sarcasm was probably lost on him.

"Ah, for a very good reason," he assured her.

"Which is?" Brandy prompted.

"Laura Jones wants me to keep you entertained."

"Why would you want to do that for her? Are you in love with her or something?" Her hand was clasped too tightly for her to pull it free.

He laughed loudly at the question. "I'm doing it because that raven-haired witch is on her way to the top. Personally I don't think she has the talent to stay there, but she'll make it one way or another.

It pays to have friends at the top who owe you. She'll return the favor with interest by suggesting me for some of the more demanding roles in her future movies."

"I see," she said with disdain.

"All part of the game." Bryce smiled down. "Let's walk over to the bar and get you something to drink."

"I can find it myself." Brandy tried to pry his fingers from her hand, without success.

"Tonight I'm your shadow. You can't get rid of me, so why not make the best of it?"

She stopped struggling and glared at him angrily. "No, thank you!"

"Are you hoping the rugged James Corbett will come to your rescue?" His contempt was clear in his whispering voice.

"He did invite me," she reminded him haughtily.

"Have you asked yourself why?" jeered Bryce.

At Brandy's hesitation, he laughed and led her toward the small crowd. It had grown since her arrival and they were forced to line up at the bar. She refused the champagne Bryce tried to persuade her to take, asking for grape Snapple instead.

Holding the drink did give her a reason to free her hand from his grasp, although he didn't budge from her side. Sipping indifferently, she searched the crowd for Jim. As yet there was no sign of him.

"Forget him and enjoy the party," Bryce murmured.

"Why don't you leave me alone?" she muttered beneath her breath, and smiled politely as she and Bryce were greeted by another couple.

"I couldn't leave you alone and neglected," he said softly, adding in a louder voice for the other couple's benefit, "Have you met Tom and Marie, Brandy?"

He steered her toward the couple, making introductions but not mentioning that she was there as Jim's date. She found it difficult to just come out and say so.

At least the other couple's presence cut down on Bryce's sarcastic comments, but she still had to deal with his arm, which had leisurely drifted around her. No matter how discreetly she tried to shift away from his hold, Bryce succeeded in keeping her within reach.

He squeezed her waist to bring her closer to his side. Brandy had been listening to Marie with a smile, and she kept the expression on her face as she glanced at Bryce, the anger flashing in her eyes expressing her annoyance at his action.

Before she could get some space between them, Jim spoke behind her. "Glad to see you've been enjoying yourself."

Whirling around, she saw the cynical hardness in his dark eyes and guessed at his interpretation of the preceding minutes. Laura was with him, her diamond-black eyes sparking with malicious satisfaction. Embarrassment flamed Brandy's cheeks.

"Hey, baby," Bryce said loudly, "you shouldn't look so guilty. Jim will think there's something going on."

Brandy longed to slap the smile off his face, but enough interested looks were already turning their way. She decided the best thing to do was nothing.

"Are you finished for the day, Jim?" she asked as evenly as she could.

"Yes, I am."

"You mean you finally wrapped that love scene between you and Laura?" Bryce said with stagey disbelief.

"Yes." Laura flashed an intimate smile at Jim, who was still studying Brandy's tautly controlled expression. "Took all day, but it had to be perfect."

The thought of Jim being in Laura's arms all day made Brandy's stomach churn. It was too easy to visualize those two locked in a passionate kiss.

"Excuse us, Laura," Jim said briskly, "it's time Brandy and I offered the bride and groom our best wishes."

His announcement was unexpected. Brandy hadn't thought he would want to deprive himself of Laura's company, or at least not so soon. She seemed just as surprised and not at all pleased.

Instead of protesting, Laura smiled. "Tell Ginny I'll see her later, will you?"

"Of course," Jim nodded.

Brandy started to step forward, but at the same moment Bryce took hold of her hand and held it out to Jim.

"I give her back to your care, Jim," Bryce drawled.

As he released her wrist, he exerted just enough pressure to tip the glass in her hand. Brandy gasped at the sudden shock of ice-cold liquid spilling down her front. Blinking in surprise, she stared at the wet purple stain on the front of her lime-green dress.

"Bryce, you idiot!" Laura cried angrily, taking a

handkerchief Jim had removed from his pocket. "How could you be so clumsy!"

Marie took the nearly empty glass from Brandy's hand while Laura dabbed uselessly at the spreading stain on her front. Brandy found the actress's concern for her appearance hard to believe, yet Laura actually was trying to help.

"Hey, I didn't do it on purpose!" Bryce protested vigorously.

Laura grimaced as she looked at the futility of her efforts. "It's going to leave an awful spot when it dries. Maybe we could rinse it out with some cold water." She turned to Jim. "Your trailer's the closest. Is it all right with you if we use it?"

"Here's the key." He took it from his pocket and handed it to Laura.

"Can I help?" Marie offered as Laura started to lead a bewildered Brandy away.

"No, Brandy and I can manage," the actress said with a dismissive smile.

A travel trailer parked along the side of the back lot was their destination. Laura put the key in the lock and opened the door, holding it for Brandy to precede her inside.

"There's a bedroom in the rear," the brunette instructed. "You can take off your dress there while I run some cold water in the sink."

Brandy started down the narrow hallway, suddenly wondering if she had misjudged Laura all this time. She had been so blinded by jealousy that she hadn't wanted to see that the stunningly beautiful woman could be kind and thoughtful.

"Laura, I don't know how to . . . to thank you,"

Brandy faltered in her confusion. "I mean, for your helping me and all."

"It's nothing." The tap was turned on in the sink.

Unzipping her dress, Brandy pulled it over her head as Laura stepped into the narrow hall.

"Hand me your dress." She held out a hand, for it. "By the way," Laura added over her shoulder, "one of my robes is hanging on the hook in the closet on your right."

Opening the door, Brandy saw the scarlet satin robe and a few clean shirts and pants belonging to Jim. Suddenly she knew exactly why Laura had been so kind. Now she even wondered whether the accident had been genuine or planned.

The whole point had been for Brandy to discover Laura's robe in Jim's trailer. It wasn't hidden away, it was easy to see. Jim must have seen that scarlet red there; he must have accepted it as natural. Which meant that he and Laura were lovers. Laura wanted to convince Brandy of that.

Something died inside her. Mechanically Brandy slipped on the scarlet robe, letting the silky material slide over her bare skin. As she tied the sash, Brandy saw Laura framed in the hallway, arms crossed in front of her, a pleased look on her face.

"Aren't you going to ask about the robe?" Laura purred.

Brandy jerked the knot of the sash tight, tossing her head back proudly. "Is that what you want?"

"I thought you might wonder about finding it here."

"Why should I?" Brandy said, walking determinedly past the woman to the sinkful of water and her stained dress lying beside it. "I've always guessed you wanted Jim."

"And I'm going to have him," Laura declared.

"I think you phrased that wrong." Brandy picked up her dress and tried to rinse away the stain. "Shouldn't you have said *I love him?*"

"Of course I do. We make a perfect couple, in many ways."

Bryce's comment earlier that evening gave Brandy some insight into that remark. "What you mean is that Jim's talent and reputation would get you a long way up the ladder, right?" she asked coldly. Maybe Jim would never be hers, but she didn't intend to let the calculating actress walk all over her without scoring a few blows. "I happen to love Jim Corbett the man. Who do you love— the celebrity James Corbett?"

"What a cute turn of phrase!" Laura laughed, a harsh, unfriendly sound. "Fortunately, if you have one, you automatically have the other. And he's mine."

"If that's true, then why are you so worried about me?" Brandy challenged.

"You remind me of an understudy I once had." Venom dripped from Laura's voice. "She pretended to be all sweetness and innocence, too, but the first chance she had, she proved how devious she could be. I'm not going to give you the chance to spoil things."

"Too bad he doesn't see you for what you are," Brandy declared with open disgust. "Maybe he does though. Maybe that's why he's been taking me out."

"We had a fight. He only asked you out to make

me jealous," Laura jeered. "Only a few minutes ago he was telling me that he was sorry he'd asked you to come here tonight. He was going to say he was tired and take you home early. If you want to save yourself some embarrassment, you'll take my advice and leave now. You can use your ruined dress as an excuse."

Stubbornly Brandy kept rubbing away at the stain. "You'd like me to do that, wouldn't you?"

"You stupid little bitch!"

"That's enough, Laura." The door had opened silently and Jim stepped inside, his broad-shouldered body filling the small trailer.

Laura recovered from her astonishment more swiftly than Brandy, laughing brightly and walking toward him. She didn't appear unnerved by the harshness of his expression.

"Jim," she made an effort to sound delighted, "Brandy and I were just—"

"I know what you were just doing," he interrupted coldly. "I was listening outside."

That statement made the stunning brunette swallow hard. She glanced angrily at Brandy as if she blamed her. "I suppose you're going to take her side against me," she cried, bitterness in her voice.

"You know something, Laura?" was his even reply. "You've begun to believe your own hype. You think you can get away with anything."

"But you and I—" she protested.

"There's no you and I, except in your publicist's imagination. You came to me saying that you needed some help to jumpstart your career, and I agreed to do what I could. That's all there ever was between us," Jim said. Brandy wanted to cry with relief. "Now, I suggest that you get out of my trailer before I throw you out."

Her ego wounded, Laura seethed in silent outrage an instant longer. Then with a contemptuous toss of her raven hair, she stalked past him to the door, slamming it as she walked out.

For the first time, Jim turned to Brandy. The hard mouth crooked at the corners as he ran a quick eye over the scarlet robe she was wearing.

"That isn't your color," he observed dryly.

Unconsciously, one hand moved to the satin front. "It was hanging in the closet," Brandy swallowed, her heart hammering with joy.

"Laura wore it to protect one of her costumes today. I remembered she left it here when she stopped at lunch to give me the script rewrites. All part of her nefarious plan," Jim explained, "and I can guess what she wanted you to think."

"I'm afraid I believed it." There wasn't that much distance between them in the small trailer, but he closed it with unbearable slowness.

He looked her up and down. "Would you care to repeat the statement you made earlier?"

"Which one?" Her breath was stolen by the smoldering light in his dark eyes.

His gaze took in her shining face. "The one about loving someone."

Brandy swayed closer, her hands clasped between his. "I—I'm in love with you, Jim." The catch in her funny little voice said she couldn't help herself.

"In that case, you won't object if I tell you we're getting married in August." A slow, lazy smile softened his hard features.

Brandy wanted to jump for joy. "That's so long to wait"

"I want you to be very sure, angel." His fingers reached out to gently caress her cheek.

Tears shimmered in her eyes. "I am."

The dark head bent toward hers, the masculine mouth murmuring against the softness of her lips, "I love you."

Surrendering to his possessive kiss, Brandy wound her arms around his neck, returning his love with unrestrained joy. The Sonora sundown blazed through the trailer windows, flaming over their embrace.

Here's a thrilling preview of
SHIFTING CALDER WIND by Janet Dailey.
A June 2004 paperback
from Kensington Publishing.

A blackness roared around him. He struggled to surface from it, somehow knowing that if he didn't, he would die. Sounds reached him as if coming from a great distance—a shout, the scrape of shoes on pavement, the metallic slam of a car door and the sharp clap of a gunshot.

Someone was trying to kill him.

He had to get out of there. The instant he tried to move, the blackness swept over him with dizzying force. He heard the revving rumble of a car engine starting up. Unable to rise, he rolled away from the sound as spinning tires burned rubber and another shot rang out.

Lights flashed in a bright glare. There was danger in them, he knew. He had to reach the shadows. Fighting the weakness that swam through his limbs, he crawled away from the light.

He felt dirt beneath his hand and dug his fingers into it. His strength sapped, he lay there a moment, trying to orient himself and to determine the location of the man trying to kill him. But the searing pain in his head made it hard to think logically. He reached up and felt the warm wetness on his face. That's when he knew he had been shot.

Briefly his fingers touched the deep crease the bullet had ripped along the side of his head. Pain instantly washed over him in black waves.

Aware that he could lose consciousness at any second, either from the head wound or the blood loss, he summoned the last vestiges of his strength and threw himself deeper into the darkness. With blood blurring his vision, he made out the shadowy outlines of a post and railing. It looked to be a corral of some sort. He pushed himself toward it, wanting any kind of barrier, no matter how flimsy, between himself and his pursuer.

There was a whisper of movement just to his left. Alarm shot through him, but he couldn't seem to make his muscles react. He was too damned weak. He knew it even as he listed sideways and saw the low-crouching man in a cowboy hat with a pistol in his hand.

Instead of shooting, the cowboy grabbed for him with his free arm. "Come on. Let's get outa here, old man," the cowboy whispered with urgency. "He's up on the catwalk working himself into a better position."

He latched onto the cowboy's arm and staggered drunkenly to his feet, his mind still trying to wrap itself around that phrase "old man." Leaning heavily on his rescuer, he stumbled forward, battling the woodenness of his legs.

After an eternity of seconds, the cowboy pushed him into the cab of a pickup and closed the door. He sagged against the seat back and closed his eyes, unable to summon another ounce of strength. Dimly, he was aware of the cowboy slipping behind the wheel and the engine starting up. It was followed by the vibrations of movement.

Through slitted eyes, he glanced in the side mirror but saw nothing to indicate they were being followed. They were out of danger now. Unbidden came the warning that it was only temporary; whoever had tried to kill him would try again.

And here is a preview of
CALDER PROMISE by Janet Dailey
A July 2004 hardcover release
from Kensington Publishing.

"What happened, Laura? Did you forget to look where you were going?" The familiarity of Tara's affectionately chiding voice provided the right touch of normalcy.

Laura seized on it while she struggled to collect her composure. "I'm afraid I did. I was talking to Boone and—" She paused a beat to glance again at the stranger, stunned to discover how rattled she felt. It was a totally alien sensation. She couldn't remember a time when she hadn't felt in control of herself and a situation. "And I walked straight into you. I'm sorry."

"No apologies necessary," the man assured her while his gaze made a curious and vaguely puzzled study of her face. "The fault was equally mine." He cocked his head to one side, the puzzled look deepening in his expression. "I know this sounds awfully trite, but haven't we met before?"

Laura shook her head. "No. I'm certain I would have remembered if we had." She was positive of that.

"Obviously you remind me of someone else then," he said, easily shrugging off the thought. "In any case, I hope you are none the worse for the collision, Ms.—"

The old ploy was almost a relief. "Laura Calder. And this is my aunt, Tara Calder," she said, rather than going into a lengthy explanation of their exact relationship.

"My pleasure, ma'am," he murmured to Tara.

"And perhaps you already know Max Rutledge and his son, Boone." Laura belatedly included the two men.

"I know *of* them." He nodded to Max.

When he turned to the younger man, Boone extended a hand, giving him a look of hard challenge. "And you are?"

"Sebastian Dunshill," the man replied.

"Dunshill," Tara repeated with sudden and heightened interest. "Are you any relation to the earl of Crawford, by chance?"

"I do have a nodding acquaintance with him." His mouth curved in an easy smile as he switched his attention to Tara. "Do you know him?"

"Unfortunately no," Tara admitted, then drew in a breath and sent a glittering look at Laura, barely able to contain her excitement. "Although a century ago the Calder family was well acquainted with a certain Lady Crawford."

"Really. And how's that?" With freshened curiosity, Sebastian Dunshill turned to Laura for an explanation.

An awareness of him continued to tingle through her. Only now Laura was beginning to enjoy it.

"It's a long and rather involved story," Laura warned. "After all this time, it's difficult to know how much is fact, how much is myth, and how much is embellishment of either one."

"Since we have a fairly long walk ahead of us to the dining hall, why don't you start with the facts?"

"I suppose I should begin by explaining that back in the latter part of the 1870s, my great-great-grandfather Benteen Calder established the family ranch in Montana."

"Your family owns a cattle ranch?" He glanced her way, interest and curiosity mixing in his look.

"A very large one. And early ranch records show numerous business transactions that indicate Lady Crawford was a party to them. Many of them involved government contracts for the purchase of beef. It appears that my great-great-grandfather paid her a finder's fee, I suppose you would call it—an arrangement that was clearly lucrative for both of them."

"The earl of Crawford wasn't named as a party in any of this, then," Sebastian surmised.

"No. In fact, the family stories that were passed down always said she was widowed."

"Interesting. As I recall," he began with a faint frown of concentration, "the seventh earl of Crawford was married to an American. They had no children, which meant the title passed to the son of his younger brother." He stopped abruptly and swung toward Laura, running a fast look over her face. "That's it! I know why you looked so familiar. You bear a striking resemblance to the portrait of Lady Elaine that hangs in the manor's upper hall."

"Did you hear that, Tara?" Laura turned in amazement to the older woman.

"I certainly did." With a look of triumph in her midnight dark eyes, Tara momentarily clutched at Laura's arm, an exuberant smile curving her red lips. "I knew it. I knew it all along."